MISS RANSKILL COMES HOME

In memory of Venice
and much Werlsch.

with love,

Nina Freda
Werlsch Books.

Persephone Book Nº 46
Published by Persephone Books Ltd 2003

First published 1946 by Chapman & Hall
© The Estate of Barbara Euphan Todd
Afterword © Wendy Pollard 2003

Endpapers taken from 'Sutherland Rose', a 1946
screen-printed cotton textured fabric designed
by Graham Sutherland for Helios
© Whitworth Art Gallery, the University of Manchester

Typeset in ITC Baskerville by Keystroke,
Jacaranda Lodge, Wolverhampton

Colour by Classic Cheney Press, Banbury

Printed and bound by Biddles Ltd,
Guildford and King's Lynn

ISBN 1 903155 363

Persephone Books Ltd
59 Lamb's Conduit Street
London WC1N 3NB
020 7242 9292

www.persephonebooks.co.uk

MISS RANSKILL COMES HOME

by

BARBARA EUPHAN TODD

with a new afterword by

WENDY POLLARD

PERSEPHONE BOOKS
LONDON

To Marguerite Steen,
with love and gratitude

MISS RANSKILL COMES HOME

CHAPTER ONE

I

Miss Ranskill sat back on her heels; even that movement was an agony, driving the sand into her sweat-softened skin, but it was the torment of her hands that had forced her to stop digging. The grave was nearly deep enough. It would have to be deep enough because for two hours now she had been fighting the shale. She had tugged at it with frayed fingertips, twisting great flakes from their beds while the pinkish-grey edges of other flakes deepened in colour as they bit into her knees.

She pushed back her hair with one hand, while the other sought the comforting softness of her mouth. She was terribly thirsty, and the sand, gritting from the cracks of her torn fingernails, tasted salty. Yet before she could reach the stream she would have to pass the Carpenter. There was only one stream on the island.

Her left-hand fingers found, in their turn, the solace of her mouth and tongue. It was a child's attitude she had taken, squatting back on her haunches, her cut fingers in her mouth. She had done to the Carpenter all the things that were

1

necessary. Had done them reverently because she revered him, practically because of what she had once heard, lovingly because she had loved him, though that fact had only come to her while she was digging his grave and after she had dealt with the now inert and helpless body that had never presumed to display more vigour before her than dragging of timber, lifting of stones and thrusting through waves demanded.

I'm a boxer, look. All boxers get to be gentle. They learn to keep the strength in when they've got to – part of their training. Bruiser, that's a word makes me laugh. . . . Even a heavy-weight walks light like a cat. He learns to ballet-dance before he's learned to hit. You've never seen the ringside women, Miss Ranskill. Enough to make you sick they are, crowding round and thinking they'll get their kisses while the blood's still slippery on the gloves. Boxers don't think a lot of them. Boxers like to do their own wooing – it's part of their training, see, Miss Ranskill. A boxer's got to be a wooer all along, got to draw his man close in, seduce him like. No woman need fear to marry a boxer. Fighting and lovemaking go the same way. Boxers don't want no easy knockouts either. They like to use their skill, Miss Ranskill.

'Miss Ranskill', yes, she had always been Miss Ranskill to him since the time he had dragged her chilled water-heavy body out of the sea. The 'Miss' and her surname had made her armour against an assault that had never been hinted at. She had called the Carpenter, Reid. His surname seemed to set the right distance between them. At home, on that other island, she had always addressed the village carpenter by his surname, so the distinction had come easily enough.

She had been proud, virtuous and old maidenly. She had cherished the flower of her virginity because all the years of

2

her sheltered upbringing had encouraged that nurturing. To her, at thirty-nine, her chastity had still been a cool white flower, not to be snatched lightly and thrown away. It had remained the same all through the years on the island. She had always been proud of her integrity and of the Carpenter's also. They had made between them a greater story than the ones usually begotten on desert islands in books.

It occurred to her now, as she shifted sideways, relieving the hurt of her knees and bringing yet another new pain as the sand gritted between calf and thigh, that he had never heard her Christian names – Nona Mary. Supposing she had died first, would he have engraved MISS RANSKILL on her tombstone? But then there wouldn't be a tombstone because there were only rocks on the island. Silly. Why did all these irrelevances keep crowding in at a time like this, futile thoughts and memories when she hadn't even cried yet? This was the first time she had had time to cry, in a grave – not above it as most people do. Tears washed the sand out of her eyes and the salt stung the sore places that flicked shale had made on her cheeks. Then, as an animal consoles itself by the licking of wounds, as every child, since the world began, has solaced its own distress, she set her tongue working from corner to corner of her mouth, catching her tears and taking those outward and visible signs of the soul's distress into the body to be its comforter.

Ten minutes later she sagged on to the shale and fell asleep.

II

It was two o'clock in the afternoon and Miss Ranskill had been asleep for half an hour.

She was trying not to wake now, trying to resist the summons of an insistent fly, buzzing the last message of the Carpenter to her.

'Please, God, don't let it be true. Let it be all all right.'

Miss Ranskill kept her eyes shut to give God his last chance of working a miracle. Then she stood up slowly and, helped by the paddle the Carpenter had made, scrambled out of the grave. The paddle was split and frayed by the hours of futile jabbing at the shale. He would have been hurt to see its condition after the weeks of patience that had gone to its making.

You don't need to dig with it, Miss Ranskill. Anyone would think you was working your allotment 'stead of trying to row. You don't need to dig with it, see.

Two tears ran down her cheeks, dripped off the end of her chin and were sopped up by the thirsty wood.

It had been such a splendid paddle, considering that the Carpenter had had nothing but his knife to help hands, brain, and the skill begotten when he was first apprenticed.

Not so bad, Miss Ranskill, not bad at all considering. When I think of the song and dance I made as a lad if the steel of a plane was too soft for my liking. We could have done with any old plane here, couldn't we?

She leaned her weight on the paddle now to ease her aching back and, looking down into the grave, saw that his knife was lying there. Civilised nervousness possessed her for

4

a moment, as it often did even after four years on the island. It wasn't safe to leave their only valuable treasure there. Then she straightened herself as reality jerked at instinct. She would leave the knife where it was while she went about her other duties. It would *make the grave more homely* until she had collected leaves and grass for a lining.

Makes it more homely-like, Miss Ranskill, see.

That had been one of his favourite expressions. He used it as he arranged stones round the smoky fire, and when he handed her a shell.

Saucer, see, Miss Ranskill. We mayn't have cups, but we've plenty of saucers. Makes it more homely.

He had loved his English home in a way she had never loved a house.

Slowly, word by word, as he had once laid brick on brick, he built it again for her to see, made her free of it, invited her to the hospitality of the rocking-chair by the steel fender. She could almost smell the nasturtiums in the blue jug and the scent of the rising dough in the crock.

Yes, of course the homelessness had been worse for him than for her.

But now?

For the next hour she walked backwards and forwards from spinney to grave, carrying leaves and moss. Her mind was stilled by the tiredness of her body.

Now she must wash herself before saying goodbye to the Carpenter, who was taking his first rest for many years.

He lay straight and curiously flat in his ragged trousers and the shirt she had rinsed out that morning.

When she reached the stream she drank, dipping the drinking shell in and out of the water, gulping and gasping in the manner of hot thirsty puppies and children.

The drinking shell had been the Carpenter's idea.

Handy, if we always keep it there, see, Miss Ranskill. We'll not know ourselves soon with a drinking fountain and a bathing pool. We only need a band and an ice-cream stall to turn the beach to Blackpool.

She rinsed the shell before returning it to the ledge. They had always left it in readiness for one another.

Then she plunged her face and head into water that stung the sandied edges of her eyelids and gentled the hard tangles of her hair until it flowed into separate strands again. After that she picked up the clothes she had laid ready and walked down to the tiny creek of sand and flat rock that edged *the lady's bathing-beach.*

She stripped off her one garment, and walked into water that received her tenderly, swirling the sand from sore places, bracing and making her ready for the ordeal to come.

She let her hair dry in the sun before tugging at it with the blunt wooden comb that had been fretted out by the Carpenter's knife. He had made her a little brush of quills too – a tiny besom.

I used to make toy besoms for my lass when she was a little one, Miss Ranskill. Highly delighted she was, but her mother wasn't so pleased when she smeared cinders across the hearthstone.

On one of their Christmas Days, at least, on one of the days they thought might be Christmas, he had brought her a shell filled with powdered cuttle-fish and a sort of fuller's earth dried from the clay of the cliff. There was a pearl grey puff too, bunched from the feathers of a sea-bird. The shell and its lidding shell had been stained with the blood of the bird.

Face powder, see, Miss Ranskill. You've got to look smart on Christmas Day, makes it more homely.

She did not use the puff now: it would have broken her heart.

Presently she dressed in the brown tweed coat and skirt that were so shrunken from their waterlogging that the cuffs came halfway up her forearms and the skirt-edge brushed her knees. She had no hat. But she had dressed for the ceremony as well and suitably as she could. No more could be expected from any gentlewoman.

Then this particularly distressed gentlewoman lifted her tired head, braced her aching shoulders, and, with something of the defiant shyness of a little girl going to receive her first school prize, walked slowly, almost on tiptoe, towards the place where the Carpenter lay.

III

In her world before the island, decently brought up people had bathed once a day, washed all over additionally once a day, and sent their linen to the laundry every Monday morning. Those were some of the rules: others were that babies must be baptised within three weeks of birth and the dead buried within three days of death, or, if possible, sooner.

So she stooped down, grasped the Carpenter's armpits and began the slow dragging across the sand.

He was very heavy and his heels and flapping trouser-legs left a trail in the sand. She had not reckoned for that Man Friday marking. How would she be able to bear the sight of it when she was quite alone? She left him and tried to smooth away the sad indentation with her hands, but she only widened the track, making a mock-tactful smudging of his trail. The marks must stay there until wind and rain destroyed that memorial.

Afterwards she was to remember her last sight of him as he lay (face downwards since she had neither strength nor space to shift him) on the leaves and moss until, handful by handful, the sand covered him up while she muttered remembered snatches from the Burial Service:

I am the Resurrection and the Life.
For I am a stranger with thee: and a sojourner as all my
*   fathers were.*
Earth to earth, ashes to ashes, dust to dust.

Then, feeling nothing but the sore aching of her body Miss Ranskill filled in the grave, using the paddle when her hands failed.

Many hours later the moon laid a silver finger along the sea. It pointed towards her dishevelled form as she lay asleep.

A ship went by – the first that had been near for years. But for the first night since the Carpenter came to live on the island the fire was out.

CHAPTER TWO

I

Miss Ranskill awoke in the chill of the dawn. She shivered, and then shifted her position on the damp gritting sand. For a few moments she tried to convince herself that she was still on the edge of nightmare and that soon she would hear the Carpenter's whistle as he put fresh wood on the fire.

Thought I'd be up a bit earlier, Miss Ranskill, and make a long day of it. There's nothing left for us to do now but provision up the boat and wait for weather if we need to. Just think, it won't be long now before you'll be thinking of having an early morning cup of tea in England. No more cold water for you.

But there was no whistling, no voice, no cracking of wood, and, as every ruffle of the sea was set glittering by the rising sun, she remembered clearly and more clearly. She could not lie there for any longer, watching the sea and cheating her mind with memories. She must get up, change her clothes and occupy herself. Her limbs ached from cold and exertion, but, as she stretched them, every little nag of pain dragged some of the hurt from her mind.

She stood up now and took off her coat and skirt so as to shake the sand from it.

She was a tallish woman, rusty-haired and with jackdaw blue eyes. Her figure and type demanded tailored tweeds, good silk shirts, flat shoes and hat-shaped hats. She was one of a company whose members are to be seen going to meetings, whistling to dogs, talking to children and giving tea-parties in every English village. Her kind are at home and at their best on their own ground only, and their ground is the English countryside. They are as clean as soap, water, unheeded mud of lanes and the turned earth of gardens allow.

Miss Ranskill had always looked her best on September mornings when crisp air pinked her cheeks, when her sweaters were new and her tweeds fresh from the cleaners.

Now she stood bare-legged and bare-footed, shins and knees hacked by shale, her hair so stiffened by salt water and sand as to look wooden. She was wearing what remained of a pair of grey lock-knit knickers. They were laddered and torn: the elastic at the knees had long since shrivelled away and that at the waist was supplemented by a pair of knotted braces, whose tags, hanging down in front, suggested the skeleton of a sporran. From her waist upwards she was naked, but the blue-veined whiteness of her breasts, gleaming between the tanned skin above and below, told that they were not used to the sun.

When she was washed ashore she had been wearing two pairs of knickers (she had always been an absentminded dresser), a vest, a brassiere, a knitted jumper, and the tweed coat-and-skirt – nothing else but shoes and stockings. Somehow she had managed to make her clothes last, or, at least, hang together, by never wearing skirt and knickers at the same time except on Sundays. Her top half had been more easily covered by vest, brassiere, jumper or coat. It had taken her two years to appear before the Carpenter in brassiere with no coat. She only did it then because the vest had been used as a fishing-net, and both jumper and coat were wet. So the light and shades of her body with its dark arms and shoulders, paler diaphragm and immaculate breasts were also the chart of her modesty.

There was no need for that now that the Carpenter had gone, leaving, so far as her eyes could see, no sign of his being except a trail that led from the shuffled sand where she had slept to the mound she had heaped above him. Soon, but only for a little time, there would be another trail – a track made by her own feet and the track of the boat she would push down to the water's edge.

'But not today,' said Miss Ranskill to herself, 'and not tomorrow: perhaps not for quite a long time. I must get used to being by myself first for a bit. The sea would be too lonely yet.'

She felt more content now that she had made up her mind. She would keep the fire going, catch and dry some more fish, tidy the Carpenter's grave and recover her strength for a little while.

There was, after all, no very great hurry, and it would be sensible to check over her provisions in a seaman-like way. It would be as well, too, to take a few trial trips in the little boat.

There's no hurry, Miss Ranskill, see. You've not got a train to catch.

No, there was not any hurry, but she must see to the fire now. She picked up her coat and skirt and began to walk along the shore. Already, thoughts of occupation were renewing the elasticity of her mind.

11

It's a queer thing to say, Miss Ranskill, but I've smiled to think of all the work that the dead give to the living. Regular slave-drivers they are in their hurry to be buried. They keep us busy all right, almost as if they knew what was good for us. Mourning to get and pies to bake and all the sorting up afterwards. Wouldn't do for those that's left behind if they packed up their trunks before going, and then set out by train to Heaven.

Well, there would not be much sorting-up to do in the stone and wattle shelter that had been the Carpenter's bedroom. He had left little behind him but a blurred catalogue from an ironmonger's shop, a leather wallet of sea-stained snapshots and newspaper cuttings, an indelible pencil, a pouch that had once held tobacco, and a watch that had, by a miracle, survived its long sousing.

'I must take the watch to his wife,' thought Miss Ranskill as easily as though she were contemplating a journey from one English town to another. 'She'd like to have it.'

Queer thing about this watch is we don't know whether it's lost or gained in all these years: water plays odd tricks with works. I've never let it run down and I'd been marking down the days by it before you came along to keep me company. Still, we'll not know till we get to England if we've lost two or three days out of life or been given a few extra to play with. What shall we do with 'em, Miss Ranskill, eh, go to the pictures or what? And talking of that, let's go to the pictures now, shall we?

'Going to the pictures' had been their favourite game. It had been invented by the Carpenter one evening as they sat round the fire during the first month of their acquaintanceship.

Tell you what, Miss Ranskill. I'll shut my eyes and you tell me all about your home till I see it. Start at the beginning when you were a little 'un, and then I'll do the same for you.

He had done the same for her, building with slow words all the houses in the small Berkshire village, laying a patch-work quilting of downs, raising a church steeple, thatching the wheat straw roofs, setting out the gardens and opening the school-house door for her so that she could see a little earnest boy, kicking at his desk with rough boots while he carved his initials with his first pocket-knife.

It was the smell of the pitch-pine sawdust that started me, I reckon. I'd always wanted to go to sea, same as most boys, but carpentering was nearer to hand, and I wanted that too. I got apprenticed easy enough – there was a grant from the school.

She saw him standing boot-deep in the shavings that curled away from the flying plane, saw his sawdusty hands, the tendrils of wood that clung to his hair and the play of the muscles on his forearms.

He had gone to sea in the last war and had liked the life.

Always something to look at and something to do. It was then I started making ships in bottles so's my fingers wouldn't get clumsy. Wish we'd a bottle here, Miss Ranskill, so's I could make you one. Never mind, that'll have to wait till we get home.

After the war when the ship was paid off, he had worked for a time in the shipbuilding yards before going back to the village, where he had learned his trade, and taking over what remained of his old master's business. Then he had married.

You should have seen Annie then – pretty girl she was. We did very well at first till a new carpenter came and set up his sheds in

*the village. He could afford to wait for his money and I couldn't.
Then the old folks, the ones that knew the difference between good
wood and bad, died off, and the new customers they didn't like it if
you sent in a bill twice, and we'd the children to think about. It wasn't
so easy then.*

Miss Ranskill had known the children very well indeed.

There was Ada, so pretty that 'she couldn't be blamed for
wanting a bit of fun,' fond of shop windows and towns and
cinemas and gay clothes. It was hoped that Ada would settle
down, but the Carpenter, though loyal, was doubtful.

*I ought to have made more money for Ada since she wouldn't stay
at home or go into service. The shops don't pay enough wages for
girls that have got to find their own lodgings. I did what I could, but
it wasn't enough.*

There was Donald, who died when he was twelve, and there
was Colin, who had been 'just over seven' when his father saw
him last.

*It was just when times got bad that I went to the shipyards again
– it was regular money and no bad debts, and the missus got a lodger
– schoolteacher she was, and she could pay regular, so it seemed the best
thing to do. Then there was the chance of a sea-going job – just for
six months, and I took it just in time, before they closed down the yards.*

He had been knocked overboard on a dark night. It was
something to do with a winch, Miss Ranskill thought, but
she could never understand his sea-language and he always
went on to describe his thoughts about Colin when he found
himself alone in the dark water.

*I said to myself, it's not good for a lad to be brought up by women,
Colin needs his Dad. I'd have given up long before if it hadn't been
for that. I was just going to give up when that bit of driftwood went by.*

14

Then, as always, Colin dominated the picture. Colin, handling tools as though he loved them, Colin running down the road to meet his Dad. Whenever she thought of Colin she thought of the Carpenter until they seemed, not like father and son but like two little boys, the one stepping into the other's shoes and taking his place against the pattern of village life that was so curiously undisturbed by partings or even death, because each family produced more families to live in the same place and inhabit the same houses and inherit the same way of life.

She knew that Colin would come to think as his father thought, use his hands in the same way and see the same things.

Yes, Miss Ranskill, you'll have to see Colin.

But she had seen him already.

Go on, Miss Ranskill, it's your turn now. I want a turn at the plush seat next.

So she had made him presents of her own comfortable and carefully guarded childhood, set the brass guard round the nursery fire, conjured up the bowls of bread and milk, red dressing-gowns, the smell of soapy flannel, and all the ritual of bedtime when Nona and her elder sister, Edith, had listened to the shouts of the village children playing in the street and had envied them.

You may have been a Miss Independence, but you never thought you'd get to a desert island, did you, Miss Ranskill? Tell you what – it's all very well playing cinemas, but when we get back to England we'll have to see each other's homes, eh? There's the front bedroom that's never used only when the wife's sister comes to stay. We'd make you welcome any time, if you'd honour us by coming, Miss Ranskill.

She too had issued an invitation to stay and had enjoyed the anticipated sight of her elder sister's face when the visitor arrived. For Edith was a great respecter of persons. Miss Ranskill heard her plaintive voice, saw her rather handsome distressed mouth, slightly moustached.

'But, Nona, it's *impossible*. The man is neither fish, fowl nor good red *herring* now that you have made a *friend* of him, as it were. Yes, I *know* the circumstances are peculiar, but that makes it all the more *difficult*: people won't *understand*. We can't let him eat in the kitchen with Emma if he's a *visitor* – so unsettling for *her*, and he can't possibly feed with *us*. Yes, I *know*, my dear, but even *you* must admit it's an *awkward* situation. I don't know how it is, Nona, but you always *have* managed to do uncomfortable things. I have never before heard of *anyone* falling overboard in mid-ocean just because they'd dropped their *hat* over the railings or whatever they were. It will be difficult enough to explain *that* away without your bringing a great *lumbering carpenter* to stay in the house. Besides, it was rather a *compromising* situation, even though the man seems to have behaved very *decently*. Yes, I *know* all that, my dear, and he seems a *perfectly* steady respectable sort of man. . . . But people *will* talk in these small villages. Besides, you can't *possibly* have anything in *common* with him. You mustn't be *too* democratic.'

That anticipated attitude of her sister's had seemed as sure and certain as though it had actually been taken; so sure and so certain that Miss Ranskill had made mental retaliation.

'Nothing in common, oh no! nothing except a drinking shell and a fire and the boat we built together. He used my vest for a fishing-net, and I used his braces when my knicker elastic gave. It doesn't seem awfully odd to me to ask a man to stay when he's caught fish in your vest. As for democracy – it was more a mixture of monarchy and communism. He was a monarch – he made the rules and I had to keep them to save my own life. I didn't know the rules of tree-cutting and fishing and boat-building. I suppose we were communistic in a way – neither of us took the bigger share of fish or anything like that.'

The elder Miss Ranskill would not be embarrassed by the Carpenter now, thought her sister, as she passed the dreary ashes of the fire.

The ends of a few charred sticks showed where the flames had tired to smouldering. They reproached her until her negligence seemed disloyalty to the Carpenter, and she picked up the twig besom to brush them clear of the slab that made the hearthstone.

She remembered how the last time the fire had gone out he had whittled a pile of chips and frayed the ends of thin branches till each made a little brush to decoy and spread the flame before the maddening task of flint-striking began. She had offered to help, but he had not let her. He had always been jealous of his knife.

See now, Miss Ranskill, where'd we be if you broke the blade? Women they're all right when it comes to scissors, but it needs a man to use a knife the right way. 'Tisn't as though we could buy another at the shop.

Right way or wrong way, she must use the knife now.

For the first time since the Carpenter had died, Miss Ranskill went into the wattled shelter he had used as a bedroom. His old ragged coat lay, as he had last flung it down, on a slab of stone. In the second before snatching it up, the sight of sleeve-wrinkles, made almost permanent by the movement of his elbows, hurt sharply and unexpectedly.

The left-hand pocket was empty. There was nothing in the right-hand one but a half-handful of fish-hooks chipped from shells and the bones of birds. The breast-pocket held the familiar bulging wallet. There was nothing in the worn lining of the coat, nothing on the stone, nothing on the sandy floor.

Tell you what, Miss Ranskill, if that knife was lost we'd be just about done for. We'd never get on without it. Might as well cut our throats only there'd be nothing to cut 'em with.

She began to panic as she scrabbled among the moss that covered the sandied hollow of his bed.

Where had she last seen it?

Then with a cold sickening jerk that gave a tug to memory she recalled that she had left it in the grave. It must be lying there now with the Carpenter above it and all that fiendish sand on top of all.

Might as well cut our throats with nothing to cut 'em with.

It might have been more bearable if she had flung the knife out to sea, than to know it was lying four or five feet below where she might choose to stand at any time on any day. It would stay there now till rust fretted the fish-oiled blades and joined them to their steel compartments.

If she had dropped it in a crevice between rocks she might have tugged, and levered with other rocks till something gave – even if it were her own heart. But she could never dig in that sand again, never scrabble like a dog till she came to the Carpenter. He would not wish her to see his changing body. Honour and privacy were due to the dead. She could never disturb him now.

'Never!' screamed Miss Ranskill. 'Never! NEVER!'

As she stumbled out of the shelter, her voice shrilled until it set the sea-birds screaming. It seemed to compete with their voices. The wind caught it and blew it backwards. Then the birds came circling, muted for a moment or two by the terrible sound until again the cacophony challenged them and they shrilled and shrieked.

She screamed until her throat ached and until the sounds died to a hoarse groaning, sank to a whispering and stilled.

The silence was more shocking than its raucous prelude – empty and tense.

The birds veered seaward, sickling the blue.

'What shall I *do*?' gasped Miss Ranskill. 'What *shall* I do?'

She sobbed achingly as she staggered back into the Carpenter's room, sagged to the sand and flummocked against the stone, pressing her cheek against his hollow coat.

Pictures of knives came into her mind, of white-handled pocket-knives snug against green baize in the show-cases of superior shops, of silver knives with mother-of-pearl handles and of the very first knife she had bought for herself with her own pocket-money. It had worn through the linings of so many pockets that she had been ordered to wear it on a string

19

round her neck. With a thought she could feel the rough edge of the string cutting into the back of her neck, but the satisfactory heaviness of the knife itself, jogging against her middle as she ran, had always been comforting. She had never seen a horse without hoping that if it had to get a stone in its hoof it would get it then, so that she, Nona Ranskill, could come to the rescue with the knife that had 'the thing for getting stones out of horses' hooves with'. But never the horse and the stone and the knife all together, never once! She still had the scar left by the first cut made by the little blade on her forefinger. It was queer that the scar should remain now that there was no knife at all.

At this very moment, no doubt, in hundreds of shops in England people would be buying knives, carelessly unaware of Miss Ranskill's need. Surely, her thoughts ought to reach them, surely they should glance over their shoulders as the draught whistled under the doors, a draught that was, maybe, a tiny gust of the wind that had blown across the island, streaming Miss Ranskill's hair and blowing a tear-drop from her face. How long would a wind take to travel from wherever the island might be to the shores of England? Did winds of England travel direct to her, winds whose breezes may have been parted momentarily by a knife held in a gardener's hand as it passed through the air on its way to trim a rose-bush?

What adventures steel suffered, tempered by fire, shrunk by water, tired by use and revived by rest, keeping its vitality for longer than a man could, whether it was worked for centuries, rested in an armoury or left to rust out its virtue at the bottom of a grave!

The jack-knife had been chief servant to the Carpenter for years, and he had been its sole employer. He had oiled it with fish-oil, whetted it on carefully chosen stones. Its blade had grown thinner and narrower as the years went by. Every time it was shut, it closed upon a story. Its blade had known the resistance of ships' tobacco, codline and hemp, as well as unseasoned wood.

It had been made in Sheffield: its steel had been tempered by men who had never been out of England and who took their girls to the cinemas at nights to see pictures of desert islands.

'Coo!' they said, when the heroine (her hair freshly waved, as though by some barber of Neptune) was lifted out of the sea by an immaculate and bronzed young man. Her dress was only damp enough to cling prettily to her perfect curves. And the young man, even though his shorts might be a trifle ragged, wore a shirt that must, surely, have been put on clean that morning. That was all that the makers of steel knew about desert islands, but the steel itself had learned everything: it had mirrored cracked fingers and ragged nails. Its steel had been true and flawless, but now it was powerless to help any more as it lay close to the Carpenter's hand just as it had done through all the years of its working life.

She felt again in the pockets of the coat. There was just a chance that in her hurry she might have searched one of the pockets twice, that she had only buried the knife in nightmare, but of course she had not.

The rough tweed caressed her hand as she fumbled.

Thing I like best about you, Miss Ranskill, you never make a fuss.

Memory of the Carpenter's approval lifted her heart a little. Suddenly it became important to him as well as to her that she should not make a fuss. It would be disloyal to their friendship, a denial of the quality in her – the quality he had admired – to make a fuss now. She must continue to be the same person.

Friendship with him had changed her so that she had, in a way, become a part of him.

> Let me not to the marriage of true minds
> Admit impediments. Love is not love
> Which alters when it alteration finds.

Loyalties were important: they outlive the grave and whatever it is that we label death.

No use crying for the moon, Miss Ranskill, we've got to make shift with what we can get.

No use crying for a knife either.

She raised her head from the rough tweed and blinked at the sunlight.

From the horizon, the sea stretched like a broad scimitar, fretting and chipping the tide's edge to silver splintering. Its great curving blade took on all the blue-and-grey and white tones of tempering, with gold as well where the sunlight touched it. There was the cutting hurtful blade-edge towards her and beyond, where the blue thickened to grey, the harder less acute tempering – the safer stronger side of the blade.

Mind once more took possession of Miss Ranskill's body, easing its strain by virtue of that sudden command. She had the boat, which was all ready except for stowage – storage, what was the word? They had meant to go, anyway, and now she would continue the plan. There was work to do in England. She must use the boat the Carpenter had made. The years of his labour must not be wasted. She must find his wife and tell her the manner of his death because she had no right to keep the last years to herself. It was a pity she was so tired, but it didn't really matter. She would sleep all the better when she got home.

Beds cried out to her to come and sleep in them, cool beds in summer and warm ones in winter. China tea would be waiting at her bedside in the early morning and she would put her lips to thin-fluted china. There would be thin bread crumbling under its load of butter. There would be flowers to 'do' – pink-stemmed primroses to be gathered in woods.

Now she must hurry. She must be quick, very, very quick over everything before her mind sagged again. She must begin work now if she were to leave the island tomorrow, or the next day, or the day after that.

CHAPTER THREE

I

It was early in the morning, but Miss Ranskill had been at sea for some hours. The island would soon be out of sight now. Already, it looked no bigger than a handkerchief – a small grey-blue one with an edge of fluttering white lace.

So far, thanks to the patient instructions of the Carpenter on two trial trips, she had managed the paddles fairly well. The boat had a tiny mast but no sail – that was to have been made later from her skirt and his shirt.

Not that we'll risk a lot of sailing, Miss Ranskill. I'd not trust the stepping of that mast too much. No, we'll only have a bit of a sail for when the wind's middling lazy and we're feeling slack the same. Tell you what though, Miss Ranskill, when we do want a bit of a blow we'll stick the knife-blade in the mast. That's a sailor's trick, and they say it never fails. Yes, we'll use the knife to call the breeze up, and we'll sail along looking like mother's washing-day. Your skirt and my shirt'll make it more homely-like. Yes, the knife'll do one more good turn for us.

Without the knife there could have been no boat. The big blade, helped by fire and flint, had laid the small trees low and

24

made slits for the stone wedges before they could do their work of splitting. It had made wooden rivets, smoothed the tiller and shaped the rudder.

The boat had been three and a half years in building, for the wood had had to be seasoned and there had been all the heartbreaking hindrances of knots and splits and snaps. The ribs had been bent to shape while still green, but the longer planks had been coaxed to curving by water boiled laboriously in large shells set round the fire. Rivet-holes had been caulked with resinous tree-sap, helped by clay.

The same clay secured the tops and bottoms of the shells that lay in the stern-sheets and held Miss Ranskill's water supply. She had brought quite a lot of water, because she knew that the slabs of sun-dried fish would make her thirsty. She felt thirsty now, so she shipped her oars, slipped forward from the thwarts and grovelled for a shell. Luckily it was a calm day, even so, it was not easy to break away the clay binding without spilling the water. Some of it splashed on to her lap, a dribble trickled down her chin, and the rest tasted fishy.

And now the island had disappeared, had slipped away unnoticed while she wrestled with the shell. There seemed to be nothing left in the world but the monotonous sea, the curving sky and the golden pathway of the sun – a path she had decided to follow. An aching loneliness possessed her for a moment or two – a loneliness that must not be realised lest it turn to terror.

'There might be a ship,' Miss Ranskill comforted herself. 'There might be a ship any time now.'

But there was no ship. There was nothing. Even the birds seemed to have left the world.

'One couldn't go on for very long without seeing *anything*,' she thought. 'One must see something in time. One *must*.'

For it had always seemed to her and the Carpenter as they waited on the island, and strained their eyes with starings-out to sea, that there must be a ship just beyond the horizon, a ship or another island.

Just out of eye-shot, Miss Ranskill, just out of eye-shot, that's the devil of it.

She snatched at the paddles and began to row frantically. The faster she could make the boat travel the sooner she would be – where? If only there were corners to be turned or the top of a hill to reach. As she tugged savagely at the paddles visions of maps filled her mind, big splodges of continents, little spatterings of islands set in the immense splashes of blue. She was jerking at the paddles now in her exhaustion and presently she was obliged to rest in order to relieve her sobbing breath.

Would it be better, after all, to go back – home? What a ridiculous word, for there was no home on the island now. It took more than one person to make a home where there wasn't even a dog or cat or canary. But there was her shelter there – her shelter and a grave and a familiar stream where she could drink and wash. There was space to walk about. If the island was not home then this boat was hell – a tiny wooden hell. There was nothing between her and the deep water except a frail planking, nothing at all between her and the sky. Perhaps there were other little floating hells, dotted about, beyond any sight, on the surface of the sea. If people could fall overboard from ships as she and the Carpenter had done without being noticed, perhaps other people had done the same. There must be ships somewhere.

She began to paddle faster along the golden path (now paling to silver) that streamed eastward. Yes, she must get away if there were anywhere to go.

Easy now, Miss Ranskill, you don't need to dig, see.

II

It was noon, and the sea was still calm, monotonously interrupting and fretting by the lip-lap of its restless tongues of water. The sun was high overhead, glaring down at her with a demoniacal gold eye.

'And how do I know where to go now?' thought Miss Ranskill, 'I shan't know, till the sun begins to go west so that I can row away from it if I'm to keep an eastward course. I don't know my *way* about the sea. I don't know whether to go to the right or left.'

Naturally, port and starboard meant nothing to her.

Now, with the sea as empty as the tracing paper she had admired in childhood, before she had spoiled it with her spluttering pen, how was she to find her way?

III

It was evening and Miss Ranskill was asleep, her head against the gunwale and one arm crooked round a paddle. Not so very far away a small island deepened to indigo against the red-gold of the setting sun. She stirred her cramped legs, opened her eyes, blinked and looked at it.

It was the most beautiful island, welcome and welcoming. In that moment of half-wakefulness when she seemed roused from the horror of nightmare into the peace of a happy day, she had no doubt of its friendliness, just as when she was a child she had always been sure of recognising her own among the many mansions of Heaven and all her ancestors too. Yes, she was quite familiar with the island.

She knew that creek and the outline of rock that was like a sleeping giant. She knew that tree with the solitary lopped branch. She knew that tree very well.

'Oh, no!' She spoke the words aloud. 'Oh, no, it can't be: it mustn't be.'

But the lopped-off branch was part of the planking beneath her feet. The boat had drifted back to the island while she slept.

If the beacon fire had been alight, perhaps she would have pulled inshore towards homeliness and warming flames.

'But I can't start again,' said Miss Ranskill, 'I can't.'

She hated the island then, as she unshipped the paddles and began to pull away from the sun; and hoped to get further away this time before sleep won another battle or the currents played their alien tricks.

IV

One-two-one-two. The rhythm of rowing was beating her body and beating into her brain until it seemed she would never forget it.

A few stars were out now – small delicate hazy ones. Presently she would choose one to steer by. If she did not, she might row in a great circle for ever – the island out of sight but never any nearer or any farther away.

She must rest sometime, but the trouble was that if she slept by day she might not see the ship as it crept over the horizon. If she slept by night she would have no guiding star.

One-two-one-two-one-two.

V

There was neither sun nor star to steer by, and hard grey waves cracked and slapped at the boat.

For hours, Miss Ranskill had abandoned the paddles; and now she was clutching the tiller in an attempt to make the boat ride bow-first through the water instead of broadside on, as she had done for the sickening minutes when Miss Ranskill had left the tiller to grovel for the dried but now sodden fish.

She was terribly exhausted and frightened too, for the water seemed to crash from every direction, now cracking against the bows as though determined to split them, now leaping at the port gunwale, now hurtling at the starboard. Those sudden rushes up the sides of steep waves were terrifying, so was the shudder and humping of mounted water as it shook the small boat from its shoulder to the trough before the upward ploughing began again.

The tiller quivered and fought for freedom.

Suddenly Miss Ranskill surprised herself by a yawn, for she was not sleepy. Terror is not a soporific until after it is passed. The yawn was followed by another and by jaw-stretching successors. Something seemed to be clutching at her solar plexus: something inside her responded to the rise and fall of the sea. She felt colder than ever and realised she was going to be sick.

Her hands let go their grip and she sagged sideways into the stern-sheets.

As she did so the tiller caught her sharply on the side of the head and she was not conscious of any more movement for some time.

VI

Now Miss Ranskill was riding a horse and the animal was running away with her. It charged at a telegraph pole, but the jarring crash scarcely checked its speed. It swerved sideways and jumped a stone wall – jumped it sideways too. On it went over brooks and hedges and walls, over a cottage once – up and up, then crack on the tiles and down again.

A small boy, sitting on a rock by the sea, called out to her. *Don't dig, Miss Ranskill, you've no need to dig, see.*

She was riding a merry-go-round ostrich now, and there was whirligig music. Faster and faster, up and down, round and round went the ostrich, and it smelled of fish.

The merry-go-round spun so quickly that the bird broke away, and went striding round and round in a widening circle, until it hopped on to a swing and flapped its wings.

'Faster! Faster!' screeched the ostrich. 'We'll swing level and then we'll go over the top!'

She was slipping off its back now, and all the tail feathers came away in her hand. Down she went, splash into a pool of water, but when she tried to swim she found she was moving her limbs in glue which hardened swiftly.

Now she was in a picture-gallery and searching desperately for the Botticelli Venus because she needed the great curved shell: it was full of clear water that did not smell of ostriches.

There were a great many pictures in the gallery and nearly all of them moved. There was a still-life painting of a knife that lay on a tray with a bowl of pansies, a toy boat and an orange. As Miss Ranskill looked, the blade of the knife closed, folding up into itself the golden reflection of the flowers. One of the pansies made a face at her.

There was a picture, too, of the flight into Egypt. Joseph, the Carpenter, tugged at the donkey's bridle until it moved forward, carrying its burden of Holy Mother and Holier Child, and only stopping when its muzzle touched the heavy gilding of the frame. The next picture showed the face of another Carpenter, bearded too, but more familiar. As she looked, he died.

'Oh dear!' said Miss Ranskill, as once she had said when very wide awake. 'You should never have tried to lift that rock with your heart in the state it is.'

The Carpenter did not answer.

The next picture was the same, and so was the next and the next. There was no getting away from it. When Miss Ranskill shut her eyes it was inside her lids.

She rushed through the gallery though the cords of the pictures wound themselves about her ankles. Presently she came to the last room of all, and there was no picture – only an unglazed window opening on to a grey-blue sky with a touch of gold hinting through cloud and a white bird lazing in the air.

That was the picture Miss Ranskill saw when she opened her eyes to the sky again and was conscious of the gunwale digging into her shoulder-blades.

VII

There had been sunrises and sunsets, stars at night, birds and clouds by day, but never a wisp of smoke from any funnel.

The weather, so far as Miss Ranskill knew, had been fairly good after the first. Her head ached so that she could not remember much about the voyage except that she had finished the fish and drunk the last drop of water from the last shell, even sucking her skirt afterwards because a sudden lurch of the boat had jerked her elbow. The skirt was soaked with salt water too. She slept now and then, half-sitting, half-lying propped against the thwarts.

Nothing mattered very much any more. There were no other boats on the whole of the sea, but she was too tired to care. She did not even resent the mist that came swirling in shreds and skeins, dowsing the horizon, limpening her salt-stiffened hair and making her shiver and huddle to-gether.

If one got very cold in this mist one might die more quickly.

She got very cold but still she did not die, though the fog came down like a chilling blanket.

Suddenly there came the sort of bellowing that might have been made by a great sea-cow with colic. The bellow was repeated but it conveyed nothing at all to Miss Ranskill, whose brain was now too tired to connect sound or sight with cause. She felt faintly annoyed at having been roused from what she had hoped would be her last sleep.

She huddled herself together, drew her left foot up from the water that covered the bottom boards, and rested her aching head on her hand.

Just then the mist lifted suddenly, and, as the last shreds blew away, she noticed the ships – long grey ships in a long line. High above them, swinging buoyantly, were two silver-grey monsters, immense and bloated-looking. Their entrails dangled from them – ridiculously thin, trailing entrails.

Miss Ranskill laughed as she had not laughed for years. They couldn't be true, of course. Whales did not float about the sky like that. All the same they were frightfully funny.

She was still laughing when they took her aboard one of the destroyers of the convoy.

CHAPTER FOUR

I

'Delayed concussion, I think, sir,' reported the Surgeon-Lieutenant as he walked into the Commander's cabin. 'She's had a nasty jab on the side of her head.'

'How does she seem now?' asked the Lieutenant-Commander. 'Sit down, won't you?'

'Thank you, sir. Well, she ought to be all right soon, but she's suffering a bit from shock. We've got some soup into her and I've given her a shot, and she'll probably sleep till morning. What I can't understand –'

The young doctor hesitated and frowned. He was fresh from his medical school and the etiquette that forbids discussion of cases with the laity was strong in him. So too were the facts, so constantly impressed during his three months' service in HM Navy, that he must make his own diagnosis swiftly and certainly and then take his own responsibility for his cases. Consultants are not supplied to destroyers on convoy duty.

'Well?'

'I can't understand why she's in such a mess, sir. Her knees and legs are all hacked, and –'

'If she's a survivor from some torpedoed ship, you'd expect her to be hacked by floating wreckage or anything.'

'Yes, sir, of course, but you'd not expect gravel-rash all over her. She looks as though she's been buried in sand and then pickled in brine. There was sand under her nails and in her ears. And her breath –'

'*Must* you just before dinner? Can't you be the best friend and tell *her* when she wakes?'

'But it smells of fish, sir, fairly reeks of it.'

'She probably likes fish: some do. Any other wealth of detail about this Barnacle Belle?'

'Well, sir, her clothes – her *underclothes*. Damn it, we've picked up survivors before, and they've never been like that.'

'If you're suggesting I should give her gifts of lingerie, I won't do it. I was brought up conventional-like. Time and again my old Nanny said to me, "Never give panties to pretties unless they're legworthy." You've told me about her legs. By the way, what's she wearing now?'

'Number One's pyjamas, sir: he's the smallest.'

'How romantic, and she's in his cabin too, isn't she? Anything else you can think of to make me cast the vome?'

'No-o, sir – except – I was just wondering if she's a genuine survivor or if there's anything fishy about her.'

'Apart from her breath I should say no, but you should know more about that.'

The Surgeon-Lieutenant smiled politely. He was not yet quite sure of his dignity.

'I only meant I wondered if she was a spy. One does hear odd things.'

'I doubt if the Huns, though they have queer ideas of amusement, would hit a woman on the head, roll her in sand, feed her on bad fish and dump her into a boat. The boat's the only thing that puzzles me. I'll have another look at it now and I'll talk to the mermaid in the forenoon if she's receiving visitors.'

II

Next morning Miss Ranskill opened her eyes to fluffy white blankets and a glinting of bright-work and mahogany. Gradually her ears attuned themselves to a sort of humming rhythm.

Back in the ship, was she? Oh no, she couldn't still be pleasure-cruising: it couldn't all have been a dream. Those sky-borne whales were no nightmare. She closed her eyes because they ached so badly but opened them again three seconds later to the rattle of curtain rings.

A young man was peeping at her from under the shadow of a peaked cap.

'Good morning,' he said. 'That's splendid. Are you feeling better?'

Miss Ranskill answered the question with another.

'Am I in a ship?'

'Yes, that is –'

'Then will you please ask the stewardess to come to me.'

'If there's anything you want, I –'

'I want the stewardess, please,' said Miss Ranskill as firmly as aching throat and swollen lips would allow.

'I think I had better give you the once-over first. I'm a doctor, you know.'

The Surgeon-Lieutenant produced his thermometer.

It would, he decided, be better not to worry her with the knowledge that she was the only woman aboard. These delayed concussions were tricky things to deal with.

'By the way,' he said, after he had shaken down the mercury, 'by the way, how did you manage to get so sandy?'

Miss Ranskill answered him briefly.

'I had to bury the Carpenter.'

'Bury the Carpenter? Why?'

Suspicion made him jerk out the question in his newly-acquired voice of authority. He might have been addressing some scrimshanking rating.

'He was dead. There wasn't anybody else there.'

The Surgeon-Lieutenant attempted the bedside manner – a thing he had only heard of in lecture-rooms, read about in books and practised, whenever possible, on his admiring mother. There is not much time or space for that manner among rows of hospital beds or in the Sick Bays of the Navy.

'So you had to bury the Carpenter?' he soothed. 'Yes, of course.'

Miss Ranskill closed her eyes and then snuggled her head into the pillow like a tired dog.

The Surgeon-Lieutenant waited for a minute or two, and then, baulked by her closed eyelids from any more questioning of the interesting case or even more interesting spy, returned to the Wardroom to report that though Barnacle Belle *might* have delayed concussion or bats or both, in his opinion she was overdoing it.

'Overdoing it, my foot!' said the First Lieutenant. 'It's perfectly sane to bury a dead carpenter.'

'All right, but when she first came to she tried to kid me that she'd kidded herself that the barrage balloons were flying whales.'

'Keep it clean.' The First Lieutenant, who had given the unwelcoming hospitality of his cabin to Miss Ranskill, yawned and stretched himself. 'Don't let's have obstetrics even if you did get a first in midwifery.'

The Surgeon-Lieutenant grinned sulkily and went along to give a more modified report in the Captain's cabin.

III

Commander Wrekin was used, after long years of service, to ministering to the needs of many people, from Masters-at-Arms suffering hurt dignity to ships' boys whose swelled-headedness must be balanced against homesickness. Nor was woman business kept apart from his jurisdiction even at sea, or likely to be kept apart so long as AB's continued their requests to 'see privately on family matters'. The family matters, slowly divulged, usually meant that 'the wife had been carrying on with a friend', and that another friend had thought it 'his duty' to acquaint Able-Seaman So-and-So of the facts and always when the ship was away from home waters. The usual result was that the harassed AB, after nights of brooding in his hammock, fell foul of some Petty Officer and 'didn't seem to have heart for anything somehow, sir.'

Yes, the destroyer's commander had had to deal with 'woman business' often enough, but he found Miss Ranskill baffling.

She received the news that she was the only woman aboard the convoy with little surprise and less embarrassment, remarking:

'It will be odd to see a woman: for years there was nobody but the Carpenter.'

Little by little, as the days went by and her strength increased, so that their conversations could be longer and more frequent, he was able to piece her story together into a more or less consecutive whole.

She had been on a world pleasure cruise.

'It was just after the Munich scare and we thought it would be safe. Things were beginning to look very bad though, a few days before my accident.'

That was as much as he heard the first day, because that seemed the moment for him to tell of the outbreak of a war that had made convoys and balloon barrages necessary.

'I hope the Maginot Line is being a success,' said Miss Ranskill.

The story of the fall of France and the great evacuation of Dunkirk was as much as she could bear to hear that day.

'And we had four years of peace,' she commented. 'Stolen sort of peace. I'm glad the Carpenter didn't know. He was at sea in the last war. It doesn't seem fair for us to have had that separate peace. If I'd only believed war was coming I wouldn't have bothered about my hat.'

'No,' he said, and not interrogatively because her eyes

were closing. 'No, I'm sure you wouldn't. Well, I mustn't stay chatting any longer now.'

But before he left the cabin, Miss Ranskill raised her head from the pillow.

'Wasn't there a War of Jenkins's Ear?' she asked.

'The Peace of Ranskill's Hat,' she muttered, and the sense of irony that had lain so many years dormant roused itself for a moment before she went to sleep.

The next morning she explained herself.

'It was only a silly little pull-on felt. I didn't even like it particularly except that it generally stayed on better than the others. It was getting dusk and I was standing alone by the rails on one side of the ship when it blew off. It didn't go right overboard, I mean, not right down because it caught on a hook or something. I can't be technical, and, anyway, you don't count P and O's as ships, do you?'

'Well, never mind that though, go on.'

'I thought I could reach it, so I climbed over the rails and hung on with one hand. Then my foot skidded on some iron or something and I suppose the jerk made me let go.'

'And then?'

'Oh! all darkness and choking and then when I came up I think I lost my head and just swam desperately. I'm not awfully good, and clothes make a difference. When I did see the ship she seemed quite a long way away, and I couldn't make my voice carry. It seemed to scream back into my own face till my throat was sore. Nobody heard. . . . I tried to follow the white line – the wake, you know, and it seemed to keep stretching out like elastic, getting longer and longer as the ship went further away. . . . It was dark by then, and I don't suppose anyone could have seen me even if they'd been looking. . . . It was awfully lonely swimming in the dark. . . . I gave up trying to swim fast. . . . I don't know how long it lasted. . . . I got tired. . . . I suppose I went down because I remember choking and fighting, and then –'

Miss Ranskill's eyes were wide with horror and Lieutenant-Commander Wrekin laid a hand on the scarred fingers that were doubling up a fold of sheet.

'Go on,' he ordered, knowing that she must finish now if she were to have the peace of a mind unburdened.

'I don't remember any more. I suppose I was pretty well drowned. When I came to I was lying by a big bonfire and being sick and someone was working my arms about – a man with a beard. . . . It was the Carpenter.'

Suddenly Miss Ranskill gave a little choking sob. Before she needed it, her listener pulled a white handkerchief from the pocket of his monkey-jacket.

'Quite clean,' he said, 'and don't mind me. Here, let's get your pillows better.'

Then as he stooped over her, Miss Ranskill's hands clutched his coat-lapels, her head butted the hollow of his shoulder, while his arms, practised in such holding of his two small daughters and not so very much bigger wife, went round her quivering body.

Presently she gave him a little push and lay back on the pillows.

'It was awful of me –' she said. 'But –'

'It wasn't awful at all. Any woman would want to cry after an experience like that.'

'It wasn't that, it was talking about the Carpenter. I never cried on *his* shoulder. . . . I never wanted to – till he was dead. It's awful when a man's dead and he was the only person who could have comforted you.'

Miss Ranskill stretched out her hand for the handkerchief, but he took it, and dabbed professionally at the last of her tears.

'Do you good to cry a bit.'

'It doesn't really, at least, it won't any more.' She took the handkerchief and gave a final dab to her nose. 'Think if that young doctor had come in!'

It was not a thought that the senior officer cared to brood over, but he replied, 'Done him a lot of good if he had.'

Miss Ranskill grinned.

'It would have been rather funny. He hasn't much sense of humour.'

'No, he'd probably prescribe soup for you. As a matter of fact that's what I'm going to order now – a cup of good strong soup.'

And at once the word soup became a rescuer, relieving them both from embarrassment, changing the subject and making the relationship easy again.

'Soup,' said Miss Ranskill. 'Yes, I should like some soup. After that I'll have a sleep.'

Most of her days as well as nights were spent in sleeping: there was so much to be made up. In the intervals between sleeping and dozing she ate and asked occasional questions whose answers she digested slowly. There was a good deal of digesting to be done. Geography and history were so curiously changed and muddled. Germany had removed its neighbours' landmarks and turned the whole of Europe into

42

No-man's land. Friendly Italy had become foe; Russia, so often cartooned, was the saviour of civilisation, and France was divided against herself.

The wireless made her head ache, besides, she could not follow the news, and remarked, after her first attempt, that she felt like a kindergarten child who had been jumped into the sixth form of a high school.

She did not ask many questions about England. It would, she decided, as there had been no invasion, be very much as it had been in the last war, anxious and busy. But her sister, a permanency if ever there was one, would still be doing the church flowers and having servant difficulties. Miss Moxon and Miss Grant (two other permanancies) would still be quarrelling under the roof they had shared for twenty-five, no, for twenty-eight years now. The village children would have grown, the tiny ones plumping up and the taller ones pulling out.

She never thought of considering whether there would be any change in herself: there is not much difference in age between thirty-nine and forty-three. No, everything would be pretty much the same in the village when she, Nona Ranskill, came back, with a story to tell that would make tea-party gossip for week after week.

She was in the state known to all of us in some degree when the train has steamed out of the station – not quite here and yet not *there* either, with all the pictures of the destination as bright in the mind as coloured postcards.

Yet, some urgency of mind told her that though her own particular pictures might keep their brightness for a week or so after her arrival, they would soon fade or be superimposed upon.

'But just for a little,' drowsed Miss Ranskill, 'just for a little, early morning tea and hot baths and electric light switches and armchairs and roses. All so easy, getting into a train and going where you want to, and listening to the wind blowing outside and the rain on the window-panes, and seeing the lights blazing from the windows when you come home from a walk.'

One morning she remarked, 'It's very queer to be so safe.'

'A convoy,' replied Commander Wrekin. 'A convoy isn't everybody's idea of safety, you know. I'd meant to have a chat about that, but I didn't want to worry you after the shaking-up you've had.'

'Oh! *submarines!*' said Miss Ranskill, in a voice that might have dismissed a mouse. 'I don't mind them. It was being alone on an empty sea that I minded. One can get used to most things, but not to that.'

She was gradually getting used to the idea of freedom and plenty again, and, as mind and body were fed, desire grew. She longed not for one knife but for twenty, for dozens of silk stockings and abundance of clothes. She would have four years' income to spend.

It was not until they were two days offshore that she heard their destination was Hartmouth. Hartmouth? What did she know about Hartmouth? She shook her memory and saw a sheet of blue notepaper with a stamped address – *Hillrise, Newton Road, Hartmouth. Tel. Hartmouth* 258, looked again at the tight precise little handwriting on envelopes that reached her three or four times a year. The letters they carried brought news of the tea-parties, 'marvellous bargains' and 'wonderful' holidays of 'yours ever, Marjorie Mallison (Mottram).'

Yes, Marjorie, whose india-rubber she had shared, whose pencils she had chewed, lived at Hartmouth and was married to a doctor. Stodgy-legged, smooth-haired, rabbit-mouthed Marjorie would be glad to see her, would put her up until she could buy a trunk and a suitcase and fill them both. She would put up Edith too, if her sister came to welcome her.

She would telephone to Marjorie as soon as she was ashore and then she would take a taxi to Newton Road.

Marjorie, who had won the 'Special Prize' for 'being the most helpful alike to staff and pupils', whose reports, lacking the venom that had brightened Nona Ranskill's, were tributes to sterling and stodgy character – *very good, tries hard, good careful work, an excellent term* and (eulogy from the Head Mistress) *Marjorie sets the tone of the school and is a first-class influence* – would be the very person to help.

That was all settled then. Miss Ranskill packed up her mind for the night, pulled down the sleeves of the First Lieutenant's pyjamas, knocked her head against the edge of his bunk and turned over to sleep.

Visions of Marjorie kept interrupting, echoes of Marjorie's voice jogged her to wakefulness. It had been rather a throaty voice.

'I say,' (this on the occasion of her first Head Girl speech to the sixth form) 'I say, this isn't going to be a pie-jaw or anything, but I do sort of feel it's up to all of us to make this a frightfully specially good term because of that new school that's come to the Towers. I mean, we mustn't go ragging about in crocodile or anything. Personally, I think it would be a frightfully good idea if we were to march in step for the first half mile, or anyway till we're through the village. I know it'll be a bit of a fag but I do think it's up to us to show this ghastly new school that St Catherine's is *the* school. We'll have to challenge their eleven next week and fix up a match, and we simply must win it. But anyway, I do think it would be a jolly good idea if we were to begin by marching in croc.: Hands up everyone who agrees. . . . Wake up, Nona. . . . Nona, everyone else has put their hands up. Aren't you going to vote?'

And back through the years, surviving the death and burial of the Carpenter and threat of starvation at sea, Nona Ranskill's answer came echoing back to her:

'Well, I don't see why we should suddenly start marching about just to show off to a new school.'

'But it isn't showing off. I mean, they must jolly well know that St Cat's is the best school. It's only just keeping up our prestige sort of. I mean, I don't want to pie-jaw, but there are some things one just can't explain. I do think that marching would sort of show. Hands up again everybody. . . . Nona!'

'But I don't see why *their* school shouldn't be the best to *them*. P'raps they'll march too: then *we'll* want a band. Besides, I don't see why we should call St Catherine's the best school just because we were sent to it.'

'Nona!'

'Well, I don't. It's silly!'

Thereafter, Marjorie, perched on the edge of the row of

wash-basins in the sixth form cloakroom, had pleaded confusedly to Nona to 'back up St Cat's', had mingled the death of Nelson with dinner-jackets on shikari, linked the school song, 'Forty Years On' (taken with no sense of humour from Harrow) with 'Rule, Britannia' and 'God Save the King', and waved (metaphorically) a new National Flag composed partly of the Union Jack and, more largely, of the school badge on whose shield-shaped background a Catherine Wheel, a portcullis and the legend *Honour before Honours* were embroidered, until Nona, more embarrassed than convinced, muttered that she wouldn't mind marching so much if she didn't always start off with the wrong foot.

Marjorie's triumphant 'I knew you'd come round. I knew you were only ragging, you chump,' ended the conversation.

There followed visions of Marjorie reporting herself (with a heroism that reeked of smugness to the lawless) for absolutely necessary speech in the dormitory. 'Still a rule's a rule, and I *did* break it and it would have been rotten not to report myself, even though I *had* to tell that new girl where the bathroom was, because she said she was going to be sick.' Visions arose of Marjorie's return, absolved from shame, though the owner of a conduct mark she had insisted on receiving from the Head Mistress – 'She was jolly decent. I'm most awfully glad I reported myself. Do you know, she actually said. . . . No, I can't tell you. . . . All right, then, I will. . . . She said it was . . . well, I mean she said I could consider it more of a *decoration* than a conduct mark!'

Still Marjorie, who had always had stores of pencils and india-rubber and blotting-paper, who could read a time-table as well as a genealogical one, whose suspenders never broke and whose folded clothes were as trim as piles of sandwiches, would be the very person to advise a returned desert-islander.

IV

'Tomorrow,' said Commander Wrekin, 'tomorrow, with any luck, you'll see land.'

At last he had answered the question she had not dared to ask: the slow days aboard had taught her that queries were not encouraged.

She did not answer, for his words had given her a picture of the Needles, as she had seen them just after dawn one June morning. She remembered their mistiness and the shimmer of New Forest trees edging Southampton Water and the traffic of the wide sea-lane and how the magic of return had clutched at her though she was only coming back then from a holiday in the Channel Islands.

'Yes, tomorrow you'll see land again.'

An icy quiver ran down her spine, so, just like that she had thrilled to rare and occasional music, to the ice-clear voice of a chorister singing a carol in King's College Chapel, to a Highlander piping up Regent Street, to Reveille after the fraught silence that follows the Last Post, to a thrush in November, to the new bleating of a lamb in spring and to the sound of bells across water.

'Queer,' said Miss Ranskill, 'what a good word *nostalgia* is. It sounds like smells, I mean, one thinks of a nose at once, and it is by smells one remembers things best.'

'It means "return pain", roughly translated, and, God, how that hurts – the return, I mean, even more than the thinking about it. Don't know why, but it does. England hits me again every time I come back.'

'Pierces, I think,' said Miss Ranskill, 'if we're being particular about words.' She added, 'I shall buy a dictionary first of all. No, a knife first, then a dictionary. It's funny, I always used to read the lists of books that people made out for imaginary desert islands, but nobody ever put down a dictionary.'

'Sir!' the First Lieutenant interrupted, and after that Miss Ranskill, who was on deck for the second time only since her rescue, was left alone to plan her return to the land.

It was a blue-and-silver morning, and even the battleship-grey of the long line of ships had taken on a hinting of azure. The sun silvered the bellies of the barrage balloons and caught the wings of an aeroplane that zoomed above.

Miss Ranskill sniffed. A sailor, she knew, could smell the sea from a long way off, and she hoped to catch a whiff of land soon, for already the business of little independent fishing vessels hinted of harbours. They, she remembered, carried home-tangs with them, an accumulated reek of harbours – tar and rope, cork, and salty nets. But big clean ships only smelled of themselves – of paint and metal-polish.

Tomorrow she would smell England, but what was its characteristic scent?

Tomorrow she would watch the misty grey edge of the land absorbing slow colour as the 'return pain' smote her.

V

Next day, a dripping sea-fog made land and sea and ships almost invisible. The foghorns blared like sea-cows calving, as the destroyer, nosing into harbour, carried Miss Ranskill home.

CHAPTER FIVE

I

She was ashore at last. Her feet had touched not dry land but the slimy stones of the dockyard. There had been no great moment as she stepped from the slippery gangway into a place of slush and shouting. Mist and drizzle had stolen her own thunder. There was no colour anywhere but the gold stripes on the First Lieutenant's sleeve and her own reddened finger-tips resting on it. Grey figures moved beyond a sheeting of fine grey rain. Grey shapes varied only in bulk and in tone according to their distance from her.

'Filthy day,' remarked the First Lieutenant. 'But I think it's going to ease up.'

The misty rain was thinning as they came near to the dreary building by the dockyard gates.

And now Miss Ranskill was dialling. Two – five – eight – Her fingers slipped on the last number and she began again while the First Lieutenant chatted to the policeman in a lowered voice and incomprehensible jargon.

She could hear the blaring of the telephone in, so she supposed, Marjorie's bedroom. Then came a click, and at last a voice answered in strident cockney tones:

''Ullow! 'Ullow!'

'Is –' Miss Ranskill's own voice sounded peculiar to her, 'is Mrs Mallison in?'

'Naow, she's not.'

Miss Ranskill swallowed twice before daring to ask the next question.

'Is she away from home? I mean, she still lives here, doesn't she?'

'Naow, but she's out.'

'Could you tell me when she'll be in?'

A tooth-sucking noise was the first response, and then, 'I couldn't siy, I'm sure. Would you like to leave a message?'

'Are you the maid?'

'Ow naow.' The voice sounded rather offended. 'I'm styin' 'ere.'

'Then perhaps you could take a message?'

'Righty ow! Ow, there's the doctor just coming in. I'll fetch 'im. What nime shall I siy?'

'Miss Ranskill, Miss Nona Ranskill, but he won't –'

The barking of a dog and confused noises interrupted. Presently a male voice spoke.

'Yes, Doctor Mallison speaking.'

'This is Miss Ranskill – Nona Ranskill – I don't suppose you'll have heard of me, but I was at school with Marjorie, and –'

'I'm afraid my wife – I'm afraid Marjorie is out. Perhaps you could give her a ring later. The evening would be best.'

'Yes, but –' by now Miss Ranskill was almost shouting, 'I've only just arrived. I've been –' She hesitated. It was impossible to say to that remote voice, 'I've been on a desert island for

52

three and a half years,' so she ended flatly, 'I've been having rather a bad time, and –'

'Sorry to hear that,' the doctor's voice sounded wary. 'Well, Miss Rankin, I'll certainly give Marjorie your message, and if you could ring up after dinner this evening or –'

'Ranskill!' she shouted. 'R-a-n-s-k-i-l-l, Nona *Ranskill*. Marjorie's sure to remember me. We were in the same form at St Catherine's, and –'

'Ranskill, yes, I've got that. I won't forget: I'll write it down, and now I'm afraid –'

'Won't Marjorie be in before the evening? You see – it's all rather difficult – I – I haven't been very well, and if –'

'That's bad luck.'

The words might be sympathetic, but the tone warned her as clearly as though he had said – 'I am sorry as an acquaintance but not as a doctor. Sharing a schoolroom with Marjorie does not mean the free run of my brains and surgery. Not a bit of it, my good woman!'

Miss Ranskill interrupted his warning.

'Oh! I'm all right, *really*, but I should have liked to see Marjorie as soon as possible.'

'Quite. Well, let me think. I'm pretty certain she's got a committee meeting of some sort here this afternoon: that means she should be in to tea. Could you come along at about half-past four?'

'*Thank* you,' said Miss Ranskill gratefully.

'That'll be splendid then. Goodbye.'

There was a click at the other end of the line, but she did not put down the receiver. Her fingers tightened round the vulcanite.

It seemed a strange welcome home after all the years of boat-building, hardship and danger.

She had not expected to be snubbed in a box of a room with a bored policeman standing by and a young Naval officer anxious, of course, to be rid of her, so that he could enjoy his brief leave.

She hung up the receiver.

'My friend is out. I'm asked to tea there this afternoon. I'd better fill in the time somehow till then. I could go to the bank, couldn't I, and see if they can get in touch with my bank.'

'Better have a cup of coffee with me first,' said the Lieutenant, and to the policeman he remarked, 'You can leave it like that, I think, Sergeant. I'll OK everything.'

'Very good, sir.'

The mist was lifting, shifting and shredding away as they went through the gates of the dockyard to pavements and wan sunlight.

A Midshipman saluted, a perambulator-faced girl in khaki walked with a swagger and a slight lift back of the shoulders as she noticed the Naval officer.

A couple of trousered girls, whose curls were half hidden by turbans, stared at Miss Ranskill.

She did not notice them. She was conscious of nothing but the noise – rattle of army lorries, cars changing gear, horns tooting, a boy whistling and a couple of men shouting. But as soon as any one noise gained dominance so that it could be recognised, another one broke in. Thud mingled with rattle, squeal with blare. The only familiar sound was the crying of the gulls: all the others were tiring.

A notice informed her –

'Public Air Raid Shelter 500 yards', and she turned to her companion.

'Have there been any air-raids yet?'

He returned a blue-jacket's salute before answering.

'Lord, yes! You ought to see some of the places. Still, we're giving better than we get now.'

Once again his hand went up to the salute.

'Look here, I'll try to get a taxi.'

One was approaching but its flag was down.

'There's sure to be another in a minute.'

'But I don't mind walking at all,' Miss Ranskill told him.

'Still, a taxi would get us there quicker. One gets so sick of saluting.'

By this time there was not a uniform in sight, but suddenly a shrill – 'Coo-er! Look at 'er skirt!' from a small girl told Miss Ranskill why her companion was so anxious for the privacy of a taxi.

A cluster of children edged closer and closer, nudging each other, whispering and giggling.

The young officer swung round, and advanced two steps towards them.

'Off with you!' he said. 'At the double!'

They scattered and ran, breaking into shrill laughter like a chorus of bad fairies.

'Mannerless little brutes. Look, if you don't mind waiting here, I'll do a gallop for a taxi: there's a rank round the next corner.'

He sprinted across the road but before he had reached

the opposite pavement, the children came darting back. They stared at Miss Ranskill and surrounded her.

Then one with a dirty face but a sweet and kindly expression smiled up at her.

'Where are you goin'?'

'I'm going to a shop.'

'Go on then!' shrilled the child, and put out a rose-leaf tongue. 'Go on then! Go on, can't you?'

A taxi slurred up through the mud, the young Lieutenant jumped from the running-board and opened the door, as the children scattered again.

'Don't know what's the matter with the brats of today. Dad's away and Mum's hand is too light, I suppose.'

Miss Ranskill sniffed as she sat down. She had forgotten that the inside of a taxi smells of leather, stale tobacco, oil and metal-polish. For the first time that morning she had found something recognisable. The taxi gave her assurance; she knew how to put her feet and how to rest her arm. She had not, it seemed, forgotten civilisation.

II

There were a few cakes in the window of the café and many large boxes decorated with pictures of chocolates. Miss Ranskill stared at them while the taxi-man was being paid.

She had never been particularly fond of sweets, but now her sense of taste, that had been first nauseated and then lulled to rest by the taste of fish and almost fishier sea-birds, was stirred by the sight of so many little portraits of chocolates.

One with a crinkle of violet on the top almost made her mouth water, though her adult palate had always resented the flavour of scent and cloying cream.

Now Lieutenant Maddock was at her elbow.

'Let's go in and find a table, shall we?'

The café was empty except for a few country shoppers who were having early morning coffee.

Her companion led the way to a table in a corner far from the door, ordered coffee, and then produced an envelope from his pocket.

'Commander Wrekin asked me to give you this. If you'll excuse me I'll go and wash my hands. Coffee's sure to be ages.'

As soon as he had gone, Miss Ranskill glanced at her own hands with their still sore fingers and blunted nails.

She decided it would be pleasant, no, more than that, almost exciting to wash her hands in a ladies' room, to dab her nose with tinted powder instead of the white talcum that Lieutenant Maddock used after shaving.

A notice at the foot of a staircase showed her the way.

At the turn of the stairs, Miss Ranskill saw herself full length in a looking-glass for the first time since her arrival on the far away island. The small mirror in the destroyer's cabin had been shadowed in a kindly gloom. There, her coat and skirt, pressed and darned by the ablest of seamen, had looked almost smart in comparison with its island shabbiness, though she had noticed how much he had shortened the skirt in order to cut away rags that had been six inches long in places. She was wearing a Midshipman's shoes: they were shiny enough but much too big, in spite of the extra pair of socks. His golfing stockings, even though their tops were turned up and showed the wrong side of rather wildly-coloured knitting, did not quite reach the hem of her skirt but showed an inch of bare brown leg and four strips of wide black elastic, each ending in a braces' tag. This was because the Able Seaman, a resourceful man, had made a suspender belt out of the only material he could find and had sewn trouser buttons to the golf stockings. She remembered being told how lucky she was that Midshipman Sparke's rather casual selection of a sea-going wardrobe had made the long stockings possible. But now she was not so sure.

Her coat was so shrunken that it did not meet and the soft white shirt (gift of Lieutenant Maddock) looked tactlessly clean and new. Also it bulged.

How had she managed to forget the navy blue mackintosh that he had lent her?

Her face looked old and weather-beaten, the cracked lips showed little ruckings of brown skin. Only the lines, radiating from the corners of her eyes, carried whiteness. The rest of her skin, now that the tan was beginning to wear off, looked dirty. Two tufts of hair rose defiantly from between the folds of a turban she had made from a sailor's silk.

She turned away from the mirror and slunk up the stairs towards a door marked *Ladies' Toilet*.

There were more mirrors above the rows of white washbasins. From the centre one the exquisitely-coloured face of a girl stared at her. It was a silly little face, pink and white, except for the darkened lashes, surprised blue eyes, and lips that were receiving a fresh coat of crimson. The effect was synthetic, but the expression had an insolence that terrified Miss Ranskill. She was defenceless against that stare and without woman's weapon. There would be privacy though behind that row of white enamelled doors and she tried the handle of one of them.

A woman in an overall rose from a chair, snatched a cloth from a hook and held out her right hand. Miss Ranskill, staring down at the pink palm, realised that she was expected to produce a penny.

'It doesn't matter,' she said, as her persecutor continued to display that toil-free palm. 'I mean, I haven't –'

The attendant shrugged her shoulders and sat down again. The girl smiled so that the slight movement of her mouth altered the progress of her lipstick and sent the flaming colour off the line of her upper lip. That made Miss Ranskill feel a little better.

She moved towards a table that held a powder-bowl, a box of cotton-wool pads and a sapphire and diamond ring. She could powder her nose without paying a penny, she could go on powdering it until the girl had gone. Then, perhaps, the attendant could help her to tidiness. But, before her hand could reach one of the little pads, another and scarlet-nailed hand snatched at the ring on the table.

The movement startled Miss Ranskill into dropping the envelope she had been clutching. Her own name stared up at her from the floor.

If she opened the letter, the reading of it would give her something to do. She need not look at the brutal mirror or pretend that she did not want to take refuge behind one of those white doors, or that she didn't mind being suspected of trying to steal a ring.

She picked up the envelope and slit it.

HMS Halliard.

Dear Miss Ranskill,

It has occurred to me that you may like to do a little shopping before the bank gives you facilities, so will you, please, accept the loan of the enclosed. My own movements are uncertain, but c/o Admiralty, Whitehall, London, SW1, will always find me.

I hope you will soon recover from the rough and ready treatment you received aboard, and get in touch with your friends.

With best wishes,

Yours sincerely,

L R Wrekin

Here was something kindly and warming, and something, as well, to restore self-respect. Miss Ranskill took one of ten notes from the envelope.

'I should like a clean face towel, please,' she said.

'Haven't you anything smaller?'

'No, I'm afraid not.'

'Well,' the attendant made the announcement proudly, 'we never have much change at this time in the morning, but I suppose I'll have to see what I can do.'

Miss Ranskill picked up one of the little pads from its bowl, dipped it into powder, dabbed her nose with it, looked at herself in the glass, and wondered whether to laugh or cry. Peach-coloured powder looked sad and ludicrous against her tanned skin. She dropped the pad back into its box and tried to rub the powder away with another one.

The girl looked at her disdainfully and then addressed the attendant.

'Could you give me some clean pads?'

'The box was filled with fresh ones this morning, Madam.'

'I know, but . . .' a thin finger pointed to the bowl, where the pad Miss Ranskill had used showed a peach-coloured dusting, 'a dirty one has been put back on top of them. I really couldn't use any of them now.'

The attendant made clicking noises with her tongue, emptied the box of pads into a bin, flounced to a cupboard, took out a packet of new pads and looked scornfully at Miss Ranskill.

'This is the receptacle for *soiled* pads.'

It was absurd that the scorn of a lavatory attendant and the insolence of a knock-kneed chit should have had the power, so Miss Ranskill reasoned, to make her feel as ignominious as a disgraced puppy.

What had the attendant seen of the world? She spent her days amongst plugs and taps and porcelain, her life in ministering to the lowest needs of the human body, dependent on their coppers for the price of a seat at a cinema.

And what had the girl got, apart from a slick sophistication and a second-hand complexion that must be renewed eight times a day? Her body was neat and slim – a narrow fashionable little body unsuited to child-bearing or to any other hard labour. Her knowledge of life came mostly from the theatres and light novels. The sea meant a row of bathing-huts and sun-tan cream, a desert island meant a sexy novel. The country meant new tweeds and an evening or two in village pubs where she would pretend to be 'too rurally rustic with divine yokels'. Tragedy was a spot on the chin, and 'fun' meant cocktails and screaming and dancing till dawn.

Feed the two of them on dried fish for a month, set them to boat-building and grave-digging, and what sort of shape would they make of their lives? What would they look like then?

So Miss Ranskill argued and questioned but no answer could help at this moment.

It was ridiculous that, after years of longing for companionship, her greatest wish should be to shut herself away in a lavatory, and that not because of any bodily need, but so that she could be alone – away from the people she had travelled so hardly to see.

She had heard of prisoners battering their heads against the insides of cell doors. Now she wanted to beat on one of those locked doors, force her way in and hide. If only the girl would go away, and if only the attendant, who had presumably gone to find change, would come back! The civilised scent of soap and powder began to stifle her.

She doubled up her hands in an attempt to hide scars and scratches, made suddenly shameful by a girl's glance.

You should a let me done that, Miss Ranskill. I don't like to see you roughing your hands. Doesn't seem right somehow.

Yes, the Carpenter, tired as he was, had respected her hands and what he called her 'ladyship', and the remembrance of his solicitude made a magnet for pride. Her own ragged appearance was only a phase in her life. In a week or two she would be restored. But there were people better than herself and as good as the Carpenter who would always be despised and rejected – not for themselves but because of what they wore, not because they had stolen and lived infamously, but because work had roughened their skins, because they blew on their tea or used the back of their hands for table-napkins. They were edged away from in railway carriages because their clothes smelled of their work and the sweat their work brought out, instead of reeking of the civet cat or a whale's disease.

It was more for the sake of the Carpenter and his kind that Miss Ranskill spoke now.

'Look!' she said, spreading out her swollen fingers before the girl. 'Look at my hands. It wouldn't matter being unkind if you weren't unutterably stupid as well.'

'I *beg* your pardon?'

The girl's voice had taken on the high-pitched tone used by certain people in speech to subordinates, but Miss Ranskill's overmastered it when she spoke again. She might have been a schoolmistress addressing a class of giggling stupids.

'Look at my hands and think again if your ring would be any use to me. You were afraid I might steal it, but it wouldn't go over my little finger. Look at my face! I don't rub lard into it at night.'

'I – I –' the girl edged away from the mirror. 'Really!'

Just then the attendant returned, counted out the change offendedly, put a penny in a slot, performed swift ritual with a towel and sidled away.

And now Miss Ranskill was alone and trembling in a cell six foot long by four wide. The outburst had tired her.

It couldn't really be true. Homecoming couldn't really be like this. It wasn't fair that, after all the loneliness of the island and the emptiness of the sea, she should have returned to a worse desolation of scorn.

All the comforting small pictures she had made for herself of bedroom armchairs, tea by the fireside, the welcome of friends and the safe luxury of houses had left her mind. There was nothing left of them.

Had she really come back all that way to see nothing but four white walls, the ugly furnishing of a water-closet and a roll of toilet-paper – enough paper to have made the island fire-lighting easy for weeks.

Until this moment other pictures had persisted – snapshots of England, needing only a touching-up or a toning-down.

See now, Miss Ranskill, I'd give most all I've got at home to be able to make you a cup of good hot tea. That'd make you feel different. Just you think of all the cups of tea we'll have when we get home to England.

And now, with not even a stream to cross, no further away than two flights of carpeted stairs, a cup of coffee was waiting for her, for a fool who was lucky to be between any walls at all.

She opened the door a crack and the sound of voices made her pause.

Another woman was talking to the attendant. She was a small, thin person dressed in black.

'My own girl wants to join the ATS, but I'd sooner she was a WAAF. myself. Bert'll have to register soon. He's mad to get at the Nasties after the time he had in London.'

'I thought Bert was an Objector.'

'Not now. He says they're nothing but a lot of Fifth Columnists, and that all conchies are Quislings. No, Bert's been mad to get at the Nasties ever since he was through one of the bad blitzes in London that time. It was seeing his uncle's barber's head in the gutter that changed him.'

The attendant sucked her teeth.

'How was that then?'

'Bert had been staying with his uncle near Victoria and they'd been dropping a packet. When it was over, see, they went out to look at the damage. He says you've got to see the broken glass to believe it. Well, they thought they'd go across the road to have a quick one, and while they was stepping across, Bert's uncle clutched his arm and pointed at the gutter. There was a head laying by the pavement – clean cut off by the flying glass, they thought. But what gave uncle such a turn was that the head was his barber's, the little fellow that shaved him regular every Saturday.'

'You don't say!'

'Shocking, wasn't it. Bert's mad to join the Ack-Ack now. Well, I'll have to be getting on or I'll miss my Woolton eggs. *And* I've got to get some shoes for Emma. Five coupons for a pair of gym shoes. Wicked, isn't it?'

'Wicked! Well, bye-bye.'

'Ta-ta, I'll be seeing you, Ducks. Give my love to your sister. How is she these days?'

'Never been the same since that blitzing, but she's a NAAFI now.'

'I'd forgot she was blitzed.'

'Oh! ever so long ago – three times altogether – the last was a land-mine. Luckily they was all out at the time. They'd evacuated the kiddies at the beginning, and it was her night on for fire-watching at the office. Her husband (he's a key man, you know) was out on ARP. Yes, they was lucky all right, but the house got it properly: the demolition squad said they'd never seen such a sight. Well, I must go.'

Miss Ranskill put a hand to her aching head. Had the language changed or had she forgotten words? Was she, perhaps, a trifle mad? Rip Van Winkle could scarcely have felt more puzzled than she did. What had happened in her absence that fantastic horrors could be described so casually? Even the language was secret from her, full of strange words and alphabetical sequences.

She emerged from her cell now. She must hurry or the coffee would be cold.

As she moved towards the outer door the attendant stared at her – a strangely hostile stare. How stupid! she had forgotten to tip her. She fumbled for and found two pennies among the change in her coat pocket.

'Good morning,' said Miss Ranskill, 'and thank you.'

'I'll take that roll of paper too, *if* you please,' said the attendant, and there was a bullying note in her voice.

Miss Ranskill became aware that she was clutching the roll of paper she had noticed in the water-closet.

'Oh!' she gasped, 'I am so sorry. I never noticed I'd taken it.'

The attendant pursed her lips obstinately, clattered the pennies on to a tray and held out her hand.

'I must explain,' pursued Miss Ranskill. 'You see on the – I mean where I was before I came here we hadn't any paper for fire-lighting, and I suppose when I saw so much –'

'There'd not be much for salvage if everyone went on like that. Toilet-paper for fire-lighting, indeed!'

'It was, was absentmindedness. If you had been on a desert island –'

Here the roll slipped from Miss Ranskill's fingers and trundled away across the floor under the basin, trailing a long streamer of paper after it.

'There now!' shrilled the attendant. 'We can't use that after it's been sopping up all the slop from the wash-basins. If I did my duty I'd report to the Manageress.'

'I am more than willing to pay for it, and more than willing to explain to the Manageress.'

Then the looking-glass above the basins humiliated Miss Ranskill again, and she gave a sad little gulp.

'You'll see her right enough if you come here again. The public conveniences in the town are meant for people like you.'

Shame took further possession of Miss Ranskill as she hurried down the stairs. Some day, of course, she would be able to laugh about this, but not this morning, not if she were really looking as the mirror on the stairs told her.

It seemed an hour since she had left the downstairs room.

Supposing the attendant reported her to the Manageress, and supposing, while having coffee, she was to be accused of petty pilfering?

'In mixed company, too,' thought Miss Ranskill. 'In Naval company "to the Derogation of God's Honour and the

Corruption of Good Manners."' For the first time that morning a smile cracked the parched skin of her lips.

It would be better to be accused of stealing a ring – more dignified and not nearly so humiliating.

A figure in blue uniform was standing with his back to a table by the door. Beside him, slick from ash-blonde head to silky ankles was the owner of the sapphire ring. Her voice was raised.

'Well, from your description, it *must* have been your girl friend I met when I was powdering my nose. Darling, I *do* think you're marvellous! You ought to get a GM for being seen alive with her. She's positively *septic*.'

Miss Ranskill tiptoed down the last two stairs and hurried out into the street. Tomorrow she would write a note to the ship, and make some excuse for not accepting the kind invitation to coffee.

CHAPTER SIX

I

It was better outside in the pale wavering sunlight. The wind, blowing inland, carried gallantry with it, ruffled the puddles to a mackerel shimmering, snatched the scents of a flower-shop at the corner and made Miss Ranskill the swift present of them.

She raised her head. The world would be better in half an hour, for she would be wearing silk against her skin and her shoes would fit. The tautness of her stockings would make her a woman again and her story might take on more dignity if she wore a new dress.

A flash of red in a draper's window caught her eye and she stopped to look. The sight of a jersey-suit in soft vermilion made her realise how much she had missed all the red shades of the world and how tired she was of blue and grey. But she must not begin with the frock – that must be kept to the end like the cherry on the cake. First of all she would buy some of the little trappings of civilisation.

She went into the shop and hurried towards the haberdash-ery counter where she bought a comb, a pair of nail-scissors and a tube of face-cream. Then she asked for hair-grips.

'Sorry, we've not seen one for months,' said the queenly girl who reigned behind the counter.

'Never mind, I'll get them somewhere else.'

'You'll be lucky if you do. They've all gone to tanks.'

'Tanks?'

'Tanks or Bevin or Beaverbrook, I never know which.'

'*Tanks* or *Bevin and Beaverbrooks*,' repeated Miss Ranskill carefully. 'Thank you so much, I'll try them.'

'It's a good thing someone can make a joke of it,' giggled the girl. 'You wouldn't believe how tired we get saying "No" all the time.'

A frown worried Miss Ranskill's forehead. It was all most puzzling. Still, it was better to make a fluke joke in an unknown language than be suspected of trying to steal rings or toilet-paper.

And now her great moment had come. She set foot on a stairway that led, so instinct told her, to a department where underclothes were ranged in shimmers of pink and peach and white and blue and yellow, and to another department where dresses for morning and afternoon hung shoulder to shoulder and hem to hem. Nine pounds fourteen shillings and four-pence should go far enough if she economised over shoes: a pair of cheap canvas ones would be good enough for a day or two.

A plan formed in her mind as she went slowly up the stairs, slowly because she was savouring the adventure to come. As a child she had always been reluctant to open her eyes when she was awake on Christmas morning: it had been enough to know that the stocking was there bulging in shapelessness and

70

full (just for those moments) of magic, singing loudly as the stars of the morning and all the Herald Angels.

Yes, she had a plan – she must find a friend and tell the truth, though not all of it, because she could not speak of the Island without thinking of the Carpenter. She dreaded the question, 'Were you all alone there?' She must possess herself, before she could allow the life they had shared to be touched by the new life she was to live.

She shook her head and the gesture set two cockatoo-like plumes free from her turban. Once again she saw herself in a mirror at the turn of a staircase, but the horror had passed. Better to be a Cinderella and be a Cinderella *properly* if one was to enjoy metamorphosis *thoroughly* than to be a fiddle-faddler in the brown satin rags of pantomime.

Now for the Fairy Godmother. Miss Ranskill hurried up the second flight of stairs.

When she reached the top of it, a woman in a black frock made an undulating movement towards her.

'Can I help you –' (the word 'Madam' quivered her lips, thought better of it, and retired).

'Yes, I think you can, if you will?'

For the eyes of the interrogator were kind and her mouth was finely and firmly flexed.

'I think you can. I want everything new. I've been wearing these clothes for four years, and now –'

'Yes, Madam, I know how it is. In war-time one hangs on to one's oldest clothes, but the time comes when –'

'Yes, I know, but it isn't because of the war exactly. Never mind that. You're a woman and I'm a woman. You can see the clothes I'm wearing, and my under ones are worse. I want to start underneath. I want –'

Here Miss Ranskill became aware of the comb, the scissors and tube of face-cream clutched in her right hand. Assurance left her.

'I – I quite forgot about these being wrapped up.'

'I know, Madam, it *is* awkward. Only the other day a customer bought a really lovely suede coat. In it had to go, on top of the herrings in her shopping basket, though the newspaper was sodden already. Still, I suppose we ought to be thankful to get any fish at all.'

'Should we?'

Memories of fish invaded the shop, of fish in every stage, fish with a nauseating lining that must be removed, fish half-dried by sun and going rotten in rain, greedy fish that gulped down the hooks whittled by patient labour, birds that tasted so heartily of fish that every fish, for weeks after, tasted so of sea-bird that the palate revolted, fish in the boat – soused and sodden by the sea.

'When one thinks of the risks –'

There was reproof in the voice and Miss Ranskill took her hint.

'Yes, of course.'

'You were saying, Madam?'

'I wondered if it would be possible to buy some under-clothes and put them on, and then choose a frock and some stockings?'

'Certainly. If you would care to look at the frocks and select some to try on. I can take you to the underwear department.'

'And stockings?'

'Stockings are on the ground floor, Madam. Would you like to buy them first?'

'Couldn't you possibly have a pair sent up? I don't want to go downstairs again until I'm looking – looking different.'

'I'll see what I can do, Madam, but we are very under-staffed, you know. Besides, there are still a good many shades to choose from.'

'It would be kind,' pleaded Miss Ranskill. 'I only want one fawn-coloured pair, either in a thickish silk (*not* artificial), or fine lisle thread. Perhaps I'd better have lisle.'

Memory of the nine pounds, fourteen shillings and four-pence made it seem wiser not to buy silk.

'There may be a few *cotton* pairs left.'

'I only want one pair.'

'No real silk, of course, and certainly no lisle.'

Miss Ranskill had heard the same tone of voice in her nursery days – 'Not jam *and* cake, Miss Nona: the very idea!' As she had done then, so she argued now.

'Why not?'

'Well, there's a war on.'

'A what?'

'A war, Madam. Naturally it is difficult to get *exceptional* articles.'

Shocked reproof could not have been greater if Miss Ranskill had demanded the martial cloak of Sir John Moore on a charger.

Apology seemed necessary, and was made.

'I'm sorry. I forgot.'

This time raised eyebrows and tightened lips conveyed more sorrow than anger, but more contempt than both.

'You see, I haven't read a newspaper for over three years.'

She had made everything worse than ever now – outcast herself completely.

'Or listened to the wireless except just once the other day.'

'Really, Madam. Of course, I know some people make a point of only reading escapist literature. I couldn't bear not to get the news myself, though.'

There was no chance of making friends now: an icy politeness prevailed between them as between a tea-party hostess and the guest who has made unwise comment on some relation or friend.

Miss Ranskill was led to a counter where she chose two garments in artificial silk whose sheen seemed to fade as she looked at them. Then she asked the price of the jersey-suit she had seen in the window, heard it was too expensive, chose another in meek fawn and accepted the assistant's choice of a paler toned sweater.

'Utility garments, Madam, and really it is more practical to select neutral colours when one has to wear clothes for such a very long time.'

'I shall buy the red suit tomorrow and the green one next day,' said Miss Ranskill thoughtfully, and was quite unaware she had spoken aloud.

Raised eyebrows answered her and the arrival of a girl with stockings ended the pause that followed.

Two minutes later, Miss Ranskill, who had arranged to

pay her own reluctant assistant 'for everything at the end', was alone in a mirrored cubicle.

Shan't know ourselves, shall we, Miss Ranskill, when we've got ourselves all togged up again. I'll buy a Sunday-go-to-meeting suit and wear it for a month of Sundays, and when I see you coming along I'll say to myself, 'Who's this fine lady? I'll bet she's never done a stroke of work in all her born days. Why, it's Miss Ranskill, who'd ever have thought it.' We'll smarten ourselves up one day, never you fear.

She had forgotten her figure was so good, forgotten the subtle curving and the flatness where flatness should be that now made cheap wool sliding over silkiness look expensive. She fitted the clothes: they were not cajoled into fitting her. The humble colour of the jersey exalted the jackdaw blue of her eyes and paid compliment to the sunbleached streaks of her hair. *That* was shaggy and ragged, but the comb did something to help and the vanishing cream toned down the snatches of red where the sun had caught her cheek-bones.

'But gloves, I think, as well as the canvas shoes,' decided Miss Ranskill as she doubled up her fingers.

She walked over to the window and looked down into the street. The people there were her own people, she could walk among them now inconspicuously: she had a place in the world again.

For a moment she wondered whether to leave the old clothes to be put in a shop dustbin, but as she stepped back she trod on the coat and her footfall released a salty, sandy, seaweedy odour. She would keep them for so long as the island tang lingered about them.

Just then there was a tap on the door and the assistant came into the cubicle.

'I wondered how you were getting on, Madam?'

'I'll take everything, please.'

Miss Ranskill picked up her old jacket and took the nine pound notes, some shillings and coppers from a pocket.

'I'll wear them now if you will be so kind as to have these clothes made up into a parcel for me.'

'Suit six-and-a-half, jersey a guinea, vest five-and-eleven, knickers five-and-eleven: that's eight pounds three shillings and fourpence, please Madam.'

So there would be just enough left for the canvas shoes, a very cheap pair of gloves, perhaps, and carpentering tools.

'Thank you, Madam, and –'

'Could you have these clothes parcelled up while I go to the shoe department? I'll call back for them.'

'I'm afraid I can't do that, Madam.'

Why in the world not? Miss Ranskill racked her brain and remembered the word 'understaffed'.

'Then if you'll let me have some paper and string I'll make up the parcel myself.'

'I'm sorry, but I'm no more allowed to do that than to wrap up the new clothes for you.'

'Why?' began Miss Ranskill, but as the eyebrows started their perilous raising, she said, 'It doesn't matter, I'll go to the shoe department and then come back.'

'Very good, Madam. Let me see now, eighteen, and then four for the jersey and three for the vest and three for the knickers – that's –'

'But I've paid you, you've got the money in your hand.'

'That will be thirty coupons.'

'Thirty what?'

'If you'll give me your book, Madam.'

'But I don't want you to book them: I've just paid you.'

Exasperation raised Miss Ranskill's voice and made the assistant's take on a patient level tone.

'Will you give me your clothes ration book, Madam, so that I can cut out the coupons, please.'

'I don't know what you mean?'

'You have your clothes ration book, Madam?'

YOU HAVE YOUR INDIA-RUBBER, NONA, YOUR MAPPING-PEN, YOUR ROUGH NOTE-BOOK AND YOUR PENCILS. THEY WERE ALL ISSUED TO YOU AT THE BEGINNING OF THE TERM. WHERE ARE THEY NOW?

'Clothes ration book?' repeated Miss Ranskill.

'Yes, Madam.'

'But I haven't –'

'I'm afraid if you haven't any coupons left, we can't accept your order. The new ration books do not come into use until next month, but if you have any coupons in the old ration book issued to you last June –'

'Last June I wasn't even being *Swiss Family Robinson*. I was being *Robinson Crusoe* at least *practically*.'

Blankness answered the outburst.

'I don't want to be stupid,' pleaded Miss Ranskill. 'But I simply don't understand. If you *could* explain –'

'Haven't you got a clothes ration book, Madam?'

'No, and no clothes except the ones I stood up in, and –'

'Then I'm afraid we can't serve you until you can find it. We can keep the new clothes if you would care to post the coupons.'

'You mean –' Miss Ranskill glanced at the new Miss Ranskill in the mirror and then looked down at the old Miss Ranskill's clothes lying on the floor beside the Midshipman's shoes and stockings. 'You mean that unless I can give you these coupons or whatever they are, you can't sell me the clothes I'm wearing?'

'I'm afraid not, Madam.'

'Not even if I give you the address of the friends I'm going to stay with – Doctor and Mrs Mallison, Hillrise, Newton Road?'

'I can make a note of the address, but –'

'It won't help?'

'No, Madam. I'm sorry, but we can't make exceptions.'

'Exceptions!' Miss Ranskill laughed, as she took off the coat of the new jersey-suit that had turned her into a woman again.

'I haven't got *anything*. . . . I've only just arrived in England – only this morning after three years. I didn't mean to say so because – well, there are reasons. I've been trying to learn the language, but it means nothing to me: it all sounds mad.' Off came the skirt. 'I may seem stupid to you: you may seem obstinate to me, but can't we try to understand each other? I have tried . . .' Off came the jumper. . . . 'I'm a foreigner here and I thought I was coming home. Nobody can explain or tell me anything. That seems to be the trouble with the world: nobody can tell anyone anything. I've been isolated on an island but the isolation's worse on this island just because

78

one can't speak the new language properly; it's *changed* so since last I was here.'

The stockings were off by now.

'If you'll wait just a moment, Madam, I'll go to the manager and see if he can help you.'

Miss Ranskill hardly heard the interpolation.

'Listen,' she said. 'You're a woman and I'm a woman. If you came to me – if your brother was dead and if you had had to bury him, scrabbling with a paddle in the sands and then with your hands till they were raw, I –'

'My brother *is* dead, Madam; there was nothing left to bury. If you'll excuse me for a moment.'

The door clicked behind the assistant and Miss Ranskill was left alone with the mirror's reflection of her humble self.

The dead keep us busy all right, almost as if they knew what was good for us. Wouldn't do for those that's left behind if they packed up their trunks before going and then set out by train to Heaven.

This then, this England, was to be her desert island, a place where the dead left without aforethought and where there was no reckoning but hardness, where there was no solitude for mourning, where one was prisoned (if one was a shop assistant) alone in a crowd, and the servant of women yattering for new clothes and nagging for string and brown paper. In comparison, she, on her island, had been a lotus – no, a fish-eater living with loving kindness and dying her own little death with, at any rate, no interruption to be borne from people without.

Miss Ranskill stripped the artificial silk from her body and dragged herself into the clothes she had worn before.

The Cinderella dream was a niggling fancy now.

She opened the door of the cubicle and tiptoed across the carpet.

II

'No, Madam, I'm afraid they haven't come in yet: we expect them at any moment, though.'

'But you told me you were certain they'd be in this week.'

'Well, that's what we thought. We were promised them. We didn't get our full quota last month. Everything's getting more difficult.'

Another assistant was talking to another customer as Miss Ranskill, her hair looking more than ever like the plumes of a demented cockatoo, tiptoed out of the cubicle.

A dozen similar little choruses reached her ears, but made no further penetration, as she made her furtive way out of the shop.

'Oh no, Madam, no ribbed stockings at all.'

'Nothing fully fashioned at all.'

'We shan't have any more in when the stock is exhausted.'

'I should advise you to take them while you can get them, Madam, I hear they're to be couponed soon.'

'These are slightly substandard, but they are pre-war stock.'

'Quite unobtainable, Madam, I'm sorry.'

'Well, it's a case of new covers for the chairs or new vests for me.'

'Molly's going to stain her legs with walnut juice in the autumn and go without stockings all the winter.'

'Pam's made herself some heavenly frocks out of dust-sheets.'

'I'm making shirts out of dusters.'

'I can't think how Fay always manages to look like a hundred pounds. Black Market, I suppose.'

'Not Black *Market*, my poppet – black-out material.'

'Fay?'

'No, silly, but she makes Edward's pyjamas out of curtain stuff and pinches his coupons.'

It was not until Miss Ranskill had left the shop, turned down a side-street and stepped into a puddle that she realised she had forgotten to put on the Midshipman's shoes. She might not have noticed then if she had not been wearing the stockings: her feet were hardened to sharper things than pavements, but were not yet used to squelching wool. She pictured the shoes lying toe to toe on the carpet of the little cubicle. It was not worth while going back for them: nothing was worth that. After all, the addition of a pair of shoes wouldn't make much difference to her scarecrow appearance, and walking was easier without them. Presently she would take off the stockings too.

III

The Midshipman's shoes were not in the cubicle: one was on the desk of Mr P M Ebbutt, Manager of Messrs Dimmet and Togg, and the other was in Mr Ebbutt's pudgy hand.

'Service pattern,' he said. 'No toe-cap, you see. Supplied by Gieves. Must have belonged to a Naval officer.' He adjusted his pince-nez and gave a petulant tug at the laces. 'I can't think why you let the woman go, Miss Mottram.'

'I did come up to see you, the moment I suspected anything, Mr Ebbutt, but you were telephoning.'

'Yes, well, but if you'd only use initiative. Pretty fools we'll look if we've let a spy slip through our fingers. It won't do the shop any good, I can tell you that, Miss Mottram.'

'I'm very sorry, Mr Ebbutt.'

'Well, it can't be helped. I suppose we've done all we can in letting the police know. They'll be round any minute, I suppose. Let's get the points clear. Couldn't speak English, you say?'

'She spoke it all right, but she said she didn't, and she said she was a foreigner.'

'Gimme my pencil, will you? Now then –' The gold pencil travelled slowly across the paper. 'Said she was a foreigner, hadn't read a newspaper for years. . . . Hadn't got a ration book: that's pretty damning, you know. Wanted complete change of clothes – looks as though she wanted to cover her tracks, doesn't it? . . . Said nobody would tell her anything . . . evidently she'd been nosing round. . . . I hope you didn't tell her anything, Miss Mottram?'

There was numbing silence for a moment.

'No, Mr Ebbutt, I did not.'

And now Miss Mottram looked Mr Ebbutt full in the stomach, a habit which, so she had discovered, always disconcerted him. One can turn one's face away from an unflattering stare: it is not so easy to turn away a stomach, especially so high a one as Mr Ebbutt's.

'You can send Miss Smith to me now. I'll want her to take down some notes. I'll probably want you when the police come. Meanwhile you'd better trot round the shop once more and see if anyone did notice this woman go out. So busy chattering, all of you, that you never see a thing.'

Miss Mottram removed her elegant person in an undulatory way *not* indicative of trotting, and Mr Ebbutt let his stomach rise again.

At the door she turned.

'I did give one piece of information, Mr Ebbutt.'

'Yes?'

'I don't think it matters, but as you *asked* –'

'Yes, what was it?'

'I told the customer that because of the war,' – there was a long deliberate pause – 'that because of the war we hadn't any silk stockings in stock!'

Then Miss Mottram, happy in the knowledge that in another week she would be making munitions, retired with dignity from the manager's office.

IV

In the shop, gossip fluttered like a washing-day.

Girls behind counters became human beings, suddenly changed from creatures that (so they believed the customers thought) stopped short just below the waist-line or wherever the edge of the counter chopped them.

'Mr Ebbutt's caught a spy – a German one – couldn't speak a word of English and she came to buy a disguise.'

'Who told you?'

'Miss Smith told Doris.'

Girls in cashiers' cubby-holes were livened by the tale.

'Mr Ebbutt's caught a spy – a woman dressed as a man: she left a pair of men's shoes behind her.'

'We've had a spy in here – a woman dressed as a Naval officer.'

'I say! Have you heard the latest? Mr Ebbutt's caught a spy – a German Naval officer dressed as a woman.'

'Old Ebbutt's a spy. The police have just been, and a plain-clothes man too.'

'Old man Ebbutt's arrested for black marketing and trading with the enemy. They've found out he's been selling naval uniforms to German spies, the old beast!'

'You're telling me! I always knew he was a nasty bit of work.'

V

Meanwhile, Miss Ranskill was nearing disgrace again. Hunger, though not so great as to urge her into the publicity of a restaurant, suggested a picnic lunch, and she planned the menu in her mind – rolls and a carton of cheese, a packet of sweet biscuits, a slab of chocolate, a banana and two or three Jaffa oranges to quench her thirst.

She chose a little shop in one of the poorer streets – a shop where the stock was shelved behind the counter and blacking brushes kept company with packets of cereals – almost a village shop. Here might be friendliness, and here seemed to be the beginning of friendship as the owner, in answer to the jangle of a bell behind the door, hurried out of the back room and smiled a gappy smile.

'Yes, dear?'

The rolls, rather dusty-looking, were plumped down on to the counter at once.

'We've no cartons of cheese though, only Woolton.'

Miss Ranskill nodded, not wishing to give herself away.

'How much do you want?'

'Oh! just enough for lunch.'

'Better have the three ounces while you're about it, then I shan't have to mess up your book.'

A length of greasy string did its work of cutting through a piece of cheese.

'Anything else, dear?'

'A packet of biscuits, digestive if you have them, and a half pound packet of plain chocolate, and have you any really ripe bananas?'

''*Ave* I any really ripe bananas?'

Plump red hands were placed on ploppy hips, and their owner laughed flatly.

''Ave I any bananas? Think I'm Lady Woolton, do you? Never mind, I likes a yumourist. No, Ducks –' the wheezy voice broke into song –

Yes, we 'ave no bananas,
We 'ave no bananas today!

'Funny thing, when you and I was singing that song in the old days we never knew how true it'd be, did we?'

Miss Ranskill, to whom the song had always been a puzzle, smiled forcedly.

It would, she felt, be better to say no more about bananas: evidently in this strange new world they were a dangerous and difficult topic. But the owner of the shop, after stabbing home a loose hair-pin, 'Worth its weight, *that* is!', continued:

'Funny thing about bananas, I mean the things they will carry over and the things they won't. Meself, I think it's a mistake *and* hard on the kiddies. Take my young Albert now – he's never seen a banana: it don't seem natural to think of a kiddy growing up and not seein' a banana. Give us a few bananas and not so much tinned fish, what do you say?'

'No tinned fish,' Miss Ranskill agreed from her heart – 'No fish at all.'

'That's what I say.' A grin, showing a complete *broderie anglaise* of gaps, followed the statement.

Miss Ranskill, emboldened by her puzzling success as a humourist and thankful for friendliness of any sort, unbridled her tongue.

'I'll have oranges instead of bananas – Jaffas, if you've got them.'

'Is your kiddy sick?'

Miss Ranskill heard the words clearly but they made no sense. For a mad moment she believed the question to be part of a music-hall song, and expected the woman to change voice again.

'Is your kiddy sick? I'm only asking because we're short this month. I don't want any of the kiddies to go short if I can help it, but if your kiddy's sick, poor little mite –'

Such a yearning of mother-love was in the voice, such jellying of human flesh shook the vast shoulders that Miss Ranskill gave reassurance.

'It isn't sick. I mean I haven't got a – a kiddy. I was only going to have a picnic lunch. I wanted the oranges for myself.'

'*Well!*'

Not, 'Well, fancy a great girl like you, Miss Nona!' but the tone implied it.

'Only instead of lemonade,' explained Miss Ranskill. 'But it doesn't matter a bit.'

'I've only been sparing the oranges to *sick* kiddies till we see how they go round. Anything else I can get you?'

'No, thank you.'

'Let's see now, I'll want your personal ration book for the chocolate and the other for the cheese and biscuits.'

A hand was held out in anticipation.

'Ta?'

'I haven't got –' began Miss Ranskill, and then scenting confusion, said, 'I haven't brought any books, I'm afraid.'

'Well, there now, after I've cut the cheese! It'll only go stale. We've little enough as it is, without letting that go stale.'

'I'd pay for it willingly.'

'Pay? You could pay for Buckingham Palace, maybe, but payin' won't keep cheese fresh once it's cut. Could you fetch your ration book and I'll keep the stuff till you come back?'

'I'm afraid I can't. It's – you see, I came a very long way.'

'We'll have to eat the cheese ourselves, I suppose, as our ration. You'll just take the rolls then?'

'Could I,' said Miss Ranskill, very humbly and nervously, 'could I buy something to put on them instead of cheese?'

'Fish paste?'

'No,' Miss Ranskill checked a shudder. 'Not *fish*. Marmalade or jam would do.'

'That's points again.'

'Points! Jam.'

'Jam's on points.'

'Oh!' Miss Ranskill changed a conversation that was, to her anyway, becoming absolutely idiotic. 'Never mind, I'll have them as they are.'

'You could have turkey-and-tongue paste if you like.'

So, with the rolls in one pocket and a small pot of turkey-and-tongue paste in the other, Miss Ranskill went down to the beach. There with her back against a boat, and her toes scuffling sand again, she felt more at home than she had done for weeks, even though the barricading of barbed wire behind her annoyed her by its ugliness.

There was the sea that she had alternately loved and hated. There were the waves, up to their old tricks again, frittering themselves against the rocks, teasing the seaweed, rolling and shuffling the pebbles to a shushing rhythm. There were the gulls mewing, mocking, and crying their plaints.

'It will take a lot of getting used to,' thought Miss Ranskill, referring to the new world.

She choked down the dry roll and the paste she had spread using a piece of cuttle-fish, then closed her eyes against the sun's brightness, and dozed for a little.

Presently she awoke with a jerk, startled from a dream of

the island by a sound only half familiar – the sound of crying. But it was not the crying of a gull. Sunshine dazzled her eyes so that at first she saw only a dizziness of gold shot with blue and a small figure standing near her.

A child on the island – a small living jetsam?

She was on her feet before she remembered, but memory did not check her feet. Here, at last, in her unwelcoming country, was something in distress – something that needed her.

The little boy was sandy and shabby – almost as shabby as she was. There was too big a gap between his shorts and his scarred knobbly knees. His jersey was hunched up pathetically under one ear. Tears poured down his face and he was licking them up as fast as they ran.

'What is it?' asked Miss Ranskill. 'Oh! what is it?'

'I've lost my knife, my new knife and it matters.'

'Of *course* it matters.' Didn't she know how much it mattered? Didn't she know what the loss of a knife might mean?

She was on her knees by now and the conviction in her voice sent his head bumping into her shoulder. One cold sea-wet hand found her own, the other one wriggled up between his face and her shoulder-hollow to knuckle the tears away.

'How many blades?' she whispered.

'Two and only one broke'; his voice was still choking. 'It was give me by a carpenter.'

'I shared a knife with a carpenter once, and then he – he went away and I lost my knife too.'

The head came up now, and only the rubbed lashes and a streak on each cheek showed where the tears had been.

'Did you find it?' asked the boy.

Miss Ranskill shook her head. It was queer that she could speak of the Carpenter to this rumple-headed brat.

'You can't by the sea.'

He scuffled a bare foot in the sand, took a few steps and looked about vaguely.

''Tisn't here,' he said. 'Did you lose yours here?'

'No.'

'How many blades had it?'

'Only one.'

'Mine was better.' The little-boy swagger was returning. 'Mine had two and only the little 'un broke.'

'Tell you what,' said Miss Ranskill, and the thought raised her voice to excitement and tossed her head for her. 'Tell you what –' But another thought checked her.

'What?'

'I'll tell you if you'll tell me something.'

The boy hunched up his shoulders, doubled his fists and pushed them into the pockets of his shorts.

The attitude suggested he had been had that way before and preferred to keep himself to himself.

'Dunno,' he muttered.

'Try then. Can you buy knives without ration books or anything?'

Suspicion lightened and interest increased.

''Course you can. Anyone knows that!'

'You're sure? Tell me what does need ration books?'

'Cheese, butter, sweets, bacon, soap –'

The boy's hands were out of his pockets and he was checking off the items on his fingers.

Miss Ranskill listened and tried to memorise the list. He seemed to her to be a very well-informed small boy indeed, a most superior war-child.

'Sugar, corn-flakes and marge. Oh! and oranges and meat and tinned stuff and jam. Not knives.'

'How do you know?'

'I go shoppin' for Mum. What do you want to know for?'

'Because if you'd like to, and if you know a shop, we could go and buy new knives now – one for me and one for you.'

'Coo!'

He knew a shop, of course. 'Mr Jackson's just round the corner past the quay.'

Miss Ranskill followed him. She was bare-footed and bare-headed because she had taken off the woollen stockings, the scarf-turban and the suspenders, but quite unselfconscious. Beside the Naval officer and beside the girl with the ring she had looked a figure of fun. Now, hurrying after a bare-foot boy through the poorer quarters of the town she was only a shabby woman with rather peculiar hair.

'Come on,' begged the boy as he scuttled round a corner. 'Here's Mr Jackson's.'

The little shop smelled of tar and rope, oil and new leather.

The sight of a single-bladed knife with a horn handle stabbed at Miss Ranskill's memory and her fingers curved their longing to hold it.

'Coo!' said the little boy. 'Look at that one there.'

The dream of every little boy lay there shining before his eyes – a many-bladed knife with a corkscrew, a thing for making holes in leather, and –

'A thing for taking stones out of horses' hooves!' he chanted. 'That's what that's for. That's what I want.'

'Do you meet many horses with stones in their hooves?'

'You might.'

'This is cheaper,' said Mr Jackson, who had noted Miss Ranskill's clothes. 'Quite good enough for a boy to lose.'

He fingered a two-bladed knife. The boy glanced at it for a moment. He was hunched up again now, shifting from foot to restless foot, waiting, hoping, terrified.

'You will?' said Mr Jackson, and he snapped the elastic that held the grander knife to its sheet.

Miss Ranskill paid and waited till her change was counted out before she put the knife into the boy's trembling hand.

'There you are,' she said, 'and there's half a crown to buy sugar for the horse when you've taken the stone out of his hoof.'

'Coo!'

'You'll have Lord Woolton after you,' warned Mr Jackson, 'talking like that.'

There was a scutter of bare feet on the floor and the boy was away.

Miss Ranskill went to the door and watched him running, knock-kneed, down the street. His heels flew out almost at right-angles. He jumped into a puddle and was splashed with a rainbow of spray.

'Well, I never!' said Mr Jackson as she turned into the shop again.

'No manners these days, have they? Not so much as a thank-you.'

'Knives are too important for thank-yous. Now I want one for myself, a horn-handled jack-knife, like the one there, only bigger.'

Miss Ranskill pointed to the knife she had first noticed.

'I think I've got one downstairs. I'll see, if you don't mind waiting. Beats me the manners of children nowadays, and the boy will have lost his knife tomorrow as like as not.'

'I hope not. Oh! I *do* hope not.'

Miss Ranskill answered as the man clattered his way down some stairs.

For to her the gift of the knife had been a symbol. She had thought of it as a talisman with power to save the boy from what she herself had suffered through the loss of a knife. She remembered the Carpenter's singing of the Lyke Wake Dirge –

This Aye neet, this aye neet,
  Ivery neet an' all,
Fire and sleet and candle-leet
  And Christ receive thy saul.

His whittling had kept tune.

If ever thou gavest hosen or shoon,
  Ivery neet an' all
Sit thee down and put them on
  And Christ take up thy saul.

We couldn't do much in the hosen or shoon line if a tramp was to come along now, could we, Miss Ranskill. I wouldn't want to do more

93

than give him a lend of the knife neither. By gum! though, when I get home I'll give a knife or two to some lads and learn 'em to use 'em. Where'd we be now if I'd not learned, eh, Miss Ranskill? Suppose I were a clerk?

So it was really the Carpenter's present that was jolting along in the little boy's pocket, and Miss Ranskill had begun to pay back part of her debt.

'What about this one?' Mr Jackson reappeared. 'Old stock that one is, you won't find steel like it today.'

Miss Ranskill bought it – a young knife, stiff in the hasp and shiny in the blade. It had no stories to tell, no nick to show where its life had nearly ended and no rust-bite on its nameplate. All the same it felt comforting to her hand, and she was satisfied, for this after all was what she had meant to buy first.

'Anything else?' asked Mr Jackson.

'Nails,' answered Miss Ranskill recklessly, 'three-inch and two-inch mostly and a hammer and a pair of pliers, a chisel, a spirit-level and a plane and an axe. . . .'

Here in this shop, at any rate, there seemed a chance of buying some possessions. She had not been allowed to buy what she wanted in other shops, but there would be a certain solace in owning some of the things that had been so needed by her and the Carpenter. She could not have explained, even to herself, how she could provide for the past by laying in stores for the present, but the idea persisted in her mind.

A check came again, this time from the lips of Mr Jackson. It seemed that before buying certain tools he must be certain she was engaged on necessary work. There was danger, he explained, that private customers might buy tools for frivolous purposes.

'A plane for smoothing one's cheeks, I suppose,' murmured Miss Ranskill, 'or an axe for chopping embroidery cotton! Is boat-building frivolous work?'

'Oh! if you're engaged on boat-building –'

'I've finished my boat, but I might want to make something else,' said Miss Ranskill, in an attempt to be honest, though the hammer, the chisel, the plane, the spirit-level and the axe were more desired by her than dulcimer, harp, sackbut, psaltery or any lovelier-sounding implement.

'Well, if you women aren't wonderful!' said Mr Jackson admiringly, as he began to collect the tools.

Presently she slipped the knife into her pocket, then collected her armful of ringing steel and polished wood and walked out into the street.

A clock told her it was quarter-past four and a crawling taxi reminded her that the new luggage was heavy.

'Hillrise, Newton Road, please,' said Miss Ranskill.

She felt, as she settled herself in the corner and laid the axe across her knees, that everything was going to be perfectly all right now. Her bare toes twitched against steel and the new knife satisfied her hand.

CHAPTER SEVEN

I

And now Miss Ranskill stood outside a prim house. Facing her was a most respectable-looking door and to her right was a trim patch of garden, so precise and squared, edged and tidied that she was astonished to see a row of lettuces in the narrow border beneath the window, where she was quite certain there should be lobelias. In front of the lettuces was a fringe of parsley. Then came a gravel path and another parsley-edged bed full of rows of neatly earthed-up potatoes.

'Most odd,' thought Miss Ranskill, who knew that Marjorie's idea of a garden must surely be beds as precise as a page out of Euclid, set in smooth grass.

The door was opened by a bouncing slattern, who glanced at the visitor, bounced back, shouted, 'We don't want anythink todiy,' and, with a slam that left the knocker bumping, left Miss Ranskill alone to stare at green paint.

The slattern seemed as remote from Marjorie as from the ordered garden, and, just for a moment, Miss Ranskill wondered if she had come to the wrong house. Memory of a brass plate on the gate told her she had not. She set hand to the bell again, but before she could pull it the door opened and three people came out.

Two of them carried buckets of water and the third (could she be Marjorie?) an implement that reminded Miss Ranskill of a garden hose *and* a motor pump.

'Now remember,' she was saying. (Yes, it was Marjorie: there was no mistaking the conscientious prefectorial face under the tin helmet.) 'Now remember the bomb's fallen right through the greenhouse roof. Take your stations, everyone.'

'Marjorie!' exclaimed Miss Ranskill, but the sound of her voice was overpowered by the clatter of bucket-handles.

'Don't pump till I say,' commanded Marjorie. 'It's an incendiary bomb – delayed action. I'm Number One. You're Two, Miss Sprink, and Miss Jebb's Three.'

Miss Ranskill wondered if she ought to do anything, and if so, what, but before she could open her mouth again, Marjorie pushed past her and sprinted, with much flapping of blue trousers, down the path between the parsley and potatoes. Then she dropped to her knees and began to crawl on all fours towards a greenhouse by the far hedge. A trail of narrow grey piping followed her. Miss Sprink or Miss Jebb plonked the pump into one bucket. Miss Jebb or Miss Sprink, in the attitude but not the garments of a Hebe, stood beside her with the other bucket poised.

If there were a bomb, it must be a very well-behaved one, decided Miss Ranskill. Then, remembering Marjorie's remark about delayed action, she set down her armful of tools and put her fingers in her ears. It was an ignominious gesture, but what could she do?

Had she really come home to watch, like a fiddling Nero, while her old friend crawled serenely to death, was she witnessing some charade or had she gone mad?

Marjorie butted the greenhouse door with her head, Miss Sprink or Miss Jebb pumped furiously and Miss Jebb or Miss Sprink shifted the spare bucket from one hand to another. Both of them had set, stern faces.

Miss Ranskill's mind slid back to a day years ago when she, motoring from Dorset, had seen the car in front of her slew across the road, climb a steep bank, overturn and poise quiveringly, while a whole family tumbled down into the road. The accident had not seemed real at the time: it had been only a series of pictures seen at a cinema. She had watched with more interest than horror. So she watched now. But then her hands and feet had responded automatically as she had pulled up her own car.

She removed her fingers from her ears and took a few uncertain steps towards the women by the buckets.

So might a young recruit feel, staring assishly at the hand-grenade dropped by the instructor, wondering if it was a dud or not – if he'd only make a fool of himself by chucking it out of the trench – or not. The soldier would soon know. . . .

Miss Ranskill, also worried by a trial in etiquette, was to know quite soon.

Only Marjorie's heels were visible. The pump squeaked, the bucket jangled. Were the almost domestic sounds of this strange new England to be overmastered by a crashing explosion? Was Marjorie –?

'There was a head laying by the pavement – clean cut off by the flying glass!'

Where had she heard that? Today, of course, since she came home. And she, instead of Marjorie who had a husband and two children, should be facing death.

The slam of a gate made her jump. A woman with a baby in her arms was walking up the garden path – a fresh-faced rather pretty young woman, unaware of danger. Here was Miss Ranskill's job. She ran down the path.

'You'd better go back!' she gasped. 'There's a bomb in the greenhouse.'

'Bother!' said the stranger, stooping down to pick up a woollen bootee. The ejaculation might have referred to the bomb or the bootee. 'I forgot they generally have one of these incendiary bomb things on Thursdays. I'll wait till it's over.'

She plumped herself down under the hedge that divided the garden from its neighbour and began to wriggle the baby's foot into her bootee.

The bland face of the infant urged Miss Ranskill to protest.

'Is it safe to sit there?'

'I always do.' The young woman patted the grass bank and then looked at her palm. 'It's not so damp as all that!'

As well interrupt a coronation to ask if the King's crown were real, as question this young woman about the liveliness of bombs.

'If that's how they all behave, it's how I'll have to behave,' thought Miss Ranskill, trying to affect nonchalance, as she strolled towards the porch where her tools lay scattered.

Now Marjorie, erect once more, rather flushed and with a red mark under her chin where the strap of the helmet had bitten in, was shouting at the bucket-party.

'I said last time not to stop pumping *till* I said. If it had been a real bomb we'd have been sunk. Jebb, your tunic isn't buttoned properly. Sprink, your shoe-lace is untied. You might have tripped and upset the bucket: then where'd we have been if it had been a real bomb?'

No, there was no mistaking Marjorie, the prefect, and Miss Ranskill was thankful she had made no display of her bewilderment.

Miss Jebb jerked a violent salute, and must have hurt her knuckles on the edge of her helmet. Miss Sprink's salute was elegant and nonchalant. Marjorie's hand went up smartly and descended without hindrance.

'Dismiss!' she shouted, so fiercely that Miss Ranskill dropped the spirit-level.

Marjorie came striding down the path and then paused to dust the gravel from her knees.

'Marjorie!' said Miss Ranskill, 'Marjorie.'

But her old school-friend addressed Miss Jebb.

'They've been pinching the sand again. How *are* we to win the war if people keep on pinching the ARP sand for their canary cages?'

'Do you think they're Fifth Columnists?' Miss Jebb raised a face so anxious and birdlike that Miss Ranskill thought of a sparrow in a halo.

'Everyone who gives ARP sand to canaries is a Fifth Columnist in a way.'

'Marjorie!' Miss Ranskill raised her voice determinedly, for she had not come to England to listen to chat about sparrows or references to the fifth of the Seven Pillars of Wisdom, if they were what Marjorie was talking about. 'Don't you remember me?'

Marjorie furrowed her forehead and looked her old friend up and down.

'Are you the new salvage person?' she asked, and not without reason, so Miss Jebb's tremulous smile informed the visitor.

'I'm Nona Ranskill. St Catherine's, you know. I rang up this morning and your husband –'

A crashing slap on the shoulder-blades jerked the sentence to an end.

'Nona, old thing! Of course, I remember. Harry (just like him) said a Miss *Ransome* had rung up. Of course I thought it was Kathleen Ransome – that ghastly girl with a sniff. I say, though, you're looking a bit under the weather or something. And what are you doing with all those tools?'

'I –'

'Miss Jebb, Miss Sprink, this is Miss Ranskill, a very old friend of mine. We used to have great times together. She never had a bungie (did you, Nona?), she always borrowed mine. She was a whale at borrowing bungies. I'll bet you haven't got one now, have you, Nona?'

'I –'

'Well, I'll see you tonight, Miss Sprink, and you too, Miss Jebb. Don't be late, will you. I do want our unit to set a good example to all the other fire-watchers.'

Miss Ranskill regarded her spirit-level. Whoever might have stolen the thunder had not left even a rumble for her.

She had travelled a very long way indeed to be introduced as a person who was famous for losing india-rubbers.

Miss Jebb and Miss Sprink made a clattering departure and Miss Jebb added sloppiness to hers because she had not emptied her bucket.

'I say, don't you go yet, Nona. I haven't got long, but we can have a jaw while I'm changing. Come on, I'll have to look slippy or I'll be late for camouflage nets.'

Marjorie coiled the serpentine trail of the stirrup-pump round her left arm and led the way into the hall.

The slattern appeared in a doorway. Her trouble-making face had a triumphant expression as she declared there was not a bit of fish in the town and that every slab was as bare as her arm.

'So I'll have to open a tin for tonight,' she concluded.

'No, we must keep those in case of invasion. Aren't there some sausages left?'

'One or two, that's all.'

'Well, what about toad-in-the-hole, then? You could make the batter with the rest of that tin of Woolton eggs.'

'There's scarcely a drop of milk left.'

'You can use some of the household milk then. Though *we* like batter mixed with water: it's so much lighter.'

A sniff answered Marjorie and she charged upstairs followed by Miss Ranskill.

'You haven't asked after the children yet,' she reproached as she opened a door on the upper landing.

'I –'

The ringing of a telephone on a bedside table interrupted, and Miss Ranskill flopped down on to a chair as her friend picked up the receiver.

The bedroom, except that it was larger, looked very much like Marjorie's cubicle at St Catherine's. A row of books on a shelf by the window spoke volumes, almost literally.

Miss Ranskill recognised a toffee-stain on the back of a volume of *The Road Mender*, now wedged between *St John Handbook* and *Hygiene in the Home*. P C Wren and Ian Hay were well represented, so were Beatrix Potter and the Baroness Orczy. *Puck of Pook's Hill* was there, and the selected poems of Rudyard Kipling stood cover to cover beside two books by Robert Service. A book on anti-gas protection, another on rationed meals, and a third entitled *Communal Cookery* were strangers to Miss Ranskill.

She turned to look at the walls which were ornamented with slogans. JUMP TO IT startled from the head of the bed. The injunction CARELESS TALK COSTS LIVES stood in a frame by the telephone. DON'T GIVE A LIGHT TO HITLER was pokerworked into a panel by the window. BE A SPORT AND SPARE THE SOAP glaring in red paint on white oilcloth above the wash-basin was rather baffling, for Marjorie had been a particularly clean schoolgirl.

Other maxims were more familiar. Miss Ranskill knew all about deaf, blind and dumb monkeys, and about the expectations of lame dogs, though surely these would prefer to go *under* stiles and take their own time about it.

Marjorie was talking into the telephone. Her gold-rimmed

glasses added seriousness to her face. Her mouth was still a little rabbity, though in quite an attractive way, and her chin was still obstinate.

'Well, this time I'm going to report it. I've warned them three times now. They'll jolly well have to get new curtains. I'm not going to have the whole country endangered every time Miss Jackson has a bath. If you ask me, she has far too *many* baths: it's not playing the game. I've a jolly good mind to report her to the fuel people too. There's no need for all these baths in the summer. I only have three inches of water once a week.'

Miss Ranskill glanced again at the slogan above the wash-stand, and felt more shocked than puzzled.

'Goodbye.' Marjorie plumped the receiver into its cradle.

'Now then, Nona, tell me all about yourself. Goodness! you are Spartan not to wear shoes even. I never wear stockings till November except when in uniform, of course, but I do wear *shoes*. Crumbs! I forgot to ring the butcher. Half a sec, Nona.'

She picked up the receiver again and dialled.

'That you, Mr White? This is Mrs Mallison speaking. . . . Yes, from Hillrise. I say, have you got any offal to spare because I'll be having a visitor, and I simply must keep the joint for the end of the week. Absolutely anything would do – faggots or a bullock's heart, or – Right, I'll hang on –'

Relief that she was expected to stay was slightly marred for Miss Ranskill by the assumption that anything 'would do'. It wasn't as though Marjorie's bedroom looked poor, even though the old familiar things were cherished.

'Yes, sausage meat would do splendidly, thanks most

awfully. . . . What? . . . Well, I'll try to dig out a few news-papers for you, but you know we *are* trying to hit the target with our salvage drive. . . . Why don't you try to make all your customers use old sponge-bags or beach bags like I do? . . . Yes, I know they are. Well, I wish you *were* allowed to sell horse-flesh. It's quite time we did eat it. . . . Yes, but I expect it's jolly good. After all, they're nice clean feeders. Goodbye, Mr White.'

Down went the receiver again, and Marjorie began to pull off a tunic that had the letters C D embroidered on it in yellow.

'I know it's rotten to grumble and one ought to be jolly thankful to have anything to eat, but I do hate all the waste of time. Don't you find housekeeping jolly difficult?'

'Well –'

Marjorie tugged off her trousers. She was wearing navy blue knickers underneath. Of course she was, she had always worn navy blue knickers at school.

'If only one could get more fish.'

'I've had enough fish to last me all my life.'

'Lucky thing!'

Marjorie began to trace the smooth outline of her head with a whalebone brush. There was no grey in the short golden-streaked crop. Standing there, in knickers and white cotton vest, she looked scarcely older than the sixth form prefect.

'Well now, tell me all about yourself, old thing. Where are you staying?'

'Here,' replied Miss Ranskill's mind. 'Here, surely, or why did you order offal for a visitor?'

There was no need of actual answer for Marjorie ran on:

'What job are you in? Gosh, if I weren't married I'd have faked my age and been in one of the Forces ages ago. Still, I do what I can, and I've given a son and daughter to the country –'

The last remark was made as casually as though she had said, 'I'm not sending many cards this Christmas, but I've given the twins to Aunt Hilda.'

'Harry is worked to death, poor darling: he has the hospital now as well as his ordinary practice, and that's nearly doubled. Well, tell me all about yourself. You look as though you were in a pretty strenuous job. How long have you been here and why didn't you look us up before, you silly old chump?'

'Because I only arrived today. I came in the convoy that reached here this morning.'

Nona Ranskill had hoped the statement would make some impression, but she hardly expected it to be quite so effective.

Marjorie stopped scratching her scalp with whalebone.

'I say, old thing, that's most frightfully dangerous, even to *me*.'

'Not so very – we weren't torpedoed or anything – it wasn't nearly so dangerous as all the time before.'

'Even to *me!*' repeated Marjorie, making her friend wonder what worse adventures than a four-years' marooning, a death, burial, and a voyage in a home-built boat could have left that forehead so unlined and those cheeks so smooth and pink. Was Marjorie also in the habit of finding the severed heads of acquaintances lying about in gutters?

'I expect,' she remarked flatly, 'I expect you've done much worse things than that.'

'Never! Never when men's lives depend on it. I'm an absolute oyster. You ought to know *that*, Nona. I never blabbed at school, did I?'

'But I only said –'

'Shut up! I'm sorry, old thing, but really you must know that we never mention *convoys*.' The last word came almost as a whisper. 'Of course, this time it doesn't matter.' (*But it will be an order mark next time!*) 'And nothing you say to me will go any further.' (*You can imitate Miss Baynes or the Head to me, but not before the kids: that's awfully bad form, Nona.*) 'Gosh, if I passed on everything I know, I don't know where we'd be. The way people *talk*. Personally, I just won't listen to it.'

'No you won't!' whispered a little demon in Miss Ranskill's brain.

'As a matter of fact I *did* happen to know about this morning's convoy.'

'I simply don't know what you're talking about,' interrupted Miss Ranskill despairingly. 'I'm sorry, but –'

'Just like you to shut the stable door after the cat's out of the bag. Don't you remember at school – Gosh! I mustn't stand here gossiping or they'll all be screaming for me downstairs.'

Marjorie went to a wardrobe, snatched a grey skirt from its hanger, pulled open a drawer and dragged at a white sweater.

'I'm sorry to be snappy, my dear, but I've got into the habit now of squashing careless talk. It makes people so jittery. I do think the main danger's over, but if we should have any little bother in the way of an invasion scare, it will be my job to stop panic.'

Marjorie waved the sweater as though it symbolised the Union Jack. 'How I'm going to do it *and* fire-watch and run the paper salvage, I just don't know.'

Her head disappeared for a moment or two, and then reappeared through the neck of her jumper.

'Honestly, Nona, you mustn't think another thing about it. It absolutely was my fault for asking, because obviously if you go out in convoys you must be doing some *terribly* hush-hush job, and I oughtn't to have asked. I don't generally ask asinine questions. You do believe that, don't you, Nona?'

Miss Ranskill opened her mouth to answer, but she might just as well have saved her facial muscles.

'I say, it must be frightfully exciting for you going out in convoys, absolutely thrilling. No, I'm not asking questions. Don't tell me a word. Shut me up at once if I seem to be inquisitive. I suppose that accounts for the queer sort of rig you're wearing. I do think it's bad luck that so many people who're doing really vital jobs aren't allowed uniforms, don't you?'

'Well, really I don't know.' By this time Miss Ranskill felt that she knew nothing about anything – not even the job of a sexton.

'I say, you will stay to tea, won't you?' Marjorie patted her skirt. 'Or have you got to go back on duty?'

'No, I could stay. As a matter of fact, I –'

'That's splendid. I've got to fly now and get them started on the nets. We have tea at five. Tell you what, if you want to wash or anything, don't bother to come down till then. We only have a bun and a cup of tea. After they've gone I ought to have half an hour to spare. We'll have a good old talk then.'

'I'd been wondering –'

'My dear, I must fly. Make yourself at home. There's an old school mag on the table by my bed. You'll find lots of news in that. Good old June Mathers has got the GM and Buntie's on radio-location. I *must* go.'

'Could I,' for an idea was slowly rising in Miss Ranskill's brain above all the clutter thrown there by Marjorie, 'could I use the telephone?'

'Use the kitchen stove if you like.'

The voice came from outside the door and then a series of clumps remarked on Marjorie's descent downstairs.

II

A great wish to see her sister at once had suddenly possessed Nona Ranskill. She must see someone recognisable, some-one through whose eyes she could learn to observe this new world, someone who could explain without being shocked by ignorance. Edith was tiresome and quite as conventional as Marjorie, but, at least, she had never suffered by her develop-ment being arrested midway through the last term in the sixth form. Miss Ranskill herself must begin at the beginning again and learn slowly. It was rather odd that she, who had always had an enquiring mind, should have waited until she was nearly forty-four to be sorry for the Sleeping Beauty. The kiss must have been a startler to even the most complacent of princesses.

'Sleeping *Beauty!*' thought Miss Ranskill grimly as she passed the mirror on her way to the telephone.

She asked for the old number in the Hampshire village. It was queer to hear it spoken again, and odd she should remember it so clearly.

How surprised Edith would be! Would she be pleased? What had Swinburne said, something about thanking 'whatever gods there be, that no man lives forever, that dead men rise up never, that –'

'There is up to half an hour's delay to Lynchurch. You will be r-rung later.'

And then would there be another delay? Would Edith be out exercising Whuppet, the spaniel? Memory of those flying ears and fluffily-fringed paws roused a surge of homesickness. Miss Ranskill was still holding the receiver, and she put it down grudgingly; for its length seemed just a dog's lead distance to the village so far along the coast.

But even here, she looked affectionately round Marjorie's bedroom, there was a linking homeliness.

There was the school badge with its legend *Honour before Honours* black against the buff of a paper magazine.

She began to turn over the pages. It was all much as it had always been. There were accounts of house-matches and exam-honours. There was an anæmic smug little poem written by 'Joan Burgess. Upper IVB.' This was a small world she knew, a plain stodgy safe world full of ink and blotting-paper, thick bread and butter, and stout shoes; interrupted by only an occasional stir of the heart as when a peacock butterfly brought its quivering beauty to interrupt a maths lesson, a rainbow arched over the playing-field, or a lecturer brought the tang of wine-dark seas and a riot of lovely names into the hall.

No, it was not quite the same as it had been. A few bleak little notices were sandwiched between items of school news.

OWING TO THE PETROL SHORTAGE THERE WERE NO OUTSIDE MATCHES LAST TERM.

MISS CUMMINS HAS GONE TO WORK IN A MUNITIONS FACTORY. HER PLACE NEXT TERM WILL BE TAKEN BY MISS BRAY.

Then, from the REPORT BY THE HEAD MISTRESS:

Owing to our amalgamation with St Cyprian's School when it was evacuated from the East Coast, the sixth form sitting-room had to be given up last term, and the small recreation room was turned into a dormitory. . . . Girls of both schools are pulling together fairly well, but there is still need for greater co-operation in the lower forms. . . . Less fuel was used during the term, but there is still need for great care. It has been decided that on really cold days, there shall be two ten-minute breaks during the mornings for physical drill or skipping exercises. . . . The Black-out Monitors are to be congratulated on their vigilance. . . . The Salvage Monitors are reminded to keep a keener eye on all waste next term. . . . All girls whose birthdays fall on or after June 10th will register during the holidays. . . . Parents are reminded that the Bursar still has a certain number of second-hand tunics and shirts in her store: these may be purchased coupon-free. . . . There was a gas-mask parade and inspection at mid-term: some of the Juniors' masks showed signs of rough handling. . . . Ration books must be handed in with the health certificates on the first day of term, and every girl must surrender her Personal Points book at the same time. . . . ARP practices are to be more frequent in future.

. . . Some of the older girls are learning to cut Braille. Soon they hope to send some booklets to one of the Children's Homes for the Civilian Blind. . . .

No, certainly, it was not the same. Miss Ranskill remembered her terms at school during the last war, and the excitement of that day in the summer holidays when war was declared and was no longer a thing to be read of in history books but a glory to be lived through – a thin red line rioting across Belgium. A dullness had followed: there had been knitting parties but the balaclavas and scarves had been more fun to make than flannel petticoats. The brothers of two or three girls had been killed and their names emblazoned on a Roll of Honour in the school chapel.

She remembered Marjorie's comment:

'It's lucky we'll have left before they can make new history books. Gosh! fancy having to swot up all the dates of this war as well. I'm going to write and beg Mummy to let me give up German. I'm going to say I think it's absolutely disloyal to learn a word of it. We'll never speak it after this. Why, there won't be any Germans left.'

'It might be useful if there was another war. People who know German might easily help to catch spies.'

'There won't be another war *ever*, you silly chump. This is a War to end Wars absolutely; everyone says so.'

Miss Ranskill recalled Marjorie's earnest face as she flicked over the pages, till she came to the ones that gave 'News of old girls'.

There, in repudiation of her mother's cock-a-hoop statement, was a little notice:

'Daphne Mallison (Hillrise, Hartmouth) has joined the WRNS and is enjoying her new life very much!'

Miss Ranskill read other news slowly as a child mouthing through its first story-book, missing out some words and symbols, guessing at the meaning of others. Her contemporaries seemed to be doing remarkable things.

Her finger was checked by a small obituary notice.

'Mary, infant daughter of Molly Henderson (née Matthews), by enemy action.'

The shocking little statement sent Miss Ranskill's mind harking back – Molly Matthews, of course, that small redheaded second-former with the snuffle and the squeaky voice. Always in trouble for something or other, she remembered. She felt angry as she remembered how frequently Molly had been held up to ridicule.

'The untidiest girl I have ever known. You are always losing something. First your hat, then your gym shoes, then your hockey-stick and *now* your drawing-board!'

Poor Molly, well, she had lost more than a drawing-board now.

The telephone bell rang.

III

Miss Ranskill held the receiver in a grip that whitened her knuckles.

'Are you Hartmouth two-five-eight-?'

'Yes, yes.'

'Your call to Lynchurch is through. Go ahead, please.'

'Hullo! Hullo!'

She could almost smell the furniture polish in the home drawing-room now.

'Hullo!' the voice came faintly.

'Is that you, Edith?'

'Who?'

'Edith, is that you?'

'I'm afraid I can't hear you very well.'

'Is that you, Edith?' Miss Ranskill was almost bellowing by now. 'Who is that speaking? Is Miss Ranskill in?'

'No, this is Mrs Wilson speaking.' The voice sounded exasperated. 'There is nobody of the name of Ranskill here.'

'But aren't you Lynchurch five-five-eight?'

'Yes, this is Lynchurch five-five-eight.'

'I wanted to speak to my sister, Miss Edith Ranskill.'

'This is Mrs Wilson speaking,' repeated the plaintive voice. 'I'm afraid you must have got the wrong number.'

'Please,' Miss Ranskill spoke chokingly. She was afraid of hearing that Edith was dead, so afraid that she dared not ask the direct question: 'Please, are you speaking from a house called The White Cottage?'

'The White Cottage, yes.'

'Is it, is it *your* house?'

'We are the present tenants.'

Miss Ranskill felt sure that eyebrows were being raised in Hampshire, and she continued pleadingly:

'I'm not asking out of curiosity –'

An incredulous pip sounded in her ear, followed by another and another.

'I'm asking because I've just come, I mean, I have been away for some time and I used to live in – in your house. I thought my sister was there now. If you could possibly help me.'

She would hear the truth now and braced herself to receive it. Nervousness dulled her brain so that, at first, she scarcely took in the meaning of the words that seemed to come dimly and from a far country.

'I'm afraid I can't tell you anything about your sister. We took over the house furnished from my husband's predecessor about six months ago.'

'Oh!'

'I'm afraid I must –'

Miss Ranskill's brain jumped to alertness again.

'Don't cut me off for a minute, please don't cut me off. Could you tell me is there a white rug in front of the drawing-room fireplace and a Queen Anne bureau in the corner, and –?' She suddenly realised the absurdity of the questions and said, 'I'm only trying to find out if my sister let the house furnished or if –'

'I see. Yes, there is a white rug and a Queen Anne bureau.'

'And a Welsh dresser in the dining-room?'

'Yes – a black oak dresser.'

Hope came back and with it more acuteness.

'Did you keep the maids on? Is old Emma with you because –'

'No, we've only got my husband's batman. I should think it is quite likely that your sister went away, like so many other people, when we became a prohibited area.'

'Prohibited area?' Miss Ranskill repeated the unfamiliar words.

'Yes, well, I'm so sorry not to be more helpful. Perhaps the post office here would have an address. I daresay they'd forward a letter.'

'Yes,' agreed Miss Ranskill flatly. 'I wonder –'

'I wish I could help. I *must* go now or the kettle will be boiling over. *Good*bye.'

The click of a receiver in Hampshire left Miss Ranskill lonely and homesick.

Now, at this very moment, the copper kettle in her own kitchen was bubbling its readiness to make tea for a stranger. The stove was taking the reflection of a stranger's skirt and the rag hearth-rug was soft beneath a tenant's foot. She could almost hear the tinkle of the spoon against the teapot.

Meanwhile she had no foothold in England except for an hour or so. Presently, she supposed, she would have to say goodbye to Marjorie, thank her for the nice tea-party, promise to be 'certain to look her up again' next time she was in the neighbourhood, and go. Where? Could she take a room in some hotel while a bank got in touch with her bank and a post office in Lynchurch forwarded a letter? Would any hotel proprietor take her in these clothes and without luggage, and could she bear the publicity of the public rooms, supposing one did? Would the mysterious thing called a coupon be her only passport to the hotel?

Up to now she had always thought the Saracen maid, with her bleat of 'London-Gilbert, Gilbert-London' rather an idiot, but 'Edith-England' was an even vaguer address.

116

CHAPTER EIGHT

Miss Ranskill wondered what to do next. She strolled round the room, and was again shocked by her reflection in the mirror. Then a pair of nail-scissors on the dressing-table gave a hint that she might as well trim some of the jags of her rusty hair, for there was now no need to keep it long as she had done on the island, where it had been a substitute for darning thread. The Carpenter had made the shell needles.

A woman's glory is her hair, Miss Ranskill, that's what they say. Where we'd be without yours beats me. I reckon when your old Nanny was brushing it she never thought you'd be hacking it off by the handful to coax the fire to light again. You'd have laughed though, wouldn't you, when you were a little lass to think your hair would be used to tie the bait to fish-hooks and fix on buttons! Pretty hair too, I'd like to see it smoothed again. A silk handkerchief, that's what my missus used to polish the children's hair.

All the same, she trimmed economically at first, till the hair swung free of her shoulders and showed a curved edge patterned by the scissors. In another ten minutes it only reached the tips of her ears and a sleeking of brilliantine made the rusty strands gleam. She looked younger now and less like a castaway. Marjorie's scentless face-cream and powder made more improvement.

It would be pleasant to take a book from the shelves and read herself into a different world, away from the difficult one she had left and from this new one that had no welcome.

There was another row of books on top of the fumed oak writing-table, and they included a ready-reckoner, a dictionary, and a cookery book full of potato recipes. Miss Ranskill read a few more of the titles: *Grow Your Own Food, The Kitchen Front, Food From the Garden*, and *I Was a Spy*. Then she took the last book from its place.

We'll have plenty of time for reading when we get home, Miss Ranskill, reading and writing. I'll write down all that we did on the island, I shouldn't wonder.

There was a relief-nibbed pen on the desk, an inkstand and a blotter. Somewhere in the crowded pigeon-holes there would be paper and envelopes. Marjorie could not possibly mind if she looked for them. They had often shared desks at St Catherine's.

There was plenty of paper but no new envelopes. The last pigeon-hole held a bundle of old ones, a packet of sticky labels, some ration books, and a stiff folded card bearing Marjorie's name, address and a number.

'Never mind,' thought Miss Ranskill, 'I'll ask for an envelope later.'

She sat down at the desk and began to write to her sister – 'Dear Edith –'

It was difficult to know how to begin. Stiff little sentences formed themselves in her mind. 'I hope you are very well. . . . I hope this letter will find you. . . . You will be surprised to hear from me after so long, but I have just returned from a desert island. . . . I would have written before but have been so far away from post offices.' Anything she could write would sound incredible. Her arrival might be inconvenient as well, because her death would have been presumed years ago, and Edith, as sole legatee, would have readjusted her own life, disposed of most of Nona's possessions, and settled herself somewhere in a house for one. She would be playing the part of a brave woman with a great sorrow – the shock of her sister's sudden and terrible death. The letter would steal thunder from the sorrow and set Edith to the counting of tea-cups and the pairing of sheets.

Miss Ranskill crumpled the card in her left hand and stirred up the ink with her pen.

The door opened and Marjorie strode in.

'I'll be forgetting my head next. I thought I'd got all the beastly lists. Can I come to the desk for a sec?'

Miss Ranskill got up from the chair.

'I'm so sorry,' she said, 'I thought you wouldn't mind my writing to Edith. I've just heard our house is in a prohibited area or something, and –'

'You would think,' said Marjorie, rootling through a pigeon-hole, 'that they could remember to bring their own lists, wouldn't you. No sense of responsibility – that's their trouble.'

She picked up the book Miss Ranskill had taken down and looked disapprovingly at the title. '*That* shouldn't be here.'

'I'm so sorry, I'll put it back.'

A piece of crumpled card slipped from between the visitor's fingers as she held out her hand for the book.

Marjorie pounced on it. 'I do like a clear desk,' she announced as she began to smooth out the cardboard. 'And it really is important to keep even waste-paper flat: it saves the salvage people such a lot of trouble.'

Miss Ranskill waited for further reproof. It had always been the same at school when ink or an india-rubber or blotting-paper pellets in an ink-well had stirred Marjorie to speeches.

'Gosh!' she exclaimed now. 'My identity card. My *identity* card, Nona, what have you done to it?'

'I'm awfully sorry. I think I was just fiddling with it while I was trying to write that letter. I didn't know I'd got anything in my hand. Is it something that matters?'

'Something that *matters!* I ask you!'

Marjorie's cheeks were pinker than usual, and then she gave a little jerk of the head that had long been familiar to Miss Ranskill. Better nature, self-conscious better nature and good sportsmanship were going to take the place of annoyance. Fair play would be called up at any moment.

'But, of course, it's my fault, really. Serves me jolly well right for being so careless. I always do carry it in my wallet, but I *was* a bit fagged last night. Not that that's any excuse. My being fagged doesn't matter an atom. When one thinks of Russia.'

Marjorie's chin went up and she straddled her legs slightly as though she were taking firm stance on the burning deck. The gesture suggested a salute, and Miss Ranskill wondered why it was necessary.

'Now where's that list?' Her friend rummaged in a pigeon-hole, snatched what she wanted and hurried to the door.

'Tea will be ready in two ticks,' she announced. 'If you don't hurry up, we'll have wolfed all the buns. Heavens! what's that?'

One of her competent fingers was pointing to the dressing-table with its litter of rust-red hair.

'It was so long and shaggy,' said Miss Ranskill. 'I'd meant to go to a hairdresser before I came, but –'

'Aren't you a scream!' Marjorie delivered her last speech from the doorway. 'Good old happy-go-lucky Nona. So long! See you at tea. After that we'll have no end of a jaw.'

The door shut with a bang and Miss Ranskill began to collect her rags of hair from the toilet-table. Before she had finished, the telephone-bell gave a brief tinkle and she snatched up the receiver.

She had always been one of those people who never see a telegraph boy, even in a strange town, without expecting delivery of an important wire, and so it never occurred to her, even when a man's voice asked, 'Is that you, darling?' that the call was not for her. 'I say, this is rather important. Are you alone?'

Before Miss Ranskill could open her mouth she heard the unmistakable voice of Marjorie replying, into a mouth-piece in some other room. 'Yes, yes. What is it, Harry?'

Here Miss Ranskill should, and would, had she not been for so long a stranger to the land where people of her kind do not read other people's letters or listen to other people's telephone conversation, have hung up the receiver. But her mind was clumsy in this queer new world just as her feet were awkward on a carpeted floor, so she listened as a child might have done.

'Have you a visitor with you?'

'Yes, an old school-friend, Nona –'

'Still in the house?'

'Yes. Why?'

'Thank God for that. Now listen. You've got to keep her. Make any excuse you like. Get her to stay the night.'

'But, Harry, it's Mrs Bostock's night out *and* I've got my fire-watching *and* there's scarcely a thing to eat.'

'How queer,' thought Miss Ranskill. 'Doctor Mallison didn't seem to want me this morning: now he does, and Marjorie doesn't.'

It was impossible now not to go on listening. She must discover if she were expected to say goodbye after tea and go. Go where? It didn't matter so much as all that. She had slept on sand before.

'I can't help that. You've got to keep her. I've just seen White.'

'White? Oh! Harry, did he give you the sausage meat? I did ring up and he said he'd try to deliver, but –'

'I don't mean White, the butcher, I mean White, the police inspector.'

'Harry! Whatever for?'

'Well, I don't want to say too much about anything on the telephone – but – Sure you're alone?'

'Yes, I'm speaking from the surgery. Go on.'

'Well, your old school-friend is wanted by the police. She's been talking rather oddly in the shops and this morning she did a bolt from the Navy.'

'Do you mean she's deserted from the Wrens? Oh! Harry!'

'I'll be round as soon as I can, and so will the police.'

'Harry, I just can't believe that any St Cat's girl – It's too beastly.'

'It's not too pleasant for me either. Bye-bye, dear, see you soon.'

A receiver clicked downstairs and the one held fast in Miss Ranskill's grip became as silent as a sea-shell on a mantelpiece.

What had she said and what had she done and what did the term 'running away from the Navy' imply? How could she explain that she had run away from nothing but the sight of her own face in a mirror and the embarrassment it might bring to a nice young man! Marjorie had hinted at desertion, but did women who were rescued from the sea join the Navy automatically? Had the law become an absurdity? Miss Ranskill knew none of the answers, but she was frightened and her head began to ache badly.

She had expected life to be simplified by clicking of switches, striking of matches, and turning of taps, but the faces of her own country-folks were less friendly than the sneering profiles of the sea-gulls on the island.

The sound of steps on the landing reminded her that it was time to move away from the telephone. Then the door opened and a new strange Marjorie came in – a Marjorie turned wary, an overgrown schoolgirl trying to be a sleuth.

'I say,' she began, 'I meant to ask you before, only there's been so much to do; you will stay the night, won't you? You simply must.'

She had only glanced once at her school-friend's face and now she was addressing its reflection in the mirror. Miss Ranskill answered a reflection too.

'Thank you very much,' she said.

'Are you – were you going to stay in Hartmouth for long?'

'No, I – I've got to make other arrangements as soon as possible, get in touch with my sister and buy some clothes; I haven't any but these.'

She touched her threadbare skirt and glanced down at her bare feet.

'You mean you've no other clothes at all?'

Miss Ranskill shook her head.

'Why not?' Suspicion edged Marjorie's voice.

'I tried to get some this morning but they said I must have coupons or something. I hadn't got any, of course.'

'Why, *of course?* People in the *Services*' (there was slight emphasis on the last word) 'don't have coupons because they have everything given to them. Everyone else has a book of clothing-coupons. Of course, if you've lost yours, or used them up, it's your lookout.'

'I thought perhaps you could have helped,' said Miss Ranskill. 'I asked in the shop and I gave your name. I didn't think you'd mind, but it wasn't any good.'

'Of course I'd like to help.' Marjorie's fingers were fiddling with the tufts of her old friend's scattered hair. 'You ought to know that. Only there are some things one just can't help over. I mean, it's so frightfully difficult to explain, I mean –'

'I know what you mean,' said Miss Ranskill, because quite suddenly she did. 'You mean that if I were a Cavalier and you were a loyal cottager, you'd hide me up the chimney until the Roundheads went by, but that if I were a modern spy or –'

She stood up, because the relief of having hinted that she knew what was thought of her stimulated her tired limbs and she was not frightened any longer.

Marjorie strode to the door and struck a Casabianca attitude with her back to it. No, decided Miss Ranskill, she was playing Kate-Bar-the-Gate now, as she snipped at the air with inadequate nail-scissors.

'I mean,' said Marjorie, 'I mean that if my puppy, and I *adore* my puppy, chewed up the Union Jack I almost think I'd have him shot. He could have my last pair of silk stockings. He could destroy anything I have but not the *Flag*.'

'Oh!' said Miss Ranskill. She flopped down on to the bed, laid her shaggy head on the pillow and burst, not into sobs for lost loyalties, but into laughter. 'I'm sorry, but if only you knew how funny you are!'

'I don't see anything funny about it.'

'Except that I haven't chewed up the Union Jack.'

For the moment Miss Ranskill had forgotten all her horror and loneliness and fear. She shook with laughter. The sight of Marjorie, looking so exactly like the Marjorie of St Catherine's, almost made her forget the torment she had been through. The link of past laughter was between them: she was the impudent mocker again, and her friend stood for dignity.

'Spiritually, you may have done. How do I know what you've done? You've behaved very oddly and now you begin laughing at things that *matter*. I mean –'

'Yes,' Miss Ranskill checked her laughter, 'but your trouble is that you've always fancied yourself as Joan of Arc *and* an out-and-out Britisher.'

'Well,' Marjorie chucked up her chin, 'what's wrong with that?'

'Nothing except historically – and it's rather a strain on the loyalties.'

'If *you* had any loyalties –'

Miss Ranskill stood up again and Marjorie braced herself against the door.

'You needn't think you can get away. I wouldn't have taken this job on if I hadn't known I was jolly strong. I've never let myself get out of training ever.'

Miss Ranskill looked at the firm straddled legs. They were muscled certainly, but there was a good layer of fat. Marjorie had not wrestled with boulders and tides, or fought for food and warmth and shelter.

Strong as most men you are, I reckon, Miss Ranskill, nearly as strong as me.

A little puff of sea-air came in through the slightly open window, fluting the curtains and soothing Miss Ranskill's cheek. What was she doing in this conventional room, bickering with an old friend?

Your friends will be mighty glad to see you when we do get ashore, Miss Ranskill. When I think what you've been to me. Lots of friends, anyone like you must have.

For years she had lived and thought in freshening sea-air. She must try to think clearly now: she went to the window and pushed it up.

'Not that way!' shrilled Marjorie. 'You can't get out.'

'I wasn't going to,' said Miss Ranskill wearily. 'I thought you'd asked me to stay the night. Didn't you?' She gasped a little as she returned to her seat on the bed. 'I'm not used to being shut up in rooms. I only wanted some air. If I did go away I've nowhere to go.'

For a moment or two there was silence in the room. Then Marjorie's lips began to tremble like a troubled baby's.

'This is perfectly beastly,' she gulped. 'You don't know how I'm hating it. When I think of the good times we used to have and now *you*. . . . If there's anything you'd like to tell me, I wish you would. I mean, I can't promise to do anything, but . . . I don't know how to put it. . . . We were pals at school . . . if you'd sort of give me your parole.'

Miss Ranskill made no reply.

'Haven't you anything you could tell me that would make it easier?'

'Nothing, really,' said Miss Ranskill, 'except that I only came back to England this morning. I've spent nearly four years on a desert island.'

'A desert island? But there aren't any now.'

'There is one, because I've lived on it.'

'Was it a British possession?'

'I don't know: there wasn't anything to show. It wasn't coloured red, if that's what you mean.' Miss Ranskill nearly explained that sea-gulls do not sing national anthems, but she restrained herself.

'And were you quite alone for four years?'

'No, there was a carpenter there as well.'

'A *carpenter*. What sort of a man was he?'

I never was much to look at, Miss Ranskill, but I've always been well set up. Seems to me if you're born with a good body it's right to

127

use it right, keep it clean and healthy and don't let it sag. . . . This I can say, I've never owed a penny for a minute more'n I could help. I've never ill-treated an animal or a child or been rude to a girl. I've not been what you'd call a vicious man.

'He was a good man,' answered Miss Ranskill.

Marjorie left the door, her watch and ward forgotten for the moment.

'A desert island – for nearly four years. How frightfully thrilling. Why didn't you tell me at once. . . . It must have been queer, living there all alone with a man like that, I mean. It must have seemed a bit funny.'

'No funnier than being alone with a woman.'

Miss Ranskill's mouth shut firmly on the words.

'Oh! I know you wouldn't go in for any *Blue Lagoon* sort of stuff, but was he quite *all right* all the time, I mean –?'

There was no answer from the woman on the bed, but an unassailable expression came into her eyes and she clenched one hand slightly.

'I say, I'm most awfully sorry, I oughtn't to have asked, only I am one of your oldest friends, and it wouldn't make a scrap of difference to me. I mean, ordinarily it would, but a desert island's different. I only meant that over anything like *that* I'd have done anything I could to help.'

The voice went blundering on, as Miss Ranskill's knuckles whitened.

She was seeing a figure on the sand and a whirl of sea-gulls.

'I mean, of course, I hate anything like *that*, but I'm quite broad-minded, I suppose it's being a doctor's wife. I only wanted to help, I mean.'

Marjorie's voice tailed off, and, at last, Miss Ranskill answered.

'If you mean did he rape me, he did not.'

'Nona!'

'That was what you wanted to know, wasn't it?'

'Of course not, not put like *that*, anyway.'

Miss Ranskill made no answer. She was trying to see her island again, cool in the morning light, set in a fretwork of silver splinters, but the image was tarnished now.

'Or ever the silver cord be loosed or the golden bowl be broken,' she murmured.

'What?' asked Marjorie. 'I can't hear you.'

'Tone-deaf,' Miss Ranskill's mind made answer but her lips did not move.

CHAPTER NINE

I

The police had come and gone, and now Miss Ranskill was sitting in the Mallisons' overcrowded drawing-room.

'It's only a matter of form,' her mind repeated. 'This is a purely formal question. . . . Just a matter of routine, you know; no need to worry about it.'

She wondered if the Prince had murmured, 'Just a matter of routine,' before bestowing on the Sleeping Beauty that formal kiss that must have awakened her, also, to more practical matters than the buzzing of bees in the hedge of roses.

After each little bout of questioning, the elder had nodded to the younger, who had murmured, 'Excuse me, Madam,' and disappeared, not, as Miss Ranskill had at first imagined, to fetch suitable handcuffs, but to hold long telephone conversations.

He verified the fact that Miss Nona Ranskill, passenger in *The Coraltania*, had not been among the passengers who disembarked at Southampton a month before war was declared.

'It is so much better for *you*, Madam, that we should check up on everything. And now, if you wouldn't mind writing your signature, your usual signature, on that pad. . . . Three times, if you don't mind. . . . The *Midland* Bank, you said, didn't you? We can describe the signature by telephone.'

The younger policeman excused himself again, this time taking the pad with him; and the inquisition continued, to be interrupted by his return.

'That seems to be all right, sir. The full-stop just below the first i, and the short rising line under the signature. The Will was proved in 1940.'

'My Will?' asked Miss Ranskill.

The elder inquisitor pursed his lips and nodded gloomily, adding: 'They would be obliged to do that, of course, just as a matter of routine, but there should be no difficulty – just a few formalities.'

An hour and a half passed by, but at the end of it Miss Ranskill was in possession of her sister's address in an inland Hampshire village.

She was told that certain formalities must be observed 'merely as a matter of routine, of course', and gathered that when her identity had been established more formally, she would be given the identity card and ration books that would prove her right to exist, as well as to be fed and clothed. In the meanwhile, and, again purely as a formality, it would be more convenient for everyone if she would remain where she was for the next few days.

'Yes,' agreed Miss Ranskill. 'I must ask my hostess.'

It was then that Marjorie had made an entry and announced, while plumping uneasily on to the arm of a chair, that she had no intention of butting in.

'Quite,' replied the elder inquisitor, and saved Miss Ranskill from embarrassment by asking if she might remain as guest while matters, tiresome but necessary to routine, were completed.

'But, of course.' Marjorie hitched up a stocking and patted her sleek head. 'And, I hate suggesting it, but I do think it would be an awfully good idea if Nona, Miss Ranskill, I mean, gave her parole not to do a bunk. I mean, we were at the same school, and that sort of simplifies things, doesn't it?'

Assurance that nothing of that kind would be necessary stirred Marjorie to curious forms of activity. Miss Ranskill and the policemen watched and waited while she scratched her leg, opened and shut her mouth, tugged at her shirt collar and writhed as though the arm of her chair were a bed of stinging nettles.

'I say,' she gasped at last. 'It's no good, I simply must get it off my chest. I'd feel awful if I didn't. I mean, private loyalties and being at the same school with a person aren't absolutely everything in war-time, and so though I feel frightful and exactly like Lancelot –'

The younger policeman raised his eyebrows, and Marjorie explained:

'You know – *faith unfaithful kept him falsely true.* I'm afraid I don't go in much for poetry as a rule, I mean, there isn't time, especially in war-time, and it's mostly so sloppy, but Tennyson's different, Tennyson *and* Kipling.'

'Are you trying to tell us anything, Mrs Mallison?' enquired the elder of the men.

'Yes. It's awful, but I am. I never have been the sort of

person to say one thing behind people's backs and another to their faces, and I just can't sacrifice the whole country for the sake of one friend.'

'Of course not. Well?'

'And so,' Marjorie writhed on the chair, 'if Miss Ranskill has deserted from any of the Women's Services and my husband *did* say over the telephone that she'd done a bolt from the Navy, I somehow don't really think I could have her to stay.'

'I quite understand that.' (To Miss Ranskill's relief there seemed no need for her to say anything.) 'But I think you can feel quite easy about it. Miss Ranskill has explained to us how she and one of the Naval officers from the convoy happened to miss each other. We have been in touch with him since.'

But Marjorie's loyalties, so the activities of her legs and arms hinted, were not at rest yet.

'There's something else,' she gulped. 'I hate saying it. I'll probably never have another happy moment if I do, but if I don't I'll be a traitor.'

'What is this information, Mrs Mallison?' The policeman's voice was a little weary.

'She, Miss Ranskill I mean, tried to steal my identity card. I caught her with it in her hand, and when I came into the room suddenly, she crumpled it up and dropped it. And then she told me that her sister was in a prohibited area. If it's true that she's only just arrived in the country, how did she know that?'

She stared accusingly at her guest and then spoiled the dramatic effect by exclaiming, 'Nona, old thing, I'm dreadfully sorry, but I *had* to.'

Miss Ranskill scarcely heard the apology, for she was worn out now by explanations. Already she had rebuilt the boat with words, till her mind was as sore as her hands had been on the island. She had dug the Carpenter's grave afresh, and opened the secret places of her heart in doing so. She had conjured up the wind and the rain again, and answered questions until her head ached with remembering. Now she must reconstruct the scene in Marjorie's bedroom and explain the results of the telephone call to Lynchurch.

At last the final act was over and the two men had said polite goodbyes.

'We'll be seeing you again,' said the senior one. 'I should have a really good rest if I were you, you look pretty well beat to the wide.'

'Anything we can do to help,' murmured the younger. 'By the way, we will take charge of your boat for you, until you can decide what you want to do with it.'

'My boat,' Miss Ranskill addressed the patch of hearth-rug recently covered by black boots. 'But it isn't my boat: it belongs to the Carpenter's wife, at least, part of it does.'

Perhaps when she visited his home there would be more restfulness.

She looked at the collection of ornaments on the mantel-piece, appraising not their worth but their power of usefulness on a desert island. Those blackwood elephants would have come in handy, their tusks could have prised small fish from their shells, the lace curtains could have been turned into fishing-nets and the fire-shovel would have made a spade. The picture frames would have been better as part of the boat than as supporters of pallid seascapes. Miss Ranskill scarcely glanced at the pictures for the static waves annoyed her. She was used to changing seas, and discontented skies for ever shuffling themselves into beauty and maintaining their restless artistry by night and day.

The patterns of the chintz irritated her with the same repeated blue-bird on a bough that gushed flowers and leaves against a fawn background. The Dresden figures were no use for anything, but she resented the Lowestoft bowl on the wall-bracket in the corner. There it had stood, she supposed, empty and useless, year after year; while she had had nothing to clean fish in but a pool an eighth of a mile away from the rocky dining-table.

She shifted in the chair that was too comfortable – a hummock of sand and a jag of rock might have induced her to sleepiness, but presently she fell into a kind of waking nightmare.

There was no trust in the country. Her old friend had doubted her. Even her rescuers had been suspicious in a polite and formal way. She understood now that she would never have been allowed through the dockyard gates except under escort. The young officer had been only a courteous policeman.

II

Miss Ranskill was in bed, but she was not sleepy any more because Marjorie had been tucking her up, dragging at the sheets, pounding at the pillows, creaking on tiptoe round the room and speaking in the voice she reserved for churches.

'Harry says you're to have absolute rest and quiet and you're not to worry about anything. Sure there isn't anything more you want, old thing? You've only to sing out if there is. Are you dead-sure there's nothing you want?'

'Only peace and quiet,' answered Miss Ranskill's mind, 'only quietness, and the chance to remember the island before you rub out its memory.'

'I'm going to put this bell by your bed because it's my fire-watching night, and I've got to buzz off soon. Give the bell a tinkle if there's anything you want, and Harry will come bounding up in a sec. You needn't mind him: he's a doctor, remember, and absolutely used to seeing people in bed. I'm afraid Mrs Bostock is going out. Well, so long.'

'Good night!' said Miss Ranskill firmly.

'I'll be back about five o'clock and I'll peep in on you then.'

'Good night,' said Miss Ranskill.

'I say, you aren't still feeling huffed, are you? You do realise, old thing, don't you, that I was only doing my duty?'

Her guest, in the corner of her mind's eye, saw the island getting smaller and smaller, as it had done on the day she rowed away. Another word would scatter its frailty: it was the only place she knew now or understood.

'You do realise that I had to be beastly, don't you?'

'Of course. Yes, of course I do.'

'I say,' Marjorie plumped down on to Miss Ranskill's feet, 'I say, I've got an absolutely marvellous idea. After the war's over, we'll find out where that island of yours is exactly, and we'll all go there and spend a summer holiday. We'll take camping kit and have no end of a time. Isn't that a grand idea?'

'No.'

'Oh! I forgot you did have rather a doing there, didn't you? Still, I should have thought that in a year or so – I say, I must fly now, or I'll get it in the neck from the senior warden.'

Marjorie bounced off the bed.

'There! I'm going to put your light out and then you'll go to sleep straight away. Night-night! Happy dreams.'

There followed bumpings and bangings, and at last the door was shut.

Miss Ranskill felt breathless. There was no air or movement in the room. She missed the shuffle of the tide and the stir of the wind. Perhaps if she had more air she could sleep. She switched on the light and hurried to the window. It was queer that Marjorie, who had always described herself as an out-of-door person, should have fastened the curtains to the window-frame with drawing-pins, but perhaps it was part of the nursing programme. And why were the curtains black? Possibly Doctor Mallison disapproved of the early morning light. Even very ordinary doctors had queer fads sometimes.

Miss Ranskill flung up the window and went back to bed.

She could hear the sea now, shuffling away in the distance. A gentle flapping of the curtains told that the wind was at work too. Sea and wind would be busy with the island too, slurring out footprints – not human ones now though; there would only be the delicate patterning of gulls – coaxing the flesh from bird skeletons and making everything ready for the morning.

Perhaps this island would be better in the morning too. Always, no matter how wearily a day had ended or how fiercely the night had raged, the silver wash of morning had brought revival. It had been the same in the old life too: memories of disastrous tea-parties, smashed china and turmoil of spring-cleaning had never seemed so bad when remembered over early morning tea.

Miss Ranskill closed her eyes, content to feel that she need not open them again until the sanity of daylight freshened her mind.

'Put out that light!' Somebody was shouting in the street below, it was a menacing cry and was repeated by a voice with a snarl in it. 'Put out that light! Lights! Lights! Lights!' So might the kin of sailing men have shouted to the wreckers years ago in this very same part of the country.

'Put out that light!'

Miss Ranskill turned over and, in her half sleep, visualised the bobbing lantern and the ship drawing nearer and nearer to the rocks, while merciful men, savage in their fury against a murderer, scrambled towards him and threatened till their throats ached.

'Put out that light!'

The handle rattled, the door was burst open and Marjorie pounded into the room.

Miss Ranskill closed her eyes more firmly, and wished she could close her ears as well. Her gathering dreams would be shredded by any more conversation.

'Are you mad? Are you quite mad?'

Something clicked, darkness followed, the bed was shaken, and the end of the room near the window became noisy with bumpings and rattling as curtain-rings tinkled and things were knocked over.

'I should have thought . . . I mean, especially after what's *happened* with the police and everything. . . . This house of all houses. . . . As ARP warden I've always prided myself on having an absolutely watertight black-out.'

The room was still in darkness except for the faint torch-light that showed Marjorie's right hand as she stabbed the drawing-pins back into place.

'Do you mean I shouldn't have drawn the curtains?'

'Of course you shouldn't!'

'I'm sorry, I only wanted more air. I've been so used to sleeping almost in the open.'

'It's the people who've been used to things they won't do without, who are helping Hitler.'

Marjorie stabbed a drawing-pin home. 'I only hope the police won't hear of this or they'll think you were signalling to the enemy.'

'I'm very sorry. I didn't know. How could I know? We hadn't any curtains on the island.'

'I don't imagine you had blazing electric light either,' snapped Marjorie.

'No,' Miss Ranskill's voice had a bite in it now. 'No, we hadn't, but we had a fire that burned all day and all night.'

'Then I should have thought you'd have rigged up some sort of screen,' said Marjorie. She came over to the bedside now and switched on the light again. 'That is, unless you wanted to be neutral?'

Miss Ranskill sat up in bed and her voice took on a shrill note.

'Can't you understand,' she said, 'can't you try to understand that I didn't even know about the war till I left the island? I scarcely know anything now. I can't learn all the new rules if nobody tells me.'

'Gosh!' Marjorie's face looked very young under her tin hat. 'Gosh! how perfectly *awful* for you not to know about the war. I'm sorry I snapped, old thing: it's absolutely my fault for not telling you about the black-out. I say, I mean I just can't get over thinking of you cooped up on that island with nothing to do all day long. Is there anything else you'd like to know? I could spare five minutes, I think.'

III

It was quite quiet now that the windows were shut, and Miss Ranskill, awakened from her second sleep, wondered if it would soon be morning. Her fingers curled round the clasp of the new knife: there was familiarity in its smoothness, surety, and a certain comfort. She had taken it to bed with her just as children, newly returned from a summer holiday, tuck shells and pebbles under their pillows.

A clock in the distance struck midnight.

'It's morning at last,' thought Miss Ranskill. 'It's tomorrow.'

But now she was not longing for the day any more. Here in the darkness she was comfortable and secure. The hours of sleep had rested her, but she was not quite alive yet for her thoughts tagged about in a random way and she had no check on them. Nor had she any responsibilities or any hopes or fears.

'I'm a sort of ghost,' she thought, 'I haven't any identity and I'm supposed to be dead. But the Carpenter is really dead. . . . The island is still there. . . . Everything on it is the same as it was before we arrived except for the shelters. This morning the same big gull will light on the round rock by the stream and the others will follow.'

Let's go to the pictures again tonight, Miss Ranskill, shall we? It's my turn for the plush seat. What are you going to show me this time?

So Miss Ranskill, secure between sheets, played the island game of going to the pictures. And this time she went alone and back to the island to sit by the light of the fire, one cheek glowing from flame and the other icy cold where the wind caught it.

Something was shrieking in the darkness. It was too loud and too despairing for a gull's cry: no bird could have produced that insistent wavering whine. There was something despairing and demented about it. Miss Ranskill, struggling with sleep, imagined some half-human monster rising from the sea. Scylla or Charybdis might have moaned like that. The wailing sounded more loudly, menacing the island, and she began to fight the sheets whose smoothness affronted skin, now accustomed to the gritting of the sand. She tried to escape from their folds, fighting desperately. Was the monster itself enveloping her? Then, jerking herself from the nightmare to wakefulness, she remembered where she was. It was perfectly quiet: she had only been dreaming.

But it was quiet for no more than a moment. The banshee, or whatever it was, had followed her out of the dream. Once

141

more it raised its unspeakable voice and threatened peace. When its moaning had ended, it was succeeded by a little echo of its own despair.

A child was crying somewhere in the house.

Miss Ranskill stumbled out of bed and into the darkness. She could not find the switch, but at last her fingers met the door-handle and she blundered out into the passage.

Something dreadful had happened. The torment of the siren (unrecognised, of course, and all the more dreadful because of that) still sounded in her mind and the child's voice was raised to a crescendo.

'Mum! Mum! Mum!'

Half-way along the passage she groped against another door and pounded against it.

'Doctor Mallison! Doctor Mallison! Wake up.'

There was no reply, and the child's voice was raised more insistently every moment. At last she found a switch. Then a strange blue light showed that she was standing at the head of the staircase.

'Mum! Mum! Mum!'

Her hand was blue on the banister and her bare feet were blue too.

'It's a dream,' Miss Ranskill told herself. 'I shall wake up in a minute. It can't be true: nobody has blue lights. Nothing in England makes a noise like that.'

Then, from farther away this time, another voice raised its shuddering cry.

The turn of the stairs screened all but a reluctant gleam from the blue light, but it was enough to show her a small huddle crouching on the lowest stair. It seemed to be shapeless at first, but then a head was raised.

'Mum! Mum!' said the little boy.

In another moment her hand was being clutched by a very small one, whose owner said, ''Urry, can't you?' and tugged hard.

He had a little torch in his hand and its faint gleam showed a green baize door.

'We'd better look sharp,' said the small boy, and Miss Ranskill, her hand still held in his insistent clutch, followed as he bumped against it with his shoulder. She dreaded what she might see the other side – murder, perhaps, or torture; but there was only an empty stone-flagged passage with another door at the end.

'What's happened?' she asked, but the only answer was – 'Come on.'

Then the child opened the other door, switched on a light, and began to plop bare-foot down a flight of stone stairs.

Miss Ranskill closed the door behind her and followed him.

A square case, dangling from a strap, was slung over his shoulders. He was wearing blue-and-white striped pyjamas and his gold-streaked hair was ruffled at the back of his head.

Now they were in the cellar, but it was not at all an ordinary sort of cellar. There was a strip of carpet on the floor. Three camp-beds, each with a bundle of rugs, were stretched along the length of one wall. There was a paraffin stove and a little oil-cooker and a couple of deck-chairs, in one of which was a rather grubby Teddy Bear.

A set of shelves by another wall held a row of books, a row of tins and a white-painted box with a red cross on it. Another shelf made a home for saucepans, a frying-pan, a kettle, crockery and a teapot.

There were candles and a box of matches on a table.

The little boy curled himself into one of the deck-chairs, nuzzled his face against the Teddy Bear and remarked:

'We're in time tonight. Mum'll go to the pictures once too often.'

There were traces of tears on his face, his eyes were shining and a tiny pulse beat under the blue veining of his temple. But now that his crying was over, he was perfectly assured and at home. If he had rubbed his torch and summoned a wailing banshee to appear in a blaze of blue light, Miss Ranskill would not have been more amazed, for, to her, this cellar was an Aladdin's Cave of delight. If it could have been moved to the island, she and the Carpenter would have had all they could possibly have needed. Here was simplicity and everything that was necessary – all the furnishing in perfection for a desert island.

'Better light the stove, 'adn't you, and a candle case the lights go?'

The striking of a match and the shielding of its wavering flame was better to Miss Ranskill than all the electric light switches in the world. She felt a sense of ritual as she lit the stove. Now she was compensating herself for all the fire-lighting struggles on the island. She set match to candle, too, before asking, 'Why should the lights go out?'

'Power Station might cop it,' answered the boy. Then he

added conversationally, 'We brought down two Fokker-wolfs Thursday – that was the night our own flak killed Mr Coppinger.'

'Oh!' Once again Miss Ranskill was made aware of the new English language. She asked another question.

'What was the noise – that awful whining noise before we came down here?'

The boy fidgeted and rubbed his chin against the Teddy Bear's head. His face flushed as he answered, 'I've not created for a long time now, but I'd bin dreaming.'

'Created?' repeated Miss Ranskill. Was the boy a ventriloquist? No, it was impossible that that eerie outpouring of misery could have proceeded from his small throat.

'Kick up a row,' he explained. 'But 'Arold woke me up and I'd bin dreaming, and I didn't know if Mum was in. I knew the doctor 'ad a went out some time since. I'd heard the night-bell.'

'Who's Harold?' asked Miss Ranskill.

''Arold's our siren – the one that sounded first. The second one we 'eard was Minnie from Larkford.'

'Sirens?' Miss Ranskill's mind was snatching at a story – the story of a cruel-faced beauty luring sailors to the rocks. So might a siren have wailed across the water enticing the brave to the sound of distress.

'Air-raid warnin's – *you* know.'

'Do you often have them *here?*' She emphasised the last word as disguise for her ignorance.

'Not so much as we did, but they mean something now. Early on when we did 'ear the siren we didn't get bombs. When we did get bombs we didn't get the siren.'

He was about eight or nine years old, Miss Ranskill decided, terribly wise in his pathetic generation. His face was grey with sleeplessness, and his hair clung limply to his forehead. He shivered a little, and she changed the subject.

'What have you got in that box round your neck?'

'Go on! You know!'

'I don't.'

'Go on with you!'

'Show me then?'

Grubby fingers groped at a fastening and dragged out something with rubber straps. Then with a duck of the head and a jerk of the fingers the little boy was transformed into a pig-faced monster, a sort of synthetic goblin. His voice sounded muffled as he spoke.

'Mrs Mallison always makes me bring it down in case of leaks from the gas. She don't think 'Itler'll use gas 'cept in the big towns. They mike us tike 'em to school though, just in case.'

Rows of pig-faced goblins paraded before Miss Ranskill's mind's eye – a ballet of child-goblins dancing to the tune that Hitler played and capering to the death-call of Harold and Minnie, the sirens. So this was England now, and she had looked forward to picking primroses.

The child pulled off the pig-face and began to stuff it into the cardboard container.

'I've a tin 'at too,' he told her. 'Bought it at Woolworth's last Christmas.'

'Do you take that to school too?'

'No, that's only a bit of fun. It might keep a bit of shrapnel off of my 'ead though. D'you think there'll be bombs tonight?'

His eyes darkened slightly.

'I –' said Miss Ranskill, helpless against the look that awarded her a false omnipotence. 'I – surely not tonight.' There was pleading in her voice too.

'I don't mind all that much. After there's been bombs, Mrs Mallison gives us cups o' cocoa and biscuits.' He glanced at the row of tins on the shelf, and went on reminiscently.

'Arter we was bombed out in Plymouth that time, they give us bully beef and cocoa made with Nestlé's. You don't get that now – not unless you've been bombed out.'

'Don't you?'

Miss Ranskill was remembering the iron tonics of her childhood and the rewarding chocolate 'to take the taste away'. Was bully beef just compensation for the iron tonic of the bombs?

'I liked Plymouth better'n this. When the blitzing started we used to go and sleep out in the fields all night, and walk back in the mornin'.'

'Who did?'

'Most of us along our street. I used to get a ride on top of a pram sometimes. It was all right in the summer. Then our street got an 'it. Our kitten and me Aunty got killed and Mum said she 'adn't the 'eart to get any more furniture together, so we come 'ere. I missed the kitten.'

Having given his wordless picture of 'Aunty', the boy continued:

'Worst time was when they got the school. *We* was all right though, me and about fifteen more, but some in my standard was killed.'

He broke off and his knuckles whitened as he clutched the Teddy Bear.

'D'*you* think there'll be bombs tonight?'

Miss Ranskill looked at the ceiling for answer, but found none there and none in her mind either. She asked another question.

'Did you always live in Plymouth?'

'We was in London till the war.'

'And was that lovely?'

She longed to turn his mind to something childlike, to the Lord Mayor's Show or a school-treat in Epping Forest or a glance at the Crystal Palace from the top of a bus.

The boy scowled at the question.

'Dad was out of work.' There was a little pause, and he added, 'Dad was killed at Dunkirk.'

He twiddled the Teddy Bear's ears while Miss Ranskill considered these two chapters of a life-history. The phrases united into a poor little poem –

Dad was out of work;
Dad was killed at Dunkirk.

No, it was a rich poem and a great one, worthy of a place in any sequel to the Anglo-Saxon Chronicle.

She knew about Dunkirk because Commander Wrekin had instructed her in that most miraculous chapter in any history of war. Listening to him she had thought of two other sea occasions and the phrases that governed them – one: 'He blew with His winds and they were scattered'; the other – 'Peace, be still.' She knew how the waters had been lulled in the Channel,

148

so that small craft, hurrying from England, had run a silk-smooth course to the beaches where the men were crowded more thickly than any August mob in peace-time. In twenty-four hours the word 'beach' had changed in value: and lost its power to call up a holiday. The men who had come from that place would never be quite the same again.

'Dad was killed at Dunkirk.' He had died, presumably, that his son might inherit the land. The child, so far, had inherited Plymouth air-raids and his enemies had stolen his birthright of fearlessness. Miss Ranskill felt furious that anything so small could be counted as enemy.

The boy's knuckles were rubbing his eyes now and he yawned.

'Where were you before you come 'ere?'

'I was on an island.'

'Sheppey?'

His head was nodding before she could answer, his chin prodded the Teddy Bear's head and the lids closed over eyes that had seen more than any child should have imagined and would, for always, be liable to darken because of the bad news-reel stored in his mind's cinema.

He looked very frail, so easily crushable, and Miss Ranskill wished she knew more about the weight of bombs.

Suddenly, there came a sound as though a giant were slamming his door impatiently in a distant county. The sound was repeated.

The boy opened his eyes for a moment.

''Bout twenty miles off,' he remarked, and gripped the Teddy Bear more closely.

His sleep left Miss Ranskill lonely and rather frightened. If only she were not such an amateur in war. The sight of an ankle and slender foot protruding from the left leg of his pyjamas reminded her that there were rugs on the camp-beds.

She folded one round him, and he made a contented nuzzling movement.

She felt very much alone now.

CHAPTER TEN

I

Again a distant bomb suggested door-banging and brought back a memory of the last war, when the droppings of Zeppelins had menaced Miss Ranskill's world. Perhaps the German machines would not come any nearer to her than those had come then, but she felt she should make some preparation.

The light from the stove made a gold-barred pattern on the ceiling and the reassuring smell of paraffin suggested warmth and comfort.

If only we could have a nice hot cup of tea, Miss Ranskill, we'd get through anything. Tea's the thing we miss most of all.

There, on the shelf, was a kettle, and the cups were beside it. For the next few minutes she was happily busy. Fingers and thumb realised again the dry rustle of tea, and her nose appreciated its savour. This was better than the bedside tray or the tea-shop: this was a picnic and the island as it might have been. She filled the kettle from a bucket, put it on the stove and arranged the cups and saucers on the table. There was pleasure in setting each handle in line with a blue flower on the saucer, in placing the jug exactly two inches on one side of the teapot and the bowl that held granulated sugar two inches away on the other side. She took one of the tins from the shelf and shook it, recognising, after four years, the rattle of biscuits. She might never have been away except that each sound and movement was now joy.

The door of a low cupboard moved an inch or so, scraped against the bricks, and a green-eyed white and orange face peered out. The face was followed by a stripey body as a tortoiseshell cat, big with kittens, but still walking delicately, rubbed itself against Miss Ranskill's ankles. This was another thing she had almost expected, for a singing kettle should conjure a purring cat as surely as a cottage thatch lures a starling to spangle on it.

'Puss! Puss!' said Miss Ranskill, and poured out milk for it, kneeling down by the saucer so that she could hear the dainty lip-lip of the rosy tongue as it flicked the milk backwards. The silk of its fur stood out in little bushy patches from the tightly-drawn skin, and beneath it, Miss Ranskill could feel the stir of tiny lumpy bodies.

When it had finished the milk, the little cat shook a paw and took its leisurely way back to the cupboard. Miss Ranskill could hear it scratching.

Steam began to puff out from the spout of the kettle, and the little boy twitched and whimpered in his sleep. Miss Ranskill longed to wake him so that he could share in the magic when boiling water met the crisp leaves in the pot. She wanted to interrupt the maternity of the tortoiseshell cat because this should be a companionable moment.

Then, as she put the lid back on the teapot, the small boy gave a shriek. It would be best to waken him, to take him from wherever he was and bring him back to the cellar, to the comfort of a Teddy Bear and the fragrance of tea. She poured out two cups, added milk and sugar, and then moved over to the deck-chair.

'Wake up,' she said. 'Stop dreaming.'

The invitation was unnecessary.

There was a roar, a crash and a reverberation. Perhaps they were simultaneous, but Miss Ranskill would never know or remember that. Her ears were shocked into deafness and her chin hit the wooden bar of the deck-chair. Then she went blind. There was trembling even in the close air of the cellar, and then the little boy choked her with his arms. Somehow he tumbled himself out of the chair and on to the floor by her side. He was sobbing and whimpering and each sob shook his hard knobbly little body until it quivered like springing steel, tensed and flexed and tensed again. She could feel his head jerking against her collar-bone.

'I don't want to die,' he choked.

'You can't *die!*' Miss Ranskill's voice convinced even herself in the lull that came before the second crash. And now the cellar itself seemed to be shaking, as lumps of plaster fell from the ceiling, guttering out the candles and suffocating her with dust. There followed the thunderous cracking of guns and other showers of plaster shuddered down into the cellar. Something splashed on to her hand and a warm wet trickle ran down her wrist. Had the child been hurt? She lifted her wrist to her mouth, dreading the salty taste of blood that might be streaming in the darkness, resenting her blindness now instead of pitying it. Her lips were wet and her tongue was exploring, not the savour of blood, but a sickliness of sugar and luke-warm tea. A cup must have turned over, that was all.

The pain in her eyes became intolerable as the other anxiety eased. She had closed her lids down on them and the lids felt razor-sharp.

'It's the dark that 'urts,' shrieked the child as he threshed about in her arms. 'It's the *dark*. Where's the matches? The dark's making my eyes smart.'

Were they then both blind together? How else could darkness hurt?

'Listen, I must put you down for a minute, while I try to find the matches. Lie quite still.'

She fought with him till at last he lay, sobbing and quivering, beside her, his fingers clutching at her nightgown, his heels kicking against her.

'Only for a minute.'

Her own hand was trembling as she groped for the matches. Supposing, when she found them, no answering gleam followed the striking, supposing this darkness was not for a minute but for the rest of life? Her fingers splashed into wetness: they had found another cup.

Nothing like cold tea for the eyes, Miss Ranskill, that's a thing I've proved many a time when I've been stripping ceilings or been a bit too slap-dash with the creosote.

From the far island, the Carpenter was still guiding her.

Not fit to look after yourself, are you, Miss Ranskill?

154

She lifted the cup to her face and used it as an eye-bath until at last she was able to lift her grit-embedded lids, an act that required more courage than she had ever needed; not because of the pain but because she would rather have post-poned the answer to a question.

A tiny light was showing from the oil-stove, a light more beautiful than sunset or moonrise. The candle she had lit was out. She could only just see the outline of the boy, lying in a pathetic heap at her side, but she did not need much light for what she had to do. The next few moments were spent in bathing his eyes, first with the tea, and then with the hem of Marjorie's nightgown dipped in milk. His tears helped to rinse the torturing grit from under his eyelids.

'I don't want to die.'

Miss Ranskill made the same answer as before but without the same conviction.

'You can't die.'

Once again shuddering overtook the little boy. His teeth were chattering now. Presently he stiffened, his head jerked back, and he lay still in rigid terror before sagging once more into a collapsed whimpering bundle.

Rage filled Miss Ranskill, a rage that braced her own muscles till the boy gasped and wriggled and she realised she was gripping him fiercely. Then the crashing noise began again: it was louder this time, so loud that it felt as though the whole earth was cracked into pieces and was tearing the pieces into two with a horrible rending cacophony.

There was nothing to be done now but to wait and hate and hold the child in her arms.

Something was burning. A curious dry smell, reminiscent of a lime-kiln, pervaded the cellar. Was the house burning above their heads, and if so, how long would it be before it crashed in on them?

Miss Ranskill laid the limp body of the boy back into the deck-chair. The wavering light from the stove showed her the bottom step of the stairs and she hurried up them. Even if the house were on fire, there might still be time to escape. It would be better to face the horror of the bombs than the terror of being burned to death.

The door at the top of the stairs resisted her. She tried to rattle the handle, but it would not even turn. She set shoulder to the panels, but made no impression on them. She felt in a non-existent pocket for the new knife, but her fingers only met the folds of Marjorie's nightgown. Of course . . . she had left it upstairs in her bed. Last time she had left it in the Carpenter's bed – in his grave. Because of that she had come to England, purposely, it seemed now, to meet this child whom she might have saved if she had not left another knife in her bed.

Not fit to look after yourself, are you, Miss Ranskill? Now if this knife was lost I reckon we'd be in Queer Street, eh?

Not fit to look after a child either. She made fresh and stronger assault on the door, but it was unrelenting. Perhaps there was something in the cellar that would be strong enough to batter a panel to splinters. A table-leg might do, but she doubted if she could make purchase enough with four legs fixed to a table.

The cellar seemed hotter when she returned to it. Then she noticed that something on top of the stove was glowing and smouldering and that the dry smell had increased. She groped for and found the teapot, took off the lid and poured the contents on to the stove. There was a hiss and a splutter, darkness and a choking smell. Then she trod on the match-box, and in another minute the Christmas-tree smell of candles had overwhelmed the menace of fire, and the candle-lit dust turned golden in the air.

The child had fallen asleep again in the swift strange manner of all young creatures, though he was still twitching a little. Miss Ranskill covered him up again and then spent some minutes in cleaning and drying the stove with the edge of Marjorie's nightgown. When it was alight once more and with the refilled kettle on the top of it, she sat back on her heels for a moment or two and considered what was the next thing to be done. She was dazed and exhausted. Sometime soon, she must battle with the cellar-door again, but she would have a cup of tea first; and when the child was awake she would make him cocoa. She was still hazy with shock, but another vague responsibility nagged at her mind. What was it she had to do? A tiny scuffling sound from behind the cupboard door reminded her, and, taking a candle, she crossed the cellar to see if everything was well with the little cat.

The star of the candle illumined a rumple of paper, a little mother cat and three sleek newly-licked kittens. They lay in a row, their blunt heads half hidden in their mother's fur, their absurd tails towards Miss Ranskill, and they pulled and tugged in rhythm. The little cat's eyes were shining, but there was anxiety in them as she rubbed her head gently against Miss Ranskill's outstretched hand.

Now she added proud purring to the rhythmed tugging of her babies. She flicked her tail with a nonchalant air and it seemed to Miss Ranskill that she almost simpered.

'*Good* little cat. If only I'd known. Poor little cat!'

For it was a very young creature and the small number of kittens showed that they were probably a first family.

Sometime, during the shattering crashes of the night, the little cat, suffering its unheeded pains, had gone quietly about its business of kitten-bearing, had dealt with them and loved them, its love conquering fear. And somehow those blind babies, unaware that there was anything strange about their welcome to the world, had crawled to the warmth of their mother and the milk that was ready at exactly the right time. There they lay in a neat row, one black, one tortoiseshell, and one tawny striped black, their heads sleeked and shining as the heads of any nanny-pampered schoolroom children: three tiny creatures, born in disregard of Germany and all its works. The mother-cat curved a protecting paw as Miss Ranskill's finger went towards her babies.

'All right, it's quite all right. Nothing shall take them from you. These ones shan't be drowned, I promise you.'

So, in the cellar, Miss Ranskill guaranteed succession to a long line of cats and kittens. It was a tiny contribution to the triumph of life over death.

'No bucket-party for you,' she said, as she returned with a saucer of milk and warmed water.

The cat shook herself free of her war-babies and lapped hungrily.

Miss Ranskill had lost her own desire for tea. Exhaustion

was overwhelming her. Only sleep would bring comfort. She rolled a rug round her.

II

Miss Ranskill opened her eyes to see a low-hung star, so criss-crossed with bars as to suggest that it was suffering a strange eclipse. She blinked at it, puzzled by the new wonder above the island. Then, in a second or two, she remembered events, concisely and unemotionally as though they had been chapter-headings from a book – the death of the Carpenter, the voyage from the island and all the bewilderments and terrors of day and night. This, then, was her first awakening in England, not to sheets and fine china, a bedroom nosegay and birdsong in the garden.

Things aren't what you'd think, Miss Ranskill, never have been yet. Seems as though there's always someone having a game with us. Like as not when I get home I'll find my little lad's got the mumps so I'll not know the shape of his face for a month of Sundays.

The barred light was not a star but the reflection from an oil-stove. She was in a cellar, and she did not know if it were night or morning since she was imprisoned against the light from sun or moon that, with the tides, had been her time-keepers. She groped on the floor until the rattle of matches in a box bespoke an old familiarity.

It must still be night or very early morning, for, when she had lit the candles, she saw that the boy on the bed was still in heavy sleep. Children, she knew, awakened lively as sparrows and at about the same time.

Her throat was dry. There was grit on her teeth and dust on herself, the child, and everything in the cellar. The sharpness of it on her lips recalled her struggle with sand on the day she had buried the Carpenter.

The silence was rather frightening, for the whisper of the boy's breathing did not reach her, and there was no mockery of gulls to add truth to the Carpenter's maxim that *There's always someone having a game with you.*

Presently the little cat rustled out of the cupboard and reminded her that there were six instead of two to share in this present isolation and three mouths to be fed from the stores. It insinuated itself between her leg and a chair bar and purred cajolingly. It curved itself against the milk-bottle in feline worship, and Miss Ranskill began to count the rows of tins on the shelf opposite. There were two, four, six, eight that held milk. While one part of her mind made mechanical note, another part of it was astray. Eight tins would be enough for more than a week. Supposing that last bomb had been an infernal device, killing everyone else in the country? The four flat tins looked as though they held sardines. . . . They would get out of the cellar some day, of course. It was only a question of chip by chip, like hacking down a tree, but working at brick not timber. The round tins held soup and the bigger ones salmon, enough, so she calculated, for another week. England would be strange as a deserted island. She remembered reading a book about the last survivor of the world, his tour through the empty shops, his possession of all things and of nothing. Perhaps there would be mice for the cat until they could free themselves. Then there would be a different motor car every day, new clothes and no posterity. The boy could have the Crown of England as a hoop to trundle down the wide emptiness of Piccadilly – rattle, rattle, rattle until moss grew in the streets, though a hoop snatched from a toy-shop might run more smoothly and be just as valuable. The big square tin held tea.

Today or tomorrow (and it might, so she calculated absurdly, be either of those days now) she must count the stores and ration them. Meanwhile, she would dare to be generous to the cat. She filled a saucer full of milk and then crossed the cellar to the shelf where the candles were stored. Light would be the most important thing in this new desolation, where there was no spendthrift sun or wiser moon to lavish and withdraw their gold and silver.

There was more provision in the cellar than there had been on the island, but fewer promises. Its infertility was horrible.

When she had counted the candles in the packets, Miss Ranskill made a detour round the cat so as not to disturb its lapping. So, in the island days, she had always, however tired she had been, moved gently or taken a longer path if the shorter had led past a gull's feeding-place. She, when hungry, had known despair when a hooked fish had escaped her, and had learned to respect the hunter for food.

She did not know that always in the future she would pause on a pavement till a sparrow had finished its crumb, and that the sound of a thrush breaking snails on a rockery would still her movements.

She wondered if the boy had a large appetite. He was lying very still, his head on the crook of his arm, and his smile told that he was not a prisoner.

There is something terrifying in the isolation of anyone who watches a sleeper, and Miss Ranskill, looking at the slumbering boy, wondered about the feelings of wardens as they glanced through the grilles at night and saw the bodies, meaningless as bolsters arranged by practical jokers, and no more occupied than the clothing in second-hand shops. Sleep, for all prisoners, is the time of triumphal escape. She had sometimes seen the Carpenter lying in his freedom, had wondered if he were at home by the fireside or taking stocks of his tools in the shop with the carpeting of wood-curls, or at sea or still on the island. Sometimes he had been able to tell her in the morning. She had often wondered where the final dream had taken him when he lay, still breathing on the beach, his body performing its mechanical work until the empty exertion exhausted it too much.

It seemed, while she watched, as though the boy too had stopped breathing: the blanket scarcely moved above him. Then a little pucker of his lips told her that his dream was changing and she felt exasperation instead of fear. Children were always selfish. The Carpenter would have been up and about and helping her.

She picked up the cat's saucer and then rearranged the cups. Whatever the time, one might as well be busy now that sleep had gone. There was no need to be particularly silent either. The other prisoner might just as well be roused.

Two heads are better than one, Miss Ranskill, even if the second's an addle-pate.

162

III

'Coo!' The boy sat up and rubbed his eyes with dusty knuckles. 'Are we going to have cocoa now? What time is it? How did the cat get down 'ere?'

'The cat's had three kittens,' Miss Ranskill told him. 'And we're going to have cocoa.'

He scrambled out of bed through a cloud of dust released by the scattered blankets. Except for the dirt that covered his head and pyjamas, he seemed unmarked by the night's experience. A bomb had mattered a few hours ago: a cat and her kittens mattered now, and there was no more or less excitement over the one than the other.

When Miss Ranskill had refilled the kettle, and while the boy was still half in and half out of the cupboard, she went once more up the cellar stairs to see if the door were as tightly jammed as she had thought. As she pressed her shoulder against the stubborn wood, the voice of the siren was raised in a long gruesome wail that seemed unending.

She hurried down the steps, expecting to find the boy in a state of terror, but, though the monotonous wailing continued, he did not withdraw his head from the cupboard. He was lying on the floor, his dusty legs waving in the air, his toes curling happily.

'That's Jane,' he remarked as Miss Ranskill stooped over him.

'Is Jane the cat?' Miss Ranskill tried to sound interested, but her ears were alert for bombs and not for cats' christenings.

'Coo! You don't know much, do you?' The boy wriggled backwards. 'Jane's the All Clear.'

'The All Clear?'

'You know, the siren that sounds when the bombing's over and Jerry's gone 'ome. We always calls 'er Jane. I'd an aunt just like 'er, always kickin' up a dust about nothing. Mum 'ates Jane. She can sleep through the Alert, and then Jane goes and wakes 'er after it's all over. Doctor Mallison says the All Clear's like the man that shuts the stible door arter the 'orses are gone. What shall we call the kittens?'

'Shall we call one Tibby?'

The suggestion came from that section of Miss Ranskill's brain that was not entirely bewildered, but she scorned herself as she spoke.

'I shall call 'em Montgomery an' Eisenhower and Beveridge.'

'Why?'

There was contempt in the boy's eyes as he replied, 'Most cats and pups that's not strays gets called Beveridge or Montgomery or Eisenhower, same as most all dogs is called Winston. That kettle's boiling now.'

The boy chatted while Miss Ranskill made the cocoa.

'If Mum was at the pictures she'll be back soon now the All Clear's gone. Tell you what,' he edged closer to her, 'tell you what, let's bolt the door at the top of the cellar stairs so she can't come down till we've had the cocoa.'

'Why shouldn't she come down?'

'She'd only want me to wash. Let's bolt the door and keep 'er out.'

'All right then, we'll keep her out.'

The boy's eyes showed amazement at such unexpected agreement.

'We'll keep her out all right. You stir the cocoa and I'll go and see to the door.'

But before Miss Ranskill could hand over the spoon, the boy was scuttering and squealing across the cellar floor: He was up the stairs before she could think of a word that might stop him.

He would discover the state of the door and be frightened, and the fear would be driven from one to the other and grow quickly and increase in quality. It was better where there were two people that only one should be afraid, else there were no consolation and dominance nor any of the pretence that is the only weapon against terror.

'Cocoa!' said Miss Ranskill feebly. 'Come and give the kittens some cocoa.'

But the boy was pounding on the door already, and she followed up the stairs.

She heard a new voice from the house side of the door as she reached the top step.

'Is that you, mater? Are you coming up or shall I come down?'

It was a male voice, quick, and of a light tense quality. Miss Ranskill answered it absurdly.

'It's I, and the door's jammed; we can't get out.'

There was a thud on the other side of the wood.

'I think I can do it. You'd better stand clear of the stairs though, in case the door comes down with a wallop.'

CHAPTER ELEVEN

I

He was a thin, swiftly-moving young man, with none of the bull-headedness that Miss Ranskill would have expected from Marjorie's son. His eyes were restless and his hands never quite still. They tensed and flexed in between all the definite movements of stroking the kittens, brought to him one after another by the boy, flicking ash from his cigarette and stirring his cocoa.

From his jerked replies to the boy's questionings, Miss Ranskill understood that he had been on night operations for the last three months and that that meant dropping tons of bombs on Germany.

'Bet you killed masses of people.' The boy's cocoa-moustached lips grinned admiringly as he spoke, and he crossed his legs swaggeringly.

'Shut up!'

'But you said last time –'

'Even a butcher wants a Bank Holiday.'

'But you *said* –'

'Will you shut up. You don't know what you're talking about. I –' Marjorie's son turned to Miss Ranskill, 'I don't mind anything but the leaves.' His light voice was raised in fury. 'It's the leaves that are so bloody awful – Sorry! It's all nag and questions and tactfulness, and let's give him a jolly time. And they make special things for you to eat and watch you eating it with a sort of Last Supper look in their eyes. And, just before you go off again, they pile on the heartiness and talk about all you'll do on the next leave though *they* know what *you* know. If they'd only be ordinary about it: it *is* quite ordinary, at least it is to us. And then kids like that –!'

He was interrupted by the shrilling of a female voice.

'Sissle! Sissle! Where are you, Sissle?'

'That's Mum,' said the little boy.

Mum, so Miss Ranskill discovered when she had hurried the little boy up the stone stairs, was half angry and half tearful; and her anger was directed not so much against Hitler and the German bombers as against an unspecified body who had allowed her (Mrs Bostock) to suffer inconvenience. 'They' had left a piece of wire-netting lying about at the entrance to the ARP shelter so that her stockings had been laddered in two places – 'and that's qpons, mind you!' 'They', being what 'they' were, would be most unlikely to refund the shilling she had paid for her seat in the cinema, although the siren had sounded halfway through the 'Big Picture', *Desert Theme Song*. 'Ever so lovely it was. If we had our rights, they'd let us go back and see it all through tomorrow. Robbery, that's what it was. And I've half a mind to go back now this very instant and give them a piece of my mind.'

'Who?' asked Miss Ranskill, and was answered by a dark look that made her feel responsible personally for all the happenings of the night.

'We was all singing in the shelter,' continued Mrs Bostock triumphantly. 'It was "Roll out the Barrel" at first and then those of us that had been at the picture started up with the song Babe Fenelly sings when she's sitting all alone in the desert, and she thinks her boy's been killed, and all the while he's lying gagged and bound be'ind a palm-tree with a nasty-looking Arab gettin' ready to knife 'em.'

Mrs Bostock raised her voice and sang in a piercing tremolo:

You diddun say 'Goo'bye,'
You weren't that sorta Guy,
    You only whispered 'Cheerio! So-long!'
And only you and I
Beneath the great blue sky
    Knew what you meant the day you said 'So-long!'

Tears poured down Mrs Bostock's face as she continued –

My dear, I will not cry,
I'll look up to the sky
    Where sun and moon and stars shall keep me strong,
But always, all the while,
Although my lips may smile
    My heart is echoing 'So-long, So-*long*.'

'Ever so pathetic it was, and they kept on showing you close-ups of the young man's face as he listened from be'ind the palm-tree. She was dressed in white.' Mrs Bostock paused, and added: '*Pure* white,' as vehemently as if she feared that some doubting thought of Miss Ranskill's might sully the film-star's garments. 'White, from top to toe. You ought to have heard us singing in the shelter – that ought to show Hitler something if nothing else does. He ought to be a fly on the wall in some of our shelters, that's what he ought to be.'

'Then we'd swat 'im, wouldn't we, Mum?'

A small hand tightened its grip of Miss Ranskill's and she remembered the child.

'I think perhaps the little boy ought to go to bed now if it's safe. I heard him crying and took him down to the cellar –'

But Mrs Bostock continued her story relentlessly.

'These air-raids aren't run like the Plymouth ones was, and it's no use saying they are. We'd plenty of canteens there and the tea was 'ot, 'ot *and* strong. You'd think they put straw in it 'ere. Well, as I was saying, after the All Clear went, and they let us out, you'd think that was enough, but was it? Oh! no. You'd think They thought we 'adn't 'ad enough, sitting like sardines singing in a damp shelter.'

What horror was coming next, wondered Miss Ranskill.

In the flashing light from the torch, waved so erratically by Mrs Bostock, her son's face looked white and strained.

'Do you think we should put him to bed: he's not had very much sleep?'

'He'll not sleep if he goes now neither: too much excite-ment; he always was highly-strung,' answered the mother. 'Well, as I was saying, I'd gone right the length of Maddison Avenue when they turned me back for an unexploded bomb. I'd a gone on, mind you, if they'd not got ropes right across the road and a coupla ARP men guarding it.'

Even to Miss Ranskill's unwarlike mind an unexploded bomb sounded dangerous and the attitude of its warders not unreasonable.

'But perhaps –' she began.

'I'm not saying anything against the unexploded bomb, *what* I'm getting at is They ought to have put up a notice at the turn into Maddison Avenue, not let us walk all along and then turn us. They don't *think*, that's what's the matter with *them*. I told them strite, I said, "You don't think!" I said, "You can't never be fathers yourselves. How would you like it," I says, "if you was a mother and didn't know if your boy was alive or dead and you was turned back by a notice that ought to have been set up a quarter of a mile back? And like as not," I said, "thanks to you," I said, "I'll be too late to hear the last dying words of my little son." Come 'ere, Sissle.'

But by now Cecil too was in tears, and he clung desperately to Miss Ranskill and wailed, 'I don't want to die! I don't want to die!'

''Ark at 'im!' said Mrs Bostock, proudly, but making no attempt to comfort her responsibility. ''Ark at 'im, and no wonder! A lot They care! I knew just how he'd be when they turned us back in Maddison Avenue. I said, "he'll be shouting for his Mum, screaming himself into a fit most likely." A lot they cared!'

Encouraged more than ever he had been by the shattering of bombs, Cecil's voice, raised more and more loudly, seemed to offend his mother's ears.

'Give over now,' she threatened. 'Give over at once or I'll give you something to cry for as'll make 'Itler seem soft.'

Miss Ranskill began to feel more and more a foreigner. Was there any *truth* in this strange island where laddered stockings, a lack of notice-boards and an illiterate song had more power to rouse emotion than death and destruction and the smashing of bombs! Had it been worth while to take the sea-lane to a wonderland where young men resented their leaves and their mothers kept up the conventions of the fifth form?

'Come on, Sissle, we'd best go and see what the kitchen's looking like. I come in by the side door, and I've not looked round yet. The light's gone though, so if they think they'll get 'ot breakfast sharp at eight, they'll have to think again.'

Miss Ranskill would have returned to the cellar, but the boy's fingers were clinging to her own and they tugged urgently as he followed his mother through the green baize door.

The kitchen, seen by electric torchlight, was fantastic, more like a half-witted property-manager's idea of what a kitchen might look like after a raid than anything Miss Ranskill could have imagined in sanity.

The table was laid with a clutter of plaster from the ceiling, but in the middle of it stood a Cona coffee-machine, its frail bubble rising among chunks and chips of ceiling and layers of dust. The black blind was jagged to shreds and arrows of glass were embedded in the white panelling of a cabinet.

A posy of pale grey flowers in a pale grey bowl on the dresser astonished Miss Ranskill. They looked exactly like Dresden china; and not till she had touched one, releasing a shower of fine dust from the petals, did she realise that they were marigolds. The wall by the fireplace was bulging, a

171

cupboard door hung squalidly from one hinge and a plate on the mantel-shelf lay in two half-circles.

'Well!' said Mrs Bostock.

Then, clear and cool, crowding a woodland into a mad kitchen, sounded the voice of the cuckoo. For an instant Miss Ranskill felt moss at her feet and the stirring of wet leaves against her cheek. This was one of the things she had travelled to hear: the kitchen was gone and May was alive in England.

'Cuckoo! Cuckoo! Cuckoo!'

'They'll not get their 'ot breakfast. They can't expect it!' declared Mrs Bostock. Her torch swung round again and shone momentarily on her red face and tawdry hat.

'Cuckoo! Cuckoo!'

Parody skeltered through Miss Ranskill's mind.

'A slattern and a cuckoo's song will never come together again.'

'They'll have to get help to clear up this mess.' Light from the torch glinted on the jagged daggers of glass low down in the woodwork and the tiny body of a mouse scurried across a lit circle of floor.

'Cuckoo! Cuckoo!'

Miss Ranskill fancied she smelled hawthorn blossom, but the scent of singeing candle-wick took its place as Mrs Bostock flung down a match. Was it possible that the woman didn't hear?

'Cuckoo!'

A tiny wooden door clicked above the face of the clock that hung on the wall behind Miss Ranskill.

'Wrong as usual: it's nearer two,' said Mrs Bostock, and added aggrievedly: 'You'd have thought They might have stopped the clock while They was about it, wouldn't you?'

II

Miss Ranskill was back again in the cellar and once more she was in the company of a sleeper. Marjorie's boy was lying in a deck-chair. His cigarette had fallen to the floor and the fingers of his right hand seemed to be fumbling for it.

The voice of the wooden cuckoo had exhilarated her, but now she felt tired, helpless and impatient. She was lonely too, and in need of speech.

We'll have plenty to tell each other, won't we, Miss Ranskill, after we've both got back to our homes. I'll write to you and you'll write to me. We won't have to think what to say. I'll not have to chew up my pencil then, same as I used to, thinking what to say.

Yes, she must write to the Carpenter and tell him about coupons and bombs, a cuckoo and a cat, cellars, laddered stockings and the blackness of a house by night. News thrust itself into her mind before she could remember that he was dead. Then she tried to imagine him living and alone on the island and receiving, perhaps by carrier pigeon, the letter she would write from the world – a world that now seemed more fantastic to her than ever the island had been. Her thoughts were harking back now instead of forward. She felt like a country child who, in the middle of a whirling day in London, was thinking, not of the treats and new excitements to come, but of the little village station whence the start had been made, of the station-master's wallflowers and the safe familiar seat by the luggage trolley.

'Flowers in their wounds,' muttered the airman, 'that's what she couldn't get over, flowers in their wounds, flowers.'

It was a strange remark, strange enough to send a whole series of pictures flashing through Miss Ranskill's mind. There was a wayside Calvary she had once seen in France. It had been newly painted, and with such realism that the tall foxglove growing beside it had seemed a spear, piercing the Wounded Side with brutal tenderness. There was a poster done by a young artist during the last war, a poster showing a wounded man lying among the Flanders poppies. There was a dying harvest rabbit whose blood had stained a patch of vetch and stubble by the side of a field. There was a blind man smelling a bunch of carnations held by his wife – 'Are they red or white ones, darling? No, don't tell me, I must follow my nose now.'

A ballad jigged into her brain –

'And out of Lord Lovel
There grew a red rose
And out of his lady, a briar.'

She hummed it, as she began to wipe the dust from the table. Marjorie might return at any time now, she supposed, and though seven maids with seven mops might not clean the house in half a night, the cellar might be made habitable. While she was sweeping the dust into a saucer, the airman gave a sudden shout and opened his eyes.

174

'Gosh! I woke myself up. Have I been asleep long?'

'I don't think so,' said Miss Ranskill.

'I say, will you tell me something, please?'

'If I can.'

'Have I been talking in my sleep?'

Miss Ranskill hesitated. The remark about the flowers in the wounds became embarrassing as she thought about it. She guessed that a young man would not care to have his dreams overheard by a strange woman.

'I've a reason for asking – it's important, really it is.'

'You muttered something a little time ago.'

'What was it? I know doctors and nurses always lie, and swear that you haven't uttered under anæsthetics, but *you might* tell me.'

'You only said –' again she hesitated.

'Was it something indecent? If it was, you needn't repeat it. Just give me a hint.'

'No, it was only – I expect you were having a queer dream, you only said something about flowers in their wounds.'

'Flowers in their wounds.' He looked blank for a moment and then nodded his head. 'Oh! yes, I remember now. It rather impressed me, I don't know why. I'd better tell you or you'll think I'm bats.'

'Don't,' said Miss Ranskill suddenly, 'don't tell me if you'd rather not.'

Marjorie's son looked grateful.

'I might as well. It's not the sort of thing I could tell mater: she'd think it so frightfully unhygienic. You see, I went to see one of our chaps in hospital today – a friend of mine. As a matter of fact, he died before I got there. It's all right, you needn't be sorry or anything. It wouldn't have been any good, anyway, if he'd lived, I mean. He was too badly burnt. Blind, you know, and that's not so much fun. Well, I met a nurse at that hospital who'd been out in Algiers when the big do was on there, and she said she couldn't understand why it was that all the wounded, who kept coming in from one particular sector, had flowers in their wounds. She said it was quite uncanny. It turned out that they'd all copped it on one particular bit of road, and the wayside had been lined with flowers. Nothing in it, of course, really – only in war-time! I mean, she said it seemed queer, to see all those big wounds simply stuffed with little wayside flowers. It – I suppose it impressed me a bit. I don't know why it should, simple enough really. I mean, if they'd fallen on to a muck-heap one wouldn't have thought anything about it. Funny thing to talk about in my sleep?'

He looked at her enquiringly, but Miss Ranskill guessed that silence would be the best answer.

He gave a little gulp and asked, 'Did I say anything else?'

'No.'

'Are you absolutely sure? Cross your heart and say die?'

Miss Ranskill, supposing that he was afraid he might have given some important secret away, paused, while trying to choose the words that would reassure him.

'Everyone lies to us. It's so silly, when we are the people who know most of the truth. *We* must get a clearer view and see things in better proportion than *they* do. And yet they lie and lie and go on lying in their teeth about our chances of coming through and everything else. And when we want to marry they talk about war-weddings (war-weddings, my foot! Plenty of *us* are the result of those) and say there'll be plenty of time to settle down after the war. They look at us and see divorce courts and orphans, and think we don't know what they're seeing.'

He lit a cigarette, peered at Miss Ranskill through a smoke-puff and repeated his question, 'You're sure I didn't say anything else in my sleep?'

'No.'

'You see, it's important because, well, because I'm going to be married this morning and my dreams aren't very pretty sometimes, and I don't want to scare Lucy. The mater doesn't know about the marriage, I mean I might have told her if it hadn't been for all this horoosh, but when she comes back and finds the house in a muck she'll be too busy organising and sort of forming threes. Besides –' he paused, 'besides, the mater won't like Lucy as a daughter-in-law. She won't think she's suitable.'

A procession of unsuitables paraded before Miss Ranskill's mind's eye – a predatory widow went undulating by, a barmaid flaunted her blowsiness, a chorus-girl shrieked, a vamp ogled, a married woman appeared unmistakably misunderstood. Possibly the young man saw them too, for he said, 'She's not a bit what you'd think.'

'No,' thought Miss Ranskill, 'they never are,' but she only said: 'What is she like?' and wished she need not hear the answer.

'She's,' the airman puffed violently, 'she's so damned ordinary you wouldn't believe in her.'

'Then that's all right.'

'Oh! no, it's not, not with the mater: you ought to know that, if you were at school with her. If Lucy were a duchess that would be all right, and if she were a dustman's daughter that would be all right too, more or less, because the mater would enjoy putting a jolly good face on it. But Lucy's father is Brown of Brown and Gilson's, the second-best ironmongers in Hartmouth, and she only scraped into the Tennis Club because she'd been sent to a fairly good boarding-school. The mater only just knows Mrs Brown on Committee Meetings, and says she's "a nice little woman". She thinks Lucy's a "nice well-brought-up little girl" too: so she is, bless her! She doesn't exactly say "pardon," and she hasn't got an accent, but the mater will spot "a tone".'

'Tell me about her,' interrupted Miss Ranskill. 'I don't mean about her accent and tone and that sort of rubbish. Tell me what she's like really.'

'She, she's *comforting*,' answered Marjorie's unexpected son, 'I don't mean comforting like a nurse, but you can't feel fussed when you're with her, because she isn't afraid of anything. You see, she's never been badly hurt. I think she believes that when we marry we'll live happily ever after until we're quite old and suddenly pop off together. I don't think she's ever thought I might be killed. So far, nobody she's known *has* been killed. None of her relations, except sort of ancestors like grandparents and things, have died, either. You see, it is rather comforting to be with somebody like that when so many of one's friends are being killed. You do see that?'

Miss Ranskill nodded.

'There's only one thing – I've thought about that, of course, I don't want to go and hurt her awfully by being killed. But – it's difficult to explain – if she's got to be hurt it would be better for me to do the hurting, because I love her. If she got burned or anything I'd want to dress the wounds because I'd think I'd be gentler than anyone else. I suppose one can't be gentle over dying?'

'Perhaps one can,' Miss Ranskill remembered the benign dead face of the Carpenter.

The young man said, 'Yes, that's what I thought,' and continued his description in jerks. 'She's middling pretty (rather lovely goldeny eyes) and middling clever and middling good at games. She laughs a lot, and she won't make scenes. When I come home on leave she won't want to go rushing about to parties every night; she'll talk about the jumpers she's knitting and silly things like that. She thinks I'm marvellous because I can put her sewing-machine right, but I bet anything you like that if she flies after the war she'll never let *me* take her up. It'll have to be a proper pilot who understands civil machines. She's working at one of the Ministries in London and, for some reason or other, they haven't hoofed her into any of the Forces. That's a thing the mater won't like either: she won't like a daughter-in-law who isn't in uniform. It'll be rather a relief to me though to have a wife who hasn't got a tin hat and a kit-bag. I'd hate to get our uniform mixed up. Don't know why I've been telling *you* all this.' He looked rather fierce. 'P'raps you could sort of put it to my parents and explain. P'raps you could say it's become a habit with me now to drop bombs and turn tail. You can say

I'll be coming back on a reconnaissance flight one of these days, will you?'

'I'll try,' said Miss Ranskill. 'But –'

'I know: not easy. I would have told them tonight, I think, if things had been normal. But, you see, the trouble is the mater's never grown up, and she won't believe that I have either. She's playing at soldiers all the time, but I'm a real airman. And yet,' he laughed, 'she doesn't mind air-raids a bit, and I'm scared stiff of them when I'm on the wrong side of the bombs. I like to be well above 'em: much safer.'

The booming voice of the Carpenter filled Miss Ranskill's mind.

> One night there was a hurricane,
> The sea was mountains rolling
> And Barney Barton chewed his wad
> And said to Billy Bowline:
> "A strong Nor' easter's blowin', Bill,
> Hark! don't you hear it roar now?
> Lord help 'em how I pities them
> Unhappy folks on shore now."

Automatically she continued the song herself:

> "And, as for them that's out all day
> On business from their houses
> And late at night returning home
> To cheer their babes and spouses,
> While you and I, Bill, on the deck
> Are comfortably lying,

My eye! what tiles and chimney-pots
About their heads are flying."

'Jolly good show!'
The approval came, not from Marjorie's son, but from
Marjorie herself. Her voice came rollicking down the cellar
stairs.

'Good old Nona! Do you remember the sing-song we had
at St Cat's the night of the big thunderstorm? Your voice
hasn't changed a bit.'

Yes, Miss Ranskill remembered, and continued to remember so vividly that if the feet, clattering down the steps, had
carried a crocodile of schoolgirls into the cellar she would not
have been surprised.

Marjorie was followed by two other people. One was
middle-aged, plump and fair, the other was little and slim.

'Rex!' shouted Marjorie. 'Darling, wherever did you spring
from? Grand to see you! Nona, I don't think you know – may
I introduce Miss Ranskill – Mrs Brown – Miss Lucy Brown.
Nona, Mrs Brown's house has just been blitzed and she's
magnificent about it, simply magnificent. Mrs Brown, Miss
Ranskill is an old school-friend of mine. She has just returned
from one of our islands.'

'Really,' said Mrs Brown, 'I do think it's splendid the way
women are turning up from all parts of the Empire to help in
our war effort, really I do.' Her voice was a little tremulous.

'You must get her to tell you all about it,' added Marjorie.
'Rex, it *is* wizard to see you. Have you seen Daddy yet? Have
you had any good prangs lately?'

III

The cellar was very full of people who were all talking at once. Mrs Bostock had joined the company and was shouting descriptions of the quantity, the quality, and the permeating powers of the dust in the kitchen.

Doctor Mallison had returned from the candle-lit bedroom of a woman who had given birth to twins. He was now trying humbly and eagerly to bridge by words the great gulf of years that lay between him and his son. He longed to know him as one man knows another, to forego all relationship, and make a new friend, but he could only sound patronising. Once, when the boy was four, he had looked up from his porridge bowl and said, 'Hullo, Mallison!' through milky lips, and, as his father had replied with a grave 'Hullo, Mallison,' he had had a vision of a day when they would talk as equals and exchange opinions, forgetting that the years would not lessen the division that lay between them then.

'What about a whisky and soda?' he suggested.

'Bit too early in the day for me, thanks, Dad.'

Sixteen years ago the father had refused toffee for the same reason.

'How you *can* eat that muck at this time in the morning!'

He remembered his anger on the day when the boy had spurned his own profession.

'There's no future in the air. You'd have fun for a few years and then be done for – nothing to do, but idle your life away.'

'Depends if there's a war or not. Anyway, I want to live while I can.'

And now there was a war and the boy *was* living – while he could.

Doctor Mallison tried to make amends now for all past misunderstandings by saying – 'I'd give a lot to be doing what you're doing now.'

The younger man, wary of sentiment, replied. 'Oh! I don't know. Better stick to your baby-snatching, Dad, it's more profitable than bombing them.'

Mrs Brown spoke from her seat in a deck-chair.

'I'm certain you never bomb babies, Rex. I'm sure none of our boys do.'

Marjorie took up her Casabianca stance.

'My son must obey his orders, whatever they are.'

'Oh! they don't send us out to bomb crèches. Funny, though, we must be lining the pockets of the Hun doctors. Still, I don't suppose Jerry does Dad's practice much harm. Bought any boxes of fur coats lately, mater?'

'Darling,' begged Marjorie, 'don't, even in fun, suggest that I could ever be a war profiteer.'

'Twenty-five years ago,' said Doctor Mallison, 'if I had been making what you're making now . . .'

'Oh! I don't do too badly as a hired assassin.'

'Now, Rex,' Mrs Brown wagged a plump forefinger, 'you won't get any nice girl to marry you if you talk like that.'

'Rex likes engines better than girls,' announced Marjorie. 'All the same, he doesn't mean a word he says: he's as proud of his uniform as I am of mine.'

Rex gave a slight shudder, and his mother continued:

'Now, we'd better see about making up beds. Even if the

Browns' house has been blitzed and ours badly shaken we're not going to give Hitler the satisfaction of keeping us up all night.'

'You never said their house had been blitzed,' said Doctor Mallison.

'Didn't I?' said Marjorie casually. 'But, that's why they're here, of course. Mrs Brown was magnificent, quite magnificent. And now we're not going to talk about that any more, are we, Mrs Brown?'

'I don't seem to realise it yet. I'm bound to suffer for it later though, and have a reaction. I'm like that. I always have been. I remember when –'

'Well, you won't *this* time,' Marjorie's voice was fierce. 'Action and reaction are equal and opposite, so we won't think about them. Come along now, Mrs Bostock, you and I will go and make up some beds: that will take us out of ourselves.'

'Mike up beds at this time of night indeed!' shrilled Mrs Bostock. 'Have you seen the stite of the rooms?'

'Oh! please don't bother about beds,' begged Mrs Brown. 'If I could just have a blanket I shan't need anything else. I shall be perfectly warm in my siren-suit.'

She pushed her hands into the pocket of a blue-serge garment that reminded Miss Ranskill of the one-piece pyjama suits worn by small children.

'I'm sure I don't know what I should ever have done without this one, though my husband did pretend to be shocked when I bought it. "You'll be going into rompers next," he said. Rompers, indeed! "Never you mind," I said, "the time may come –" Well, the time has come,' she sighed. 'Yes, indeed it has.'

Now the girl spoke for the first time, addressing, so Miss Ranskill knew, not the two women but Marjorie's son.

'I haven't anything in the world but what I stand up in – not a single thing.'

She was wearing a brown tweed skirt and a white sweater. Her bare toes showed through the strapping of her childish sandals. Her straight brown hair had a nursery look.

'You're luckier than I am,' said her mother. 'You've all your London things safe in Town.'

'But I haven't. I brought them all back.'

'Whatever for?'

The golden-brown eyes flickered and then looked wary.

'Oh! just to mend and – and sort over.'

'If only you'd been in a uniformed job everything would have been easy,' announced Marjorie. 'You'd only have had to ask for a new issue of everything.'

'Yes, and now I haven't got a rag.'

'You look –' began Rex, and then checked by his mother's stare, supplemented 'all right' for the word in his mind. 'You look quite all right.'

'But not for *always*.'

The girl stood in her wedding garments, a Cinderella of a bride.

'It seems,' she said, 'it seems so funny to be The Enemy. Fancy *my* things being bombed.'

Miss Ranskill had seen that look before in the eyes of a very young rabbit early one morning. It had stopped nibbling clover, raised the dewy quivering nose that could catch a hint of menace more surely than the pink transparent ears. The rabbit's eyes had spoken. 'Then there's something more in my world than clover and dew and mother and all the rest of us. Something *bad*.' Then it had terrified itself to a flurry and its white scut had flashed out signals of reproach all the way from the clover-patch to the burrow.

'Fancy *my* things being bombed. Somehow I never –'

'Come on, and let's dig out blankets,' said Marjorie, deaf to the words behind the words – 'Fancy *my* man being vulnerable!'

CHAPTER TWELVE

Two of the kittens were beginning to open their eyes, but the third, a tortoiseshell, maintained blind indifference to the light that gave shape to the wickerwork around it. In a day or two now, its sisters would discover, by diffident paw-pats, that shapes can be felt, that looming straws can become enchanting playthings, and reward by strokings more pleasurable than the licking of a mother's tongue. The tortoiseshell kitten was in no hurry, the warmth of its mother delighted it; that was enough for the time.

Miss Ranskill, in her corner of the third-class carriage, felt in much the same mood. Two newspapers lay unopened on the lap of her new grey skirt. Presently she would try to understand their contents, but for the moment it was enough to watch the landscape flicking past, to see the flourishing of the may-flowered hedges and be dazzled by the fields of the cloth of gold.

But what went ye out for to see? But what went ye out for to see?

The engine chugged out the tune insistently and a loose button on the sleeve of the woman opposite joggled on its thread in rhythm. *But what went ye out for to see? But what went ye out for to see?*

Green and gold willows edged a stream. *But what went ye out for to see? A reed shaken with the wind?*

A re-eed shaken with the wi-ind, a re-eed shaken with the wi-ind. The chant of the engine was so clear to Miss Ranskill that she felt the other occupants of the carriage must interpret it too.

Ten days ago she had shuffled away the broken glass below Marjorie's spare room window, had looked through the empty frames to see Lucy Brown running hatless and bare-legged down the path on her way to a wedding. Before that, the girl had talked to her for a few minutes.

'Rex says you know about *us*. Nobody else must till afterwards. Rex is being awfully sweet about it. He says he likes me better in these things. Mummy would be horrified. She'd always planned a white wedding and never in May either. But you can't wait for June in war-time when – when we may only have one week of May ever – for all our lives.' The goldeny eyes had shown fear for a second time. 'Rex doesn't think about what – what might happen. I don't think he's ever thought he mightn't be lucky. Boys don't when they're that age: it's only the women who know. So we laugh a lot and I don't think he ever guesses.'

A re-eed shaken with the wi-ind, chugged the engine, *But what went ye out for to see?*

Now the carriage window framed a seascape and then a tangle of barbed wire made Teignmouth beach ugly. The red rocks of Dawlish had kept their shape and the waves were scudding inland. Miss Ranskill remembered journeys taken to the West Country as a child, her first sight of the sea and the thought that the waves were hurrying inland to cool the hot tired wheels of the train so that it could run faster to the land of buckets and spades, sandy buns, jelly-fish and seaside lodgings.

The label on the kittens' basket flapped in the salty breeze. There had been trouble about the kittens. The clank of a bucket-handle on the morning after the air-raid had reminded Miss Ranskill of a promise she had made in the cellar.

'Oh! well,' Marjorie had looked cross and tired. 'Oh, well, I suppose if you promised Cecil, we'll have to keep one. I suppose we shall get a lot of mice from the bombed houses. All the same –'

'Can I draown the kittens?' the request came from Cecil, 'lemme draown them!'

'There you see, he doesn't want a kitten at all. No, Cecil, nice little boys don't drown kittens. Your mother can do it properly. You'd better do it now, Mrs Bostock, but I suppose you'd better keep one or the cat will be ill.'

'But, Marjorie, I didn't promise Cecil.'

'I thought you said you did.'

'I promised,' and here Miss Ranskill hesitated because it was quite impossible to say in the presence of Mrs Bostock, 'I promised the cat.'

She did not feel sure that, even to one with as high a sense of honour as Marjorie, a promise made to a cat would count. Anyway, it would sound idiotic, and was unreasonable. She would never be able to explain the instinct that had forced her to guarantee cathood for three blind kittens.

'Oh! well, I suppose Rex wants them for mascots or something. If you promised him, we'd better keep them. They'll have to stay where they are though. You know we've got to go to a hotel for at least a fortnight while the windows and things are repaired.'

Later, feeling guilty because she was using part of the money lent by Marjorie, Miss Ranskill had bought a basket, big enough for the cat and her unweaned kittens.

The days that had wrought such a change in them had altered Miss Ranskill too, and brought her knowledge.

She was now recognised as a citizen and had an identity card to prove her right to exist. She had three ration books, one for clothes, one for food, and a third that enabled her to buy three-quarters of a pound of sweets each month.

But what went ye out for to see? A reed shaken with the wind or three ration books?

She had an identity disc too – a parting present from Marjorie, who had delivered a speech when she gave it.

'You won't think me morbid or anything, will you, old thing? But honestly it's the most practical present I could think of. If you should cop it in a blitz, it would save an awful lot of fag to the people who'd dig you out. I mean, nowadays when time's so precious one really oughtn't to go on giving bother after one's dead. Besides, if there should be an invasion, and I honestly hope, I mean, I think there *may* be one, it might save you being shovelled into a Hun grave. Because, after all, there'd be some women among the invaders, nurses and things. Besides, there'd probably only be odd bits of you left and a few scraps of clothes. Honestly, I can't think of anything more ghastly than being buried with Huns – enough to make you turn in your grave, if you'd anything left to turn, I mean.

And, I say, old thing, I've had the school motto engraved on the back of the identity disc to make a sort of link between us.'

The patch of her wrist that lay underneath the identity disc began to itch a little and she scratched it, rubbing out traces of the embossed legend, *Honour before Honours.*

'Anyway,' she thought, 'if I am blitzed and am due for a George Medal, they won't bother to give it to me if they read the school motto, and they won't think I've been looting shop-windows either.'

For by now Miss Ranskill knew a little about the war, just enough to keep her as quiet and wary as the occasional rider of a hired hack should be, if ever he were daring enough to allow himself to be shown round a Newmarket training-stable. She knew England had won the Battle of North Africa, that it was no longer 'done' to bewail Communism, that the Government Evacuation Scheme had been a failure, but that it had laid bare the most appalling pocks in our civilisation. She knew what 'V' stood for, and what ARP meant. She knew that it was smart to be shabby, and that it was also rather clever to turn coloured linen bedspreads into dresses and to imagine that the Government didn't know. She knew that Lord Woolton ruled flesh, fowls and a few good red herrings. She knew just as much about the Battle of Britain as little Wilhelmine had known of Blenheim, but had learned to be as loyal as old Caspar to Marlborough's successor.

Yet, in spite of identity card and disc, three ration books, a third-class ticket to Hampshire, a suitcase, a collection of carpentry tools, three kittens and a cat, Miss Ranskill was a woman whose will had been passed for probate three years ago.

Marjorie had been generous and had lent money for clothes and the journey and at least a week's future expenses.

If, retaining her present knowledge, she could put back the clock, return to the island and (her heart lifted at the thought) talk to the Carpenter, what would she have to tell him? There they had struggled for food against the wiles of that food and the elements. Here, they must submit to the dictates of bureaucracy before being allowed to buy food and clothing. There the dying of the beacon fire had been a tragedy: here the showing of a light by night was a crime. On the island two people had done the work of two. In England a thousand might do the work of four thousand or ten do the work of two. On the island, they had obeyed the rules they had made, in this other island, in spite of the need for weight-pulling, in spite of the equal need to win the war, thousands were employed to see that the rest did not cheat. What would the Carpenter make of that?

I tell you this, Miss Ranskill, I tell you this, we might be a lot worse off than what we are here. Fancy trying to live anywhere else with nothing but what we've got here. We think now we'd be grateful for a roof over our heads, wait till we've got it and then see how we'll clutter up the rooms. Wait till you see the shops, Miss Ranskill. You're pleased with the powder-puff I made you, but it'll only be fit for the dustbin by the time you've looked in one shop-window. Too much or not enough – that's what it is all over the world and nobody knows when they've got enough, that's how it is, Miss Ranskill.

A fidgeting in the carriage compelled her mind to return from its sea-lit voyage. The woman opposite was groping in her handbag. Since the beginning of the journey she had read a few pages from one book and a few from another, had written down one or two crossword puzzle clues and done several rows of knitting. Now she had lit a cigarette and was turning the contents of her handbag out on to her lap. There were two boxes of matches: those were still invaluable to Miss Ranskill's eyes. There were two handkerchiefs, a cigarette-case, a lipstick, some orange sticks, a pocket-diary, a tiny mirror, a book of stamps, a railway ticket, an identity card, a powder compact and a letter.

Only the handkerchiefs and the matches would have been the slightest use to the Miss Ranskill of the Island. Only the handkerchiefs, the identity cards and (well, yes) the powder compact were much use to anyone in a railway carriage. Miss Ranskill was beginning to feel superior until a fluttering label attracted her and she remembered the kittens and the set of tools.

You've got to keep a sense of proportion, Miss Ranskill, there'd be nothing to laugh at else.

She too was a fool in the company of at least one other fool, and for the first time during the journey she felt the warmth of companionship.

The young airman in the far corner of the carriage was asleep. There were dark shadows under his eyes and his mouth was restless. It must be odd to him to be travelling like this. He and his kind were evolving slowly into a race apart. Engendered just before the last war, they were already incomprehensible and remote. They had seen what none but their generation could see – cities burning below them and the bowl of the stars above. The wings of Icarus melted when he was still young. What would happen to these men when the money they had been used to burn in the air was dissipated to other purposes? How would they, who had seen the ten-acre meadows as inch-wide patches for a county's quilt with the warp and weft of streams and hedges no thicker than rows of stitching, keep the bounds of a counter in the years to come and employ their fingers to cut patterns of crêpe-de-Chine for customers?

Miss Ranskill remembered their fathers in the days after the last war. So many of them had journeyed through the valley of humiliation, worn smooth by the steps of commercial travellers; and had waited diffidently on doorsteps to sell vacuum cleaners and gimcrack gadgets. Fingers that had gripped joy-sticks had closed gratefully on the tips of war profiteers at petrol-filling stations.

To the young airman, asleep in his corner, the war must be a dream – half nightmare, half enchantment: perhaps even now he dreamed of the awakening.

The sailor beside the airman was leaning forward a little so that his view through the window was not interrupted. He was not such a puzzle to Miss Ranskill. She too had looked at the sea until her eyes had ached for the grey of a ship to break the greater grey of water, and her own eyes now showed the same network at the corners. He had the scoured look that makes every seaman ashore appear more immaculate than his civilian fellows. The unconfined muscles of his neck showed arrogantly above his collar and the straight line of his flannel. He was taking his fill of the land, but he looked rather bored by it. Suddenly Miss Ranskill remembered that in all her life she had never seen a sailor in a field. She wondered if there were any sea-superstition that banned meadows as unlucky, wondered what the sailor would reply if she asked him, imagined the astonishment of the other passengers supposing she did, and laughed out loud.

Now on a desert island one may laugh as freely and inconsequently as one chooses, and very slight things serve to amuse. The expression of a gull may remind one of a woman in the village at home, its gait and consequential air of someone about to open a bazaar. The astonished eyes of a crab may seem funny. Memory too plays such an important part in desert island life that one is ready and eager to be amused.

When we've given over remembering how to laugh, Miss Ranskill, we'll be no better than the fishes. Many's the time I've laughed out loud before you was washed ashore to cheer me up, and many's the time I burst out laughing still even when I'm in one cove and you're in another. Laughter's the only thing that keeps one sane to my way of thinking.

A desert island is a more suitable place for laughter though than a railway carriage in England. Miss Ranskill realised this truth, as she was made self-conscious by the alarmed gaze of the woman opposite. The sailor found her more interesting than the meadows he had been watching. He turned to look at her, and his sudden movement awakened the airman, who blinked amazedly.

A three-year-old child, on its mother's lap, pointed a sticky finger and demanded, 'Do it again!' The elderly civilian at her side coughed rather peevishly.

Some explanation seemed necessary. Since Miss Ranskill

found it impossible to give one, and equally impossible to keep silence throughout such concern, she compromised by saying, 'I *do* apologise!' in a voice that was very much louder than she had meant it to be.

Instantly all the eyes, except those belonging to the small child, were averted from her. Had she been naked, she could not have been treated with such severe seemliness.

'Do it again!' repeated the child.

"Ush!' said the mother. 'Give over looking at the lady,' and she dumped the child round on her lap until it shared the view through the carriage window with its embarrassed elders.

And now Miss Ranskill was very much alone, reproved and excommunicate from the society of her fellow-beings. She sought consolation by looking at the identity card, which did not do much to reassure her, though it should have assured any official that Ranskill Nona M/FURL/2388/2 was a British citizen and had a right to existence.

The child turned round to glance at her but was again twisted into position by its mother.

'Miaou!' said the little cat from the basket on the rack, 'Miaou! Miaou!'

Once more the occupants of the carriage stirred to look at Miss Ranskill. Some peeped furtively, some glanced once and then away.

'Do it again!' cried the child.

'Miaou! Miaou!' repeated the cat obligingly.

The extremely perturbed face of the child's mother suggested that she thought it bad manners to practise ventriloquism in a train.

Miss Ranskill sighed, as she stood up and took the basket from the rack.

From the moment she opened the lid she stopped being an alien. She and the little cat and the kittens became the most popular travellers.

'Did you ever!' said the mother of the baby. 'What little dears!'

The sailor raised the chin of the black kitten with a forefinger until the milky eyes blinked at him.

'We'd one the spit of this in the ship,' he said. 'It fell overboard off Gib – a bad day's work that was. Might have been this little chap's twin.'

The airman plucked the tortoiseshell from Miss Ranskill's lap and laid it in the palm of his hand.

The woman opposite became confidential.

'I'd a lovely cat at home, orange with a great white ruff,' she traced the tawny stripes of the smallest kitten with a scarlet fingernail. 'I had to give him away when I went into digs and started office work. Then I found my landlady would have looked after him for me, and I've been kicking myself ever since.'

'Kitty! Kitty!' shrilled the child.

'The very spit of this one,' repeated the sailor. 'I wouldn't mind being a ship's cat myself. Want to come to sea, do you?'

He addressed the black kitten and Miss Ranskill answered for it.

'Would you like to have it? If you would I could send it to you as soon as it can leave its mother, if you give me your address. It might be lucky.'

'What about making a few flights over Germany, eh?'

The airman was questioning the tortoiseshell but the child's mother reproved him.

'All very well, but suppose you was shot down, what happens to the kitten then?'

'I hadn't thought of that,' replied the airman humbly.

The man by Miss Ranskill's side spoke for the first time.

'We are a truly remarkable people!' he declared. 'I have always maintained that if the Speaker kept a supply of puppies to be produced in the House at appropriate moments, the most heated debates would end amicably. In fact, if the Germans were dog-lovers there need have been no war. An International Kennel Club could have done much more than any League of Nations. You, Madam, who can anticipate so glibly the tragedy of a kitten's death and ignore what to you is, presumably, the minor accident of the loss of a man's life, prove my point.'

And now, the man in the waterproof took Miss Ranskill's place as outcast.

The child's mother sucked her teeth ostentatiously, and muttered, 'Well, I mean to say, poor dumb animals!' and turned her offspring's back on the brutal speaker.

'Poor little beggar,' said the airman, as he stroked the kitten under its golden chin.

'If you *was* wanting a home for the black one,' suggested the sailor.

In five minutes, Miss Ranskill had found homes for all the kittens. Three slips of paper, bearing addresses to which they might be sent as soon as they could leave their mother, joined the identity card and ration books in her handbag. Once more she was a person of some consequence, a giver of gifts with a place in society.

The man by her side craned a vulture neck to peer at the huddle of kittens in her lap.

'A remarkable people,' he repeated. 'You, Madam, have probably drunk milkless tea for the last few years and sacrificed your butter ration for the sake of a cat's paws. You would think it generosity to take meat from the mouth of a child and give it to your lap-dog.'

'For the last few years,' Miss Ranskill told him, 'I have not tasted milk *or* tea *or* butter. I've robbed gulls' nests and snatched at the fish they dropped from *their* mouths whenever they were fools enough to open them.'

And now she was in isolation again, outcast with the man who had no truck with kittens. The females in the carriage looked uncomfortable, the males, except her partner, incredulous.

'Sounds like a desert island,' he muttered.

'It *was* a desert island.'

Miss Ranskill turned her face to the window but she did not see the rushing landscapes. She was wondering if she would ever be able to remember that her truth was shocking and evidently not to be borne by a people who, though they had suffered air-raids and mutilations, the destruction of their homes and the death of their kin, yet could not bear to hear oddly-timed laughter or statements of facts beyond their immediate knowledge.

Presently the train had swept past the scarred outskirts

of Bath and the crowded station, where men and women in every kind of uniform jostled each other like sheep or stood forlornly by kit-bags.

Then there were more ravaged buildings and then little housebound roads thrust themselves out towards the country. At last there were only farms and grey villages with the green of Somerset in between. The lanes, like all lanes seen from train windows, led to nowhere in particular. The houses only existed as pictures for the benefit of travellers. One might as soon live in one of them as inhabit a cottage in a water-colour sketch. The villages were as fantastic as all railway villages are, the children who waved from the sidings had no existence at all, and it was impossible to think of anyone stepping on to one of the wayside platforms in order to go home. Yet there was a difference – there was something lacking, and for a long time Miss Ranskill wondered what it could be.

When, at last, she remembered, she was rather shocked. It was all very well to play the railway game with villages and stations, but *they* were going a little too far when they began to play back. It was as baffling as though a baby whom you had addressed as 'there's a pretty lamb then' had suddenly leaped on all fours and followed its mother, the sheep.

She forgot her disgrace and spoke urgently.

'Why have none of the stations got names?'

'Because,' said her neighbour at last, 'because we do not believe that the Hun has learned geography. A few of us have maps of Germany, but we do not believe that there are any maps of this country outside the British Isles. We removed the names from railway stations on the same glad day that we painted the sign-posts white. We decided it would be a good idea for the invading Hun to mistake Huddersfield for London. We thought it would be a joke to hear him sing, "Oh! Mr Porter, whatever shall we do? The Fuehrer's taken Birmingham and he thinks he's taken Crewe."'

'Oh!' said Miss Ranskill. 'Then how?'

'It's perfectly easy, really, because the porters bawl out the names. We do not believe that any of the invading Huns will understand English, nor, of course, will the spies. As a matter of fact, none of our porters speak English either – rather a vicious circle, don't you think?'

CHAPTER THIRTEEN

The inhabitants of the garden were declaring war and peace in their several ways.

'Buzinezz as uzual!' buzzed a bee as it blundered against a spray of lilac before flying down to settle on the velvet of a wallflower, 'Buzinezz as uzual!' Its action released two scents, the sharp of the lilac, the soft of the wallflower. Each, as it drifted through the air, maintained for a moment the peace and permanence of village gardens. Then the bee-swung wallflower flicked against a clump of chives that edged the bed so that a stronger fragrance gave a taste of war. The chives stood stiffly for battle, so did the garland of parsley round the rose-bed on the lawn, and so did the seedling lettuces under the windows of the low red cottage. The aviary that had once sheltered budgerigars told a sad empty little story of the famine that had lasted a week too long for short lives.

The thrush on the rockery rapped out a grace with his snail-shell. The wagtail on the lawn flicked an insolent tail. There was nothing wrong with his world, so the tail remarked with frequency.

Even if the swallows had seen untoward sights during their crossing, their arrow flights suggested no mechanised progress since Crécy. A spider arranged its larder between gate and gate-post with the skill used by its ancestors before any child had learned to say 'Fee-fi-fo-fum'.

The entry of Miss Ranskill caused some stir in the garden. The spider's web snapped. The thrush left its snail-shell, the wagtail flicked indignation as it left the lawn; and the bees bumped irresolutely from flower to flower, releasing so many tiny gusts of scent that her nose might have been bewildered if she had not been concentrating so hard on seeing.

So this was where Edith lived, in this contented cottage on an island of flower-bordered lawn. This was where she would live too, she supposed. At any moment the white door might be opened or a window flung up. She put down the cat's basket and turned to the gate, where stood the boy who had carried her suitcase and tool-bag. She must give him his sixpence so that he could go before the door opened.

But there was no stir from the house, even when the gate had clicked, even while she walked crunchingly up the path, or when her footsteps made the scraper jangle on the flag-stone.

She cried, 'Edith! Edith!' while her right hand fumbled for the bell-push and her left pounded at the knocker. The clangour of the bell went on for too long: she wanted to hear the running of feet and the creak of the opening door. The silence that followed was too long also, and very unwelcoming. Could she, but then how could she, have missed Edith on that tiny deserted platform? Edith had said in her letter that she would meet the train: the cottage was only two minutes' walk from the station.

Miss Ranskill rang again, and now the crying of the bell's voice through emptiness was almost frightening. She knocked until echoes interrupted echoes. Then she went round to the back of the house.

She followed a path that led between shrubs to a small drying-green bordered by currant bushes. Pegged out on the line, as the first proofs of Edith's habitation, were some underclothes, two striped shirts that she recognised and (signal this time of Edith's belief in her own death) a very much worn and rather shrunken cardigan of her own. Its colour had faded since the days of peace; it had been clear blue when she had left it behind at home. The little nosegays of flowers on the pockets had been picked off and bright patches showed where they had been. It was all right, of course. It was sensible and practical of Edith to have made use of her clothes. All the same, she need not have flaunted the cardigan on the very day of her homecoming.

'She's worn it for a long time too,' thought Miss Ranskill. 'She must have begun wearing it almost as soon – anyway, blue never suited her; it always made her look rather sallow. She takes sixes, so she can't be wearing my shoes.'

She knocked on the back door, rather more sharply than she might have done if she had not seen the line of clothes.

There was something wrong about the ensuing silence. Even if the knock stirred no householder, there should have been the scutter of paws and a bark, sharpened to ecstasy as her voice was recognised. There should have been a bowl of water by the doorstep and a cloth for the drying of feathered pads. Edith was always finicky.

Miss Ranskill stooped down and lifted up the door-mat, but there was no key there. Then she remembered that the door-mat had always been *her* key-cover and that Edith had used a flower-pot.

'A door-mat's so obvious. It's the first place a burglar would look.'

'People don't always think of the obvious. A burglar could get in *any* way.'

'A flower-pot's safer. He'd probably hunt for a bit before smashing the windows.'

'If he's going to smash the windows *anyway*, why not leave the key in the door?'

A butterfly flicked on top of an inverted bee-skep near the door. If she had been a burglar, thought Miss Ranskill, it would probably have given the same delicate hint. She stooped and picked up the key.

The kitchen was very clean, very tidy, but empty of life. She noticed, with a pang, that the old nursery tea-canister with its painting of Queen Victoria, stood on the mantel-shelf. A scar ran across the face of the Queen. She remembered her tears on the day that the new flakes of paint had been sprinkled on the nursery fender. It seemed a very long time ago, and the Queen looked old and more faded now. There was nothing else that she recognised except a little lustre jug standing on a tray on the kitchen table. There were two trays, each with its small sugar basin, jug, teapot, plates and toast-rack.

Her heart warmed towards Edith. Here was the first sign of welcome. The sight of a dish marked 'PUPPY' was heartening too, unless, of course, the spaniel had a successor.

Two places were laid in the little dining-room, but the flat bowl of flowers in the middle of the table puzzled Miss Ranskill as much as the mock Jacobean sideboard. It was unlike Edith to behead monthly roses and cram them together in a shapeless mass like so many dollops of pink blancmange. They had always cut sprays of the monthly roses and set them among the sincere blue of forget-me-nots and the lace of cow-parsley. Edith had added a buttercup or two – 'pink needs yellow.' They had arranged flowers as though they were growing – 'I like to bring the garden indoors.'

The sitting-room was almost frightening in its ugliness. It had yellow-washed walls and powder-blue chair-covers. 'Sunday school blue,' thought Miss Ranskill, quoting from her mother and the objections she had raised over their choice of summer ginghams in the nursery days. A mock Jacobean 'what-not' was decorated with a scattering of Indian silver knick-knacks. There were anæmic water-colours on the walls. There was an insipid mauve carpet and shiny mauve cushions in the chairs. There were more dollops of flowers – purple and yellow pansies, this time in a black bowl on a walnut occasional table. The sight of her great-grandmother's sampler suspended from the silver-embossed sheath of a scimitar enraged Miss Ranskill. Edith might have been obliged to take a furnished house, but surely she could have 'played houses' in it better than this.

Something was very wrong.

Something else was wrong too. In her stupid disappointment over the colouring of a room and the emptiness of a house, she had forgotten the cat and the three little kittens, still humbly crowded into their basket by the gate. She ran out of the house and along the laurelled path. A countryman was walking down the road that led past the cottage. His shoe-leather creaked, and so did the straps below his knees. 'A hedger and ditcher,' thought Miss Ranskill as she noticed the bill-hook laid against his shoulder. Soon, she knew, he would be more than a hedger and ditcher: he would be old so-and-so. She would know all about his family and they would pass the time of day together.

''Mornin', Miss.' A finger jerked up to his cap peak and Miss Ranskill felt comforted as she returned the greeting. He had come alive through one war and was too old to be touched by this one, except through stabs from the wounds and death of the younger generation; and he had seen too many births of spring and too many deaths of winter to be much affected. The hedges increased and shrivelled, leaf by leaf and fall by fall, and he was as persistent as an old cart-horse. *All in good time, all in good time*, his footsteps beat out a steady rhythm till the sound of them faded away. A swift shadow from a Spitfire's wing darkened the chalk of the road ahead of him, but he did not look up as the machine whizzed overhead in its rollicking hurry and dipped a wing towards the fields below.

The kittens were mewing in the basket. Soon they and their mother made a little dappled hearth-rug on the patch of carpet before the fender. The room looked better now.

The telephone bell rang sharply and suddenly and Miss Ranskill looked round the room for it. The jangling summons sent her running into the hall, but it was not there nor in the dining-room. Meanwhile, Edith must be ringing up to explain why she had not met the train.

She ran upstairs, pushed through the half-open door of a bedroom and was greeted by a louder shrilling, which ceased as she snatched the receiver from its hook.

'Oh! is that you Mrs Phillips?'

Of course it wasn't Mrs Phillips. Who was Mrs Phillips?

'Mrs Phillips, I just wanted to make sure –'

'This isn't Mrs Phillips.'

'Oh! is it you, Miss Ranskill?'

'Yes, yes.'

'I wonder if you'd be so very kind as to tell Mrs Phillips that the meeting is at half-past two on Thursday, *not* at three-thirty. And we do so hope that you'll be able to come too.'

'I don't think –' began Miss Ranskill.

'Oh! what a pity! But I know it is your glove-making day. Well, if you *will* tell Mrs Phillips – thank you *so* much.'

One couldn't go on holding a telephone receiver and listening to the low buzzing that hinted at maddening secrecy. Miss Ranskill hung the thing up and looked round another ugly room, made friendly this time by familiar things. The mantelpiece was crowded with objects that had the facile power to bring back a spring morning or a winter afternoon so clearly that she could almost smell the lilac through an open window, and then flick away a season to inhale the scent of chestnuts roasting on a hob. There was the weathercock man and the weathercock woman, who had been prodded with hatpins on the mornings before picnics. There was the mosaic box from Capri, holding as many secrets as Pandora's casket – all the blue of the grotto and all the shimmering colours of the day. Her own photograph and her own Bible stood on Edith's bedside table; in fact, the room held more of herself than her sister.

'I had a lot of things then,' thought Miss Ranskill, remembering the powder-bowl that the Carpenter had made, and the little besom for her hair. 'I'd better find *my* room now and see if that's crowded as well.'

The room opposite contained nothing that was recognisable. The bed was turned down for the night and a dressing-gown hung on the rail at its foot. She supposed it was one of her sister's and felt grateful for the preparations, as she remembered how she had longed for the sight of a turned-down bed in the days when the wind had laid a shifting coverlet of sand in the island shelter. Here, too, was a bedside table with another Bible and another photograph on it. From its morocco leather frame the face of an elderly and rather offended-looking Army officer stared at Miss Ranskill. It couldn't be a joke, Edith's sense of humour was as orderly as her account book. Anyway, there was nothing at all jocular in that forbidding countenance.

She opened the Bible and read on the fly-leaf the inscription – 'Philippa Gilroy with love from her Godmother, January 2nd, 1900.' That told nothing.

And now Miss Ranskill was as baffled as any of the three little bears. 'Who's been sleeping in my bed?' The absurd question drifted into her brain, and she glared at the huffy face in the photograph, before opening the door again.

There was a bathroom behind the third door on the little landing, and the fourth opened into a spare room, looking spare and mean and unwelcoming as such rooms sometimes do, when one guest has left and the next is not expected yet. The bed was humpy with folded blankets, the towel-rail was bare, and there was nothing on the dressing-table except a very unbecoming mirror that reflected Miss Ranskill's baffled expression most unhappily.

'Miaou! Miaou!' The cat had left its squirming family and was coming up the stairs in search of her.

Miss Ranskill took it down to the kitchen, helped it to a saucerful of milk and returned to the drawing-room. She might as well, so she decided, get used to the room before Edith returned home. It *must* be her home, the boy from the station had led her to it at once, and there was the added evidence of possessions; but who was Mrs Phillips, and who was Philippa Gilroy, and who was the Army officer? Above all, where was Edith?

Nothing in the room could answer those questions, but the arrangement of the mantelpiece gave Miss Ranskill other things to think about.

A clock in a black marble case divided the broad shelf into two separate divisions: each of these was so crowded that it was not surprising that no one object had attracted her notice when she first came into the room.

On one side was a photograph that was twin to the one on the bedside table. Around it were snapshots, some blurred and some hideously distinct of the same man. Miss Ranskill now saw him in shorts, in plus-fours and in ordinary well-filled clothes. One silver cup made it clear that he had been a good golfer, another that he had succeeded in a gymkhana; and a rose-bowl bore witness to the fact that Major Phillips had been held in high esteem by the officers of his regiment and thought worthy of a wedding-present. There were some medals, more Indian knick-knacks and a little silver elephant.

But if one side of the mantelpiece was a shrine, the other was rival to it, and Miss Nona Ranskill herself was the heroine. She nearly trod a kitten to death as she read a framed obituary notice from *The Times* and learned that 'the beloved younger sister of Edith Ranskill' was believed to have been drowned at sea on the date when she had actually been washed ashore on the island.

A bunch of fresh flowers stood before a photograph that had flattered Miss Ranskill on her twenty-ninth birthday. There was another quite large and all too clear photograph of a stained glass memorial window. The figure in the window stood beside a magnolia tree that rose rather surprisingly from a patch of water thick with fish. Their faces gaped up hungrily and with disapproval. A magnifying-glass, which lay beside the frame, helped her to decipher the legend below the fishes. This time, it was final, though it contained a hint that sooner or later the sea was expected to give up its dead and that Nona Ranskill would be included.

A feeling of importance trickled into Miss Ranskill's mind, but it was followed by a sense of guilt. It was tactless of her to have remained alive after so much trouble had been taken. Edith, who hated any detail of a plan to be changed, must be annoyed, particularly if she had paid for the window out of her own money and not from the legacy. For Edith had a way of budgeting funds and allowed no overlapping – only sacrificial changes.

'That's my new summer dress,' she used to say, pointing to an asparagus bed, or (showing visitors the kitchen range) 'That's my trip to Bruges.'

Miss Ranskill wondered if the stained glass window was the price of her sister's new teeth, chintz covers for the drawing-room or charity subscriptions for the year. She did not want to be an object of charity, though that might be easier to bear than a new-born relationship with a toothless and martyred Edith.

'Very upsetting,' she murmured, and felt like a ghost.

Then she wondered absurdly if she could be sharing the hearth-rug with the real plus-foured ghost of Major Phillips, if he too were looking at his photograph just as she was looking at hers.

'We don't give the dead a chance,' she thought. 'As soon as they *are* dead we endue them with attributes they would have loathed.' For a moment she became as wise as the dead and aware that dissolution of the body could not mean destruction of humour and judgment and the sense of fitness.

Her hands stretched out for the hated and flattering photograph, but, before they could reach it, the latch of the little gate clicked and she turned to look out of the window.

A woman in a black and white dress was walking up the path. Before her lumbered a very fat liver-and-white spaniel.

Miss Ranskill reached the front doorstep just as the tail-end of her sister's skirt whisked round the side of the house. The spaniel, who had stopped to snuffle at a bone, heard the ring of the scraper on the stone flags and cocked up her ears.

'Whuppet!' cried Miss Ranskill. 'Whuppet!'

The stump of a tail wagged first, the bulky hindquarters wagged next, and then, lolloping, lumbering, whimpering, the little dog was home again, home in the sense that Miss Ranskill had longed to be, unquestioned, uncriticised and secure in the lap of love. Its feathered paws waved upwards and its eyes had a windblown look.

'Everything's all right!' said the eyes. 'Everything's just the same. I dreamed you were away, but you weren't after all.'

'Nona!' cried a voice from inside the house, 'Nona!' And as Miss Ranskill turned her dog-licked face, her sister added, 'You said *Tuesday* in your letter. I *know* you said Tuesday.'

The spaniel, now exhausted by ecstasy, was lying down, muzzle on paws and tail still wagging. Her bracken-brown eyes showed no awareness of stress. All days were the same to her except one day – the Dog's Day, the day of return.

'Does it matter? I suppose I got mixed: there was a frightful lot to think about.'

'I'd meant to have everything looking *so* nice.' Edith's face looked, in spite of the shadow of a moustache on the upper lip, as it had looked when, as a child, she had scowled at the rain on the morning of a picnic.

'The bed made up and *flowers* in your room and your old ornaments on the mantelpiece. I'd planned a cosy evening – just the *two* of us. I'd meant to have a *party* lunch.'

'It doesn't matter,' soothed Miss Ranskill, but it did matter just a little.

Only the spaniel was exactly the same, unaware of dates or bed-linen, confident in the assurance of her nose that her world was complete again, uncritical, accepting and jubilant, she wagged her tail.

'Come for a walk,' urged her eyes, 'don't go into the silly old house: houses don't matter. Come for a walk.'

Miss Ranskill longed to accept the invitation, to fasten the lead to the dog's collar and allow herself to be tugged back into the old familiar ways.

'Come and talk to me while I get lunch ready,' said Edith.

She was a bigger woman than her sister; and though her bulkiness had been increased by the starch and vegetables of war-time diet, so that, in spite of her constant activity, she had been obliged to let out her belts, she seemed a washed-out and nerveless edition of her. The likeness between them was provoking to each. Miss Ranskill's hair was tawnier, her eyes bluer, and her body more trim and taut.

'I'd *planned* such a welcome!' protested Edith.

Miss Ranskill felt as the prodigal son might have done if his father had not seen him from afar and if he had had to bear the reproachful gaze of the fatted calf.

'Everything would have been ready.'

'Love *is* ready,' insisted the spaniel's eyes, and the whole netherland of her body wagged violently.

'I'll get your letter,' said Edith, 'but I'm positive –'

She turned away and hurried down the passage.

It was, perhaps, the best thing she could do; since it was too late now for one to knock at the door and the other to fling it open.

Miss Ranskill felt a faint relief that was mixed with irritability.

She had never, on the island, dreamed of any conventional welcome and had always imagined *being* at home rather than going there, of slipping naturally into a world of comfort. But she was not to be allowed even to do that before Edith had been proved to be right and she to be wrong over a small matter of dates. What did Monday matter, or Tuesday, in comparison with four years? Edith would be right, of course, but what did that matter either?

Edith *was* right. She returned in triumph from the kitchen, and in her hand was the letter her sister had written – a letter full of references to a desert island, a sea-voyage and an air-raid, to police, to delays over identity cards, to official delays over trains.

'*There!*' she pointed to the postscript, 'you've got the time of the train all right, but you *do* say Tuesday!'

The carpet whispered of ease as she followed her sister out of the room, and the stairs responded to her tread. In the hall, each segment of parquet spoke of the patience and skill of men like the Carpenter. Miss Ranskill felt more alive than she had done since her visit to a war-time shoe-shop.

Whimpering, and an undercurrent of protesting squeaks told that Whuppet had discovered the kittens. So too had Edith, but though the spaniel's body was quivering with delight as she wuffled her nose among the bewildered, faintly-spitting quartette and groped with her pads and let out whines of welcome, the woman's was stiff and disapproving.

'Are they yours? I can't think what Mrs Phillips will say.'

'Who *is* Mrs Phillips?'

'I thought from your letter that you'd been on a *desert* island alone with a sort of Man Friday. And now you turn up in brand new *clothes* and a whole lot of kittens on *Monday* instead of Tuesday, and what *are* those?'

Edith pointed to the bag of carpentering tools.

'Those? Oh! It's rather a long story. Who *is* Mrs Phillips?'

'Philippa Phillips? Well – Nona, what *have* you done with your shoes? You can't walk about with bare *feet.*'

'Never mind them. Tell me –'

But Edith, grown, so her sister noticed, rather slower in her movements, stumped out of the room.

Miss Ranskill stooped and picked up the tortoiseshell kitten, now wet and tousled by the spaniel's tongue.

Edith had always been the same, and always would be. Now it was shoes that mattered – shoes for crossing the four-year-old bridge that time had set between them. Tread softly because you tread on my dreams! Must the dreams be trampled by shoe-leather? Why couldn't they sit and talk and rediscover each other, the unacquainted selves that had accumulated and discarded and experienced? That would be adventure, but Edith had never been in the very least adventurous. Her sister's mind flung back to an enchanted September morning and magic seen from the schoolroom window.

In Mr Corderoy's orchard where the boughs lavished gold against a grey-blue sky, the foot of a rainbow quivered among the tree trunks.

'Look, Edith, look! between the cherry and the pear. Come *on!*'

'You've joggled my elbow.'

'But the crock of gold. There's the very foot of the rainbow. Come *on*.'

'You said you'd do stamps today and I've got *all* the hinges ready.' Edith's voice had drifted into a whine. 'I *did* go blackberrying yesterday and got all scratched and you *did* promise and I've got all my *hinges* ready.'

'But just look. It'll be gone soon.'

For the shimmer of living colour and light was paling already, and the arch soaring above the orchard had lost a trace of its pulsing glory before Edith moved from the table.

'It's going now: they always do.'

'We might get there in time to find the crock of gold.'

'Gold! That's only a baby story. You *promised* to do stamps. It's too *bad*.'

The rainbow had nearly gone by the time Nona reached the orchard fence. It was not, after all, between the cherry and the pear, though the reluctant ghost of its splendour shimmered for a moment against the bole of an apple tree and faded before she could reach it. A spider's web did its shining best to hold the magic, so did the dew on the fallen leaves, and so did the light between the branches. But the children might have been there in time and the crock of gold might not have been a story. Nona, cheated of her birthright, the knees of her stockings wet and mouldy, her hands nettled and pricked after futile scrabbling, returned to the schoolroom. There it seemed that the very stamps had become infected by her own resentment. Their edges curled provokingly and the hinges skidded.

'I'll give you five Indians for that Hungarian; then we'll each have a full page.'

'You can't have that *as well*,' Nona's voice was savage, for was not Hungary the home of opals and was not opal cousin to rainbow?

'But we'd each have a page then.'

'I don't care.'

For years after that, the lonely Hungarian stamp, dirty at the edges and blurred by tear-stains, bore testimony against Edith, to whom stamps were reckoned by numbers; and never by the magic of their lands, to whom a rainbow lost on Monday was no more important than a pencil found on Wednesday, provided, of course, that Wednesday was drawing-day, and Monday afternoon the time fixed for 'doing stamps'.

The kittens squawked an end to reminiscence as Edith came into the room. She carried a pair of bedroom slippers and she still looked worried.

'Put these slippers on while I look at the potatoes.'

'And then can't we talk?'

'Of course. We'll talk at lunch and afterwards for a bit. A pity it's *pie* day. I suppose I could get somebody else, but I've got out of the WI Meeting tomorrow because I thought you were coming, and you know what villages *are*.'

Edith, looking as she always had done, a paler, more annotated and yet expurgated edition of her sister, stirred the heap of kittens with her toe.

'You don't have a long-lost sister returning every day!'

'Oh! Nona, and I've never even kissed you or said I'm glad to see you, or –' Edith stooped down, somehow kissed the damp kitten instead of her sister's face, rubbed some hairs from her mouth and said, 'There!'

'I suppose it would have been different on Tuesday?'

'Well, better because I'd have got everything *prepared*, and –'

'And, I suppose kisses scheduled for Tuesday can't be expended on Monday.'

'Nona!' Edith protested, but her face showed relief that her sister was beginning to understand. 'Don't be silly. Let's come and have lunch, what there is of it. Philippa won't be back.'

'Who *is* Mrs Phillips?'

The question was not answered until the pilchards had been laid out on a bed of lettuce and carried into the dining-room, where they lay for a time side by side with the bowl stuffed full of roses.

Mrs Phillips, so Edith explained and as her sister had already guessed, was the widow of an Army officer. She was the owner of the house and was very kind, very energetic and very patriotic. It was clear that Edith, who did the housework and cooking, half the garden and a certain amount of secretarial work in exchange for board, lodging and the privilege of Mrs Phillips' society, was afraid of her.

'But it works very well,' she told her sister. 'After my – our house was requisitioned I had to go somewhere and do something. I'm too old for the Forces, and I don't think I could quite stand up to munitions, and so –'

'And so you are general servant and gardener and unpaid secretary to Mrs Phillips!'

'Well, lots of people *are*, I mean, we all are these days practically.'

'Does she need so many?'

'I don't mean we're all working for Mrs *Phillips*, I mean we're all doing *something* of the sort.'

'I saw some advertisements for servants in *The Times*. Really they were more pleas than advertisements, and cooks seem to be getting about three pounds a week.'

'Yes, but it's not quite the *same*. We *share* the house and Mrs Phillips does the flowers, and –'

Miss Ranskill looked at the rose-bowl and shuddered.

'Yes, I *know*, but she likes them like that and they *are* her roses.'

'Do you get afternoons out and evenings off?'

'No, it isn't like that exactly. Of course, we can't both be out at the same time for long because of the telephone. I have to go down to the shop sometimes. I've got one or two Committee Meetings too. The arrangement works quite well, *really*. We aren't in each other's *way* too much, and I have my own things in the drawing-room. Besides –'

Here Edith hesitated.

'Besides what?'

'Oh! well, I'm always allowed to have visitors for an odd weekend or so. We *share* the spare room, I mean we *ration* our guests. Philippa has one or two nephews and nieces who come here for leaves and things, so, of course, they really have first claim.'

'I see.'

Miss Ranskill was beginning to see. She understood, too,

that it wasn't entirely Edith's fault that her unexpected arrival was, so oddly, thought awkward. Mrs Phillips had to be considered and possibly conciliated. There was only one little spare room. Leaves mattered more than the arrival home of a sister, who should have been dead, of course they did: it was Mrs Phillips' house.

'Philippa is thrilled at the idea of meeting you. All her people have lived abroad most of their lives, and she says she finds the village frightfully *insular*.'

'All the same,' persisted Miss Ranskill, 'she seems to get a good bargain in you. And if those advertisements in *The Times* are to be believed.'

'But did you really manage to get *The Times regularly* on a desert island or did you just *call* it a desert island? I've only had that one letter, you know, and I want to hear everything.'

Miss Ranskill tried, she tried very hard indeed to explain her life on the island, but lunch was finished and cleared and the washing-up was nearly done before Edith understood that there had been no ship-stores, no savages, no passing ship, no wreckage, nothing to read, nothing to sew, and no calendar.

'But you must have been so terribly *bored*.'

No, Miss Ranskill hadn't been bored. She tried to explain the games they had played and to indicate that the Carpenter had been a good companion.

'But a common – well, ordinary sort of man like *that*!'

'He wasn't ordinary.'

'Well, not educated.'

'It depends what you call education. He taught me more than I've ever learned in my life before.'

'But it must have been so *awkward* sitting down to table – well, I suppose you hadn't got a *table*, but sharing *meals*. A picnic seems even worse, so much more intimate. It must have been *dread*ful, Nona.'

'It wasn't.' Miss Ranskill's voice began to give a warning. 'And I've no doubt if I'd *asked* that he'd have waited on me first and had his own meal afterwards. You'll be surprised to hear that I didn't ask.'

'No? Well, I suppose it would have been a bit *difficult*. The trouble is that *sort* of person never seems to think about that sort of thing. Still, I think he might have let you have tea alone, *anyway*.'

'There wasn't any *tea*, and if you'd been on a desert island you would have been glad of any companion who might sometimes make you forget that the fish you were swallowing *was* fish.'

Edith hung up the dish-cloth and turned a concerned face towards her sister.

'Fish! Oh! you poor dear, and I've given you fish for lunch. Why didn't you *say?*'

CHAPTER FOURTEEN

Mrs Phillips loomed large in the cottage, the village and the nearby town. She had, so she frequently hinted, blue blood in her veins. Certainly some of it showed through the skin of her nose, which was of an aquamarine tint in chilly weather. Her politics were blue and rather bleak; so, though she admitted with generous gesture that the Russians were wonderful, she always added, 'It seems strange *now* to think how we talked about "poor brave little Finland".' For some time Miss Ranskill, uninformed in recent history, was very perplexed by the statement.

Mrs Phillips' outlook was Red, White and Blue. She stood stout and stalwart for thin red lines, for British Possessions coloured red, for white feathers (to be given to all men not in uniform), and for true blue of every shade. She believed in the flogging of boys and coloured persons, the shooting of shirkers, the quashing of Jews, the Feudal System, cold baths for invalids, the abolition of hot-water bottles, and (rather curiously) the torture of Adolf Hitler. She softened to horses and she adored dogs, whom she addressed in baby-talk.

Edith Ranskill was terrified of her and Nona Ranskill was not, though she found the frequent references to 'that man of yours on the island' almost intolerable.

Mrs Phillips took kindly to the island from the first; though she was obviously disappointed that the Carpenter had not been a native and that Miss Ranskill had not put her foot on his neck.

She admired her new friend's conduct in building and launching the boat, but so identified herself with life on the island that any listener might have supposed that *she* had shared in the perils and hardships and sustained Miss Ranskill throughout. She used the Royal 'We' when talking of the island as often as she did when speaking to children, animals and the mentally deficient.

'We don't grumble about fish, do we? We know how hard it is to catch it,' and 'Little jobs about the house are nothing to us after all we have been through.'

In time she came to inhabit the island so largely that Miss Ranskill could scarcely recall it without the added vision of Mrs Phillips, looming along the beaches and taking command of the Carpenter. But when she referred to the 'day we committed that poor man's body to the deep', Miss Ranskill snapped.

After that she was not allowed to forget her status as temporary guest and there was much hinting about the imminence of the nephews' leaves.

'But you mustn't think of going *yet*,' declared Mrs Phillips. 'We shall manage somehow.'

Edith too hinted vaguely about 'future plans', but was non-committal about her share in them.

'We might take a cottage together, of course, but cottages are so difficult to *get* and so *expensive*. Besides, I feel rather *bound* to Philippa, I promised to stay with her for the duration, though of course I didn't know then that –'

'That the sea would give up its dead at such an inconvenient time,' concluded Miss Ranskill with a glance towards the left-hand corner of the mantelpiece.

'We *must* take the photograph of that memorial window down.'

'It's a pity we can't pawn the window.'

'Nona!'

'Did it cost very much?'

'Well, you see I ordered it after your will was proved and after I'd paid the death duties. Then I was a fool about the house. I didn't like the idea of profiteering so I let it at a nominal rent. After that the dividends went *down* and the cost of everything went *up*, and I made this tiresome arrangement with Mrs Phillips. I – I didn't like to tell you before, but I signed an agreement with her. It seemed all right at the time, but *now* – And then, of course, I'm going to return your money as soon as I possibly can. We'll get back the death duty in time, I suppose, but you know what lawyers *are*. So, just at the moment, even if I could break with Mrs Phillips, there wouldn't be *enough* for the two of us in a cottage. You do *see*, don't you, Nona?'

The conversation, so long avoided, took place three days after Miss Ranskill's arrival at Mrs Phillips' house.

'Of course I see, Edith, and I expect I shall get a job quite easily. I thought if I might stay just for a week (*oh! spare me a little that I may recover my strength before I go hence and be no more seen*) till I've got my bearings? And then, I've got to go and see Mrs Reid.'

'Surely you could write to *her*.'

Edith Ranskill had thriven since girlhood on problems and

225

petty worries; the war had added its longer list – black-out, curtains, evacuees, billeted soldiers, Woolton pies, shortage of daily help, commandeering of houses, non-keeping quality of flour, rough hands, starchy diet, and now – her sister.

In the past, as one little problem grew stale, it had been succeeded quickly by another, so that her mind had not known a dull moment and even her hours of sleeplessness had been perpetually enlivened. The only impatience shown by her listeners, to whom she told her grievances, had come from the British sense of fair play that made them anxious not to miss their turn in relating their own ridiculously similar worries. Their own difficulties made them sympathetic; for they knew that if they would not listen to Edith she would not listen to them: nothing could be duller than to suffer the egg shortage in silence, in spite of the frequent assurances from America and the great of their own land that the unsung, uncomplaining housewives were being magnificent and the Kitchen Front of Britain an example to the whole world.

But in Nona Ranskill there was a problem that could not be shared. It had been all very well and even exciting at first when, as a new arrival, she had added importance to the household.

Miss Hoskins might spread her table with the grocer's madeira cake (only obtainable by going early to the shop on Friday mornings and only eatable on that day or Saturday, because, by Sunday, each slice was tethered to the main body by slender wisps of something that looked like spiders' webbing and played queer tricks with the digestion), paste sandwiches, honey and home-made biscuits. Edith need provide nothing

226

but a few stale buns, so long as Nona was there to make up, by her odd reminiscences, for the lack of butter and the weakness of tea. The guests always hoped that something rather shocking might be said about the Carpenter. It was interesting to know someone who had really been on a desert island, though Miss Blake, a keen gardener, was disappointed that Miss Ranskill had not brought any plants back with her. Miss Stocks, whose favourite topics were adolescence, inhibitions and the problems of unmarried mothers, was annoyed that there had been no assaults by savages.

Even the Woolton pies lost their age-old savour because Nona insisted on their excellence.

It was difficult to grumble in her presence about the shortage of fish or the poor quality of shoe-leather.

All the niggling annoyances that had hedged up so gradually around Edith and her neighbours were new to Miss Ranskill, who had a disconcerting way of ignoring some and kicking against the prickles of others. *She*, surrounded and almost stifled by women, did not find the war isolating: the village was too thickly populated for her liking. The variety of voices, even more than differences of opinion, fretted her mind into confusion. Inconvenience of buses was no trouble to her either: if she missed one she could walk the four miles to the town. And walk she did, with unhurried stride through dust or mud, her shoes slung round her neck by their laces, as though she were a child gone paddling.

Time was unimportant to her. What did it matter if lunch was an hour early or supper a couple of hours late?

She was difficult about food too. In Mrs Phillips' household, the rations were divided every Monday morning. There were three little pots for sugar, three little plates for butter, and three little tins for tea. If Mrs Phillips had a four o'clock guest, an extra spoonful from her tea-tin joined the other two spoonfuls in the pot. Edith, in her turn, behaved in the same dutiful way; but Nona would play no such scrupulous games. What was there, she squandered; and was content to drink cold water for the rest of the week. At least, she would have drunk cold water and eaten dry bread, had not the others preferred to victimise themselves and insisted on a martyred sharing-out again.

'You might try to *think*,' so Edith expostulated frequently, 'I don't want to seem *disagreeable*, but really it looks almost *greedy* to eat all your butter ration at one meal.'

'It seems greedier to me to make such a fuss about it and niggle it out in tiny bits. When it's there I eat it: when it's finished I go without. I don't *want* every day to be the same.'

'But it makes it so awkward for *us*. Of course *I'm* delighted to share everything with you, but it's different for Philippa and she *notices*.'

'I don't want her to, and she doesn't want to. I don't interfere with her everlasting bread-and-scrape; why should she bother if I butter half an inch thick one day and don't butter at all the next?'

'Because we happen to be living in civilised times.'

'Do we?' Miss Ranskill glanced at the headlines of the newspaper by her sister's side.

After that, she ate dry bread on six days of the week, and on the seventh, after having annoyed her sister and Mrs

Phillips by begging them to share her untouched butter ration, finished it off herself and piled marmalade on the top of it.

'Can't you see that it's better,' she insisted. 'You must see it's better to behave as if there wasn't a war for one day in the week?'

But Mrs Phillips and Edith did not see. Since they must make sacrifices, they preferred to be sacrificed daily by slow stages.

The black-out provided more argument.

'If we want to mislead the Germans and save our factory towns from bombardment, why can't we illuminate the villages – different ones every night?'

'Ours not to reason why,' barked Mrs Phillips. 'Ours but to do and die.'

'But you'd be much more likely to die if you drew back the curtains,' muttered Miss Ranskill, while Edith, who was always stirred to nervous bustling by the very mention of light, hurried away to make certain that no chink was showing between the bathroom window-frame and its curtain.

Miss Ranskill was quite aware that she was being difficult and tiresome. She tried to explain her points of view both to Edith and to the doctor, who had been called in to deal with her sleeplessness and frequent bouts of indigestion.

'You see, I thought it was all going to be the same as usual, but now that I've arrived in this country, like a new girl coming to school in the middle of the term, I feel confused. I'd looked forward for years to new clothes and bed-and-bath luxuries, but everything I have must be rationed.'

'But,' expostulated Edith, 'of course I'm sorry for you,

but *really* it is the same for all of us. We're all in this war *together*.'

'That's where you're wrong: it isn't the same for me. I've come from a primitive life where I've learned how to do without things you'd call necessities. I can still do without them easily. I can do without them *here*, just as I could do without them on the island. I can go barefoot –'

'But nobody does.'

'I can manage with two or three garments and very plain food, but I won't fiddle and faddle and niggle and naggle, and make do and mend, and turn old petticoats into blouses when I've got two blouses already: it isn't *sense*. And as for being in this war all together, we aren't. In this village we're just playing at it.'

'I'm sure' – if only Edith's moustache had been a trifle heavier it would have bristled – 'I'm sure I don't *play*, Nona. I haven't had an idle moment since the war began. I never *allow* myself to rest. If only *you* would take more interest in all the things that *are* being done in the village, you wouldn't be so *introspective* and nervy.'

'I do all I can in the garden: that seems more important to me than yattering at Committee Meetings.'

It was Doctor Fenton who had suggested garden work as a nerve-soother, and Miss Ranskill worked all day, and through the long light evenings, though every time she handled a spade she was reminded of the frayed paddle with which she had dug the Carpenter's grave.

'It should cure the sleeplessness in time,' he said, 'by taking your mind right away from the experiences you have had. Try to think of the garden when you go to bed at night. Don't let your mind dwell on that island of yours.'

'No,' said Miss Ranskill, unable to explain that the island was the one place where she could lay her mind to rest to be lulled by the memory of gulls crying, while the waves lippited along the beach, and the uninterrupting voice of the Carpenter boomed a rather tuneless song.

After the doctor had suggested light nourishing food, and mentioned the suitability of whiting steamed in milk, and had added that in normal times he would have recommended a sea-voyage, Miss Ranskill did not mention her sleeplessness again. He was a kind man. Edith was a kind woman, but incapable of understanding that if her sister could not have the gilt on her gingerbread, she would rather have bread and no ginger.

She grew a little more tired and a little thinner and a little more difficult day by day. Every evening she wrote a letter to the Carpenter's wife. Every night between waking and sleeping she pictured the postman knocking on the door, she saw the letter being fingered and opened; and she heard it being read aloud to the boy, Colin. But every morning she tore up the letter and threw it into the waste-paper basket in Mrs Phillips' spare room.

It was impossible to write: words would not carry the right picture. The story she owned was one that must be told by her under the roof that the Carpenter had raised, beside the hearth he had laid, by the light through the window that burnished the nasturtiums on the sill.

She must go soon, and the thought of her journey lifted her through the difficult days though she put off going and stored up the dream in her mind, perfecting it little by little and saving it as a refuge.

Sometimes she felt the delay was not quite fair to the Carpenter's wife, who might, long ago, have lost hope, and might now be waiting empty-hearted for the gift that Miss Ranskill alone could bring, the gift of the days of her husband's life.

Yet, surely, he could not have been dead to her through the years of his living; he had lived too strongly for that. Winds, blowing to England, must have carried his life's breath with them for so long as it lasted. True, Edith had bought a memorial window for her sister; but the link between them had never been so strong as the one which must, surely, have bound the Carpenter's wife to such a husband. So Miss Ranskill argued to herself night by night and day by day, fearful of admitting her ghost of a fear lest another dream should be tarnished or even broken.

The Carpenter's cottage shone in her mind. There she might find peace and comfort and kindliness, all of them glowing as the flowers on the window-sill, homely as the little besom on the hearth.

She might even find some sort of work in the village, enough, at least, to pay for board and lodging in Mrs Reid's cottage. Then there would be a welcome each night, and peace in which she could conjure up the island, and, word by word, restore the Carpenter to his wife and son.

You'll not have to waste time in coming to see us, Miss Ranskill.

Yet, she was not wasting time, she was cherishing what time might bring.

232

It would not, she guessed, be possible to continue for very long as Mrs Phillips' suffered guest.

In the evenings she had the middle chair before the fire, away from the light and beyond knee-warmth. She had the middle place at table, and the last bath at night. There was no hint of establishment.

Mrs Phillips was a possessive woman. She possessed her Committees, she possessed Edith and she still possessed Major Phillips, making herself the trumpet of statements, worn threadbare, even before he had uttered them, many times before his death.

She did not talk of the Country but of 'My Country', and she talked of it frequently. The bed in the spare room was never referred to as the spare room bed: it was 'my nephew's bed'. Miss Ranskill tossed in it uneasily and considered the war, as though she were turning over an album of photographs, some superimposed one upon the other, some under and some over-developed, some distorted and others freakish. As she reviewed them in her mind's eye, some of these pictures changed character, so that, at times, the village snapshots, seen through tenderness, became beautiful through their purpose and simplicity. Then she saw the village as a miniature country at war, with the Home Guard as its veteran and boyish defenders. Each cottage became a castle, each housewife obeying orders to save money (though prices had risen), fuel (though war-time joints and vegetable dishes required long cooking), clothing (though the extra work in gardens and houses racked out garments), time (though shopping and mending took longer than they had ever done before), light (though work must be continued into the night and every home was filled with evacuees, bombed-out relatives, or war-working lodgers), petrol (though all private cars had been put up long ago, buses were crowded and shoe-leather poor) became a bulwark on the home front.

At other times she saw a little petty people, strangled by red tape, nagging along, intent on their own tiny quarrels, fretting over the fat ration, playing at war and pretending to be important in their ARP uniforms and gardening dungarees.

The newspapers pandered to her bewilderment too. Side by side on the same page, she would read an account of the horrors of fighting in Russia and see the photograph of a smug child whose mother had withdrawn her from school because of the trifling injustice of a mistress.

Only the Carpenter's cottage stood secure in her mind during that first fortnight in a war-time village. Now the time was drawing very near when she must put that to the test also.

'I don't see why you can't simply *write* to that Mrs Reid of yours,' said Edith. 'You'll only harrow yourself; besides, Doctor Fenton *said* you were to take things easily for at least a month.'

'I can't write. I've tried, and there's too much to say.'

'Well, I shouldn't get *involved*. You never know with *those* sort of people.'

'I must go,' said Miss Ranskill, and, staking her future in a sentence, she added, 'I shall go next Thursday. I can get there and back in a day.'

'If I were you, I should write first,' persisted Edith.

'Don't forget,' Mrs Phillips glanced at her husband's photograph as though seeking counsel from it, and then spoke solemnly, 'Don't forget that we are asked not to hamper *troop* movements. We are asked not to travel unless it is absolutely necessary.'

'We're asked to save paper as well,' snapped Miss Ranskill. 'Whatever we do we seem to be breaking some rule. I've got a choice of breakages, anyway, and I shall go on Thursday.'

Edith looked distressed and apologetic, Mrs Phillips gave a patriotic sigh, impaled a ball of khaki wool on a knitting-needle and left the room in a marked manner.

CHAPTER FIFTEEN

The first person Miss Ranskill spoke to in the village was a
stranger there himself, and obviously proud of it. The second
gave directions so assuredly that she felt doubtful at once.

'I mean Mrs Reid, the *Carpenter's* wife,' she elaborated.

'Thompson's the carpenter now. Reid, he's been dead
these four years or more.'

'No, oh no,' her heart made silent answer. 'The Carpenter
was alive when those dahlias were in bud. He was singing
when that hedge of sweet peas was fresh.'

'Mrs Reid, though, she still lives in the same cottage
alongside the carpenter's shed. Straight along the road and
on the right; you can't mistake it.'

And now her feet were taking the road his feet had taken.
A hobnail from a man's boot lay shining in the pathway, and
she wondered absurdly if it could be the Carpenter's, until she
remembered that even broken nails do not stay for long in
village streets. Presently the sound of hammering disturbed
her thoughts; and then she saw the shed, standing flush with
the pathway, as he had described it so often. She noticed
resentfully the board with the name *Thompson*, and underneath the words 'Carpenter and Undertaker'.

Two diamond-shaped beds filled with geraniums lay behind the prim railings of the cottage, and on each side of the door.

After she had knocked, her hand sought the smooth comfort of the Carpenter's watch lying in her coat pocket. She drew it out, but its ticking insisted so loudly against the beating of her heart that she tucked it away again.

She dreaded and yet longed for the moment when the door would open. It was going to be difficult, painful, both for herself and the poor widow, but it would be easier in his house than in any other place. Surely there would be a spirit of sanity about his hearth and comfort and strength and common sense.

You've got to take things as they come, Miss Ranskill, and not get flummoxed. Troubles look big when they start, and less when you get on with them. It's the same with building a house: that looks a big job, but when you've the first two courses of bricks laid, it only seems fit for dolls, so little it looks.

A window was flung open above her, and a head, decked with curling-pins, was framed in it.

'Yes?' said a voice.

Miss Ranskill looked up into the face of buxomness turned to slattern, at tortured hair, and pink cheeks smeared with powder.

All the rehearsals failed her. You could not break news or condole when your neck was cricked at such an angle and when the face above showed such impatience. One slim hope was left: perhaps she was addressing Mrs Thompson.

'Is Mrs Reid in?' she asked.

'Yes, that's me.'

'I wonder – I, I have a message, a –'

'Yes?'

'Well, it's rather – I mean, if –'

'Are you from the gas?'

There was suspicion in the voice, but the words meant nothing to Miss Ranskill.

'From the gas?' she repeated.

'Because, if that's what it is, I've got something to say. That young man of yours read the meter all wrong. Must have done.'

'Oh no!' cried Miss Ranskill, meaning that she was not an agent from any inferno of blue hisses and stenches of tortuous pipes. 'Oh no, certainly not.'

'It's no use "oh-noing" me. I tell you he must have done, and that's why the bill's not been paid. I've a friend who can *read* meters, and I've a letter all ready written to the Management. It'll be there by tomorrow; so there's no use your waiting.'

The window was edging downwards as Miss Ranskill spoke despairingly.

'I'm not from the – from the gas. I came to give you something.'

The window shot up again.

'Beg your pardon, Miss, I'm sure, but you know how it is. They send so many young ladies round now instead of the men you don't know where you are. And talk about cheating . . . I'll be down in a minute. I was just giving myself a bit of a wash. Where's that boy?'

A frowsty black curtain blew outwards.

'Colin! Colin! There's a lady at the door. Let her in, can't you? COLIN!'

Colin's the one I want to see. He'll be getting a big lad now. The girl was all for her mother and the first boy died like I told you, but I reckon Colin'll remember his dad though he was only six then.

Steps sounded on a stairway inside the house and Miss Ranskill's knuckles grew white as her fingernails met her palms. She was used to shocks by now. Supposing the boy, with the name that suggested a sheep-dog in all its faithful steadfastness, was a snivelling brat or a cock-a-hoop or –?

The door opened and he stood before her – a little Carpenter with the same grey eyes and serene forehead, the same stocky shoulders and nervous hands. She wanted to put an arm round him and take him away to some quiet field outside the village, there to tell him stories about his father, to weave the thread of the Carpenter's eternity closer into the spiritual fabric of his son. This then was what she had come to do, not to pick flowers in woods or sip tea from thin china but to be a joiner.

Joiner and Carpenter, Miss Ranskill: there's worse things than that.

She smiled suddenly and the boy responded, making confidence between them.

'Mum'll be down in a minute. She said you was to come in.'

There was reassurance in his manner of leading the way into the small kitchen.

Miss Ranskill looked first at the hearth. It was grey and dusty. She remembered the tale of the besom made for the 'little lass'.

'You're Colin,' she said. 'You're twelve years old, aren't you?'

'Yes. How did you know?'

But she couldn't tell him that, not now and not here in this slatternly room with its filming of dust and the unwashed pans in the sink. She could not tell him anything yet: there was too much between them.

The boy did not seem to expect an answer, for his hands (his father's hands) were busy about some pieces of wood on the table.

Seems to me, Miss Ranskill, seems to me the mind moves faster when the hands are moving too. Me, in a sort of way, I was always fanciful. When I'm planing a door, I'm thinking about the grain all right, but I think most of the door when it's hung; and who it'll open and shut on. Hands carry one on when they're busy: they're always learning themselves.

She noticed how the boy's hands were being taught by the wood as he picked it up and put it, piece by piece, into a rush bag bound with webbing. He touched it in the way that some people fondle animals, communicating with them. His fingers curved, surely and gently as though the chisel had a bloom on it.

'What are you making?' she asked.

'I was building a boat, but –' he hesitated.

'Yes?'

'You need fine grain for a small one. I've only got rough bits here.'

'Would you like to go to sea?'

'Dad did.'

'What's that about Dad?'

240

The door had opened and Mrs Reid was standing on the threshold. She was dressed now in an artificial mauve satin blouse and an over-tight brown skirt. Powder covered the smeariness of her face: her hair frizzed bad-temperedly.

'I was only saying that Dad went to sea.'

From the boy's expression, Miss Ranskill guessed that the word *only* was in his constant use. It would often be necessary for him to explain that he was only doing that or thinking this, that it was quite harmless *only* he wished he could be left alone sometimes.

'Yes, he went to sea right enough, and he didn't come back. You'll stay where you are and work and get that scholarship. Now clear that clutter away and look sharp about it.' Mrs Reid turned to Miss Ranskill, 'How anyone keeps a house to rights when there's a boy in it, beats me. Dirt and litter all over the place!'

Miss Ranskill was looking at the place where the bowl of nasturtiums should have been set on the table, at the window-sill empty of the blossoming geranium, and at the rag rug where no cat lay.

A cat on the rug, a plant-pot in the window and a bunch of flowers on the side-table, they make home if you ask me, Miss Ranskill, they and a clean hearthstone. Stands to reason, doesn't it, what's the first thing you learn to read at school? The cat sat on the mat, of course, well then!

Something had gone wrong with the Carpenter's home and badly wrong too; unless distance had made him see it rosily or pride lent loyalty to his tongue. Yet he had always spoken with conviction.

My missus says I'm a rare woman in the house, a home-maker, if you know what I mean, Miss Ranskill. It's only fair to share the work.

'Look sharp, can't you, Colin? How many more times I'd like to know!'

When the boy had left them, Miss Ranskill tried to begin her story. She began by describing how she had fallen overboard and been washed ashore on the island.

'It may seem queer to you that I should come to you like this, and begin to talk about myself, but I wanted to – to break it to you that there was somebody else on that island. I expect you believed as my sister did, I mean as my sister believed about me, that your husband was drowned a good many years ago, but –'

Miss Ranskill hesitated. She was telling the story very badly. She had been trying to build up a picture, but the words had all gone wrong.

'Your husband – the Carpenter – wasn't drowned after all. Oh! *please*,' she looked up into the unmoved face of the widow, 'I hadn't meant to raise your hopes. Forgive my clumsiness. Your husband isn't alive now, but –'

'I know that,' said Mrs Reid. 'I've known that for some weeks now.'

So there had been a link between them after all. His death had stirred some extra sense or intuition in the woman.

Miss Ranskill felt humble: she need not have seen herself as newsbreaker or worried about a choice of words. The Carpenter's spirit, blowing where it listed, had ended the need for words.

Mrs Reid was the first to break the silence. She spoke conversationally.

242

'So *you'll* be the lady then?'

'The – the lady?'

'The lady that was on that island with him.'

A sudden chill jerked down Miss Ranskill's spine; for an instant her heart felt icy. By what strange communication did the Carpenter's wife know that she, Nona Ranskill, was 'the lady that was on the island'?'

She looked into the woman's eyes: they were pale, insignificant and rather wary, more the eyes of a shrew than of a clairvoyante.

'From what they said, I thought you'd have been older, but then I don't suppose you'd be feeling up to much.'

'They?' Miss Ranskill's thoughts were whirling madly, as once a flight of sea-gulls had whirled above the Carpenter's body.

Who were 'They', birds or voices, the kind of voices that the Maid of Orleans had heard?

'Yes,' continued Mrs Reid reminiscently, 'you could have knocked me down with a feather when they told me. It didn't seem natural somehow.'

No, it would not seem quite natural. And now a great curiosity overwhelmed Miss Ranskill. She leaned forward.

'Who were "They?"' she asked, and braced herself for the answer.

'He was a good husband in his way,' Mrs Reid made the statement automatically, almost as though she felt it were expected of her. 'Headstrong always, but he wasn't mean.' She looked down at her lap, then at Miss Ranskill. 'You're quite sure he was dead? You made sure of that, I suppose. You're certain he's dead all right?'

'Dead all right.' Miss Ranskill, caught back from her memory of that morning on the beach, the knife in the grave and all the abomination of desolation that had followed, felt herself trembling a little. How could she make answer to a woman possessed of the strange knowledge that 'They' had made known to her?

'He – his body was dead,' she replied at last.

'There wasn't a doctor, though, to sign the death certificate?'

'There wasn't anybody.'

'No, I was forgetting. They told me you was alone with him.'

'Who?' Again a shiver rippled down Miss Ranskill's spine. 'Who told you?'

She braced herself for the answer.

'The police, of course, not the "Special" here: he's not much use. They sent a couple of men from Lidcot. Let me see, it would be just about three weeks ago. In the morning it was.'

The shallow blue eyes were turned towards the mantelpiece and the clock, which had, so Miss Ranskill supposed, continued its indifferent ticking all through the terrible hours when she had scrabbled like a dog in the sand on the island, and all through the hour, three weeks ago, when the police had brought their information to Mrs Reid.

She ought to have realised that there could have been no 'revelations' except in the newspaper sense of that word, in a room like this.

She should have remembered how intensely the police had questioned her about the Carpenter on their visit to the Mallisons' house. Her mind harked back to that interview. She remembered how many things had been written down on the Police Inspector's pad. Of course, it had been their business to inform the widow of what had happened.

She felt drained, as though virtue had gone out of her.

Mrs Reid went on talking.

'It does seem a thing, doesn't it? I mean without a doctor or clergyman and no proper funeral or nothing. Still, they seemed to think it would be all right about my having drawn the insurance money before I should have. They didn't think the insurance people would grumble about that. Anyway, if there should be bother about that I'd have a right to his pay for all those years. I can't stand to lose both.'

She leaned forward and lowered her voice a little.

'Least said soonest mended, is what I always say. Talking won't bring him back, will it?'

'No.' To Miss Ranskill the monosyllable sounded like the first stroke of a death-knell. 'No, nothing will bring him back, I'm afraid.'

'I couldn't be expected to get into mourning twice over, could I? I mean to say I've not the coupons to spare now, and that's a fact. Besides, it would make a lot of talk. You know what they are in these villages. You see what I mean, don't you?'

Yes, Miss Ranskill saw. She had thought herself invulnerable by now, but this sudden smashing of the image created by the Carpenter shocked her so much that she felt cold and physically sick.

Could his wife think of nothing but insurance money and the neighbours? Could she not rend her heart anew just for a little while, or ask a single tender question?

For a moment the boy was forgotten, and Miss Ranskill rose to go.

'I – It was stupid of me to come and take up your time. I hadn't realised that of course the police would have told you about – about Reid – Mr – Reid.'

'Oh! you mustn't go yet. Maybe you'd like a nice cup of tea. There's still one or two things we might talk over.'

'Thank you.' Miss Ranskill felt badly in need of tea after this new ordeal. Perhaps it would pull her together, and make her feel less sick.

'I could do with a cup myself. I've been feeling a bit upset ever since the police came. Still,' Mrs Reid rose and poked the ash-choked fire. 'Still, if Harry had to die, it's a good thing it happened when it did, and that's a fact.'

She moved about the kitchen and set dusty teapot on dusty tray, blew some flecks of soot from a lump of margarine, embedded a spoon further into its jam-jar and gave a loaf of bread a shake.

Undoubtedly the man had been the home-maker.

'Funny thing,' she observed, 'to think of me in mourning all those years ago and Harry alive.'

Miss Ranskill stared in amazement at the plump body, at the show of sleek calves and the feet crammed into over-tight shoes.

This then was the woman the Carpenter had cherished. Her indifference had been shielded by the words of his loyalty. She was naked and he had clothed her; but now the garments were dropping from her one by one with every word that she spoke.

'Did he leave any last message?' she now asked abruptly.

'No, you see – there wasn't time. It happened very suddenly. He'd been working hard. He lifted a big stone. One minute he was well and strong. It was a heart attack. He didn't regain consciousness.'

Miss Ranskill covered her eyes with her hands.

'I can see you're highly-strung, same as me. I've always been a sufferer with my nerves. You'd better drink this down: it'll steady you.'

'I'm only crying because – because it *should* be so much worse for you than for me.'

'Yes, I was proper upset when they told me Harry had been lost at sea.' Mrs Reid's voice took on a tone of pride. 'I wouldn't eat a thing for days and days: not a bite passed my lips. And I can tell you I was upset again when the police came. Seemed almost like as though he'd died twice.'

She drank her tea noisily.

'But doesn't it seem better to know that he had those extra years of life, even if they were hard ones? I –' Miss Ranskill's mind groped vainly for adequate words and only snatched at the commonplace, 'I made him as comfortable as I could.'

'I'm sure,' replied Mrs Reid politely.

'He talked about you a great deal.' Miss Ranskill's voice was pleading. 'And about the boy and his home.' She looked round the room. If only her glance could sweep the dust from all those smeary surfaces and her mind's eye restore the kitchen to what it had once been to her.

'He always was like an old woman about the house. He was handy too, I'll say that for him. I had to let the place go a bit after he went. It's been too much for me altogether, but what can you do in war-time. Yes, I've missed Harry about the house, time and again I've missed him. I'll give you another cup of tea when the kettle boils up.'

Miss Ranskill, while waiting for the kettle to boil, tried to talk a little about the life on the island. It was only fair that Mrs Reid should be told as much as possible, though there was little enough to be said and less still that seemed to be understood.

'Well, fancy that now! Poor Harry!' was the widow's favourite expression. Once, she remarked, 'You'd have thought he'd have built a house while he was about it!' and once, 'Fancy him taking all that time to build a boat. He used to be reckoned a smart worker.'

Her eyes kept seeking the clock, once or twice she stifled yawns.

At the end she commented, 'I shan't say anything to anyone myself, and if I was you I wouldn't say anything neither. Folks might think it funny you and him being alone together on the island all those years. And they'd think it funny about me too; lot of Nosey Parkers they are. It's nobody's business but yours and mine and the police, is it?'

'No,' said Miss Ranskill, and hoped she was not going to be sick.

'Anyway, there's no need to say anything to Colin, might upset him, there's no knowing. It took him quite a while to get over it. Colin's fanciful. It wouldn't do to upset him.'

'But there's the boat,' said Miss Ranskill. 'I wanted him to have the boat that his father made.'

'Boat!' The tone of Mrs Reid's voice reduced the boat to the dead wood it had been before the Carpenter's skill had coaxed the planks to curving, before water and sun and air had quickened it to the resistance that the sea had failed to break.

'Boat! What should he want with a boat? Colin's the chance of something better than that. He's brains if he chose to use them. We don't want to go upsetting him now talking about his father.'

'It doesn't seem fair,' thought Miss Ranskill as she watched her hostess pouring water into the teapot. 'It doesn't seem fair to cheat him of the years his father was alive.' But she only said, 'I shall keep the boat then, I mean, I shall have it kept. Perhaps when the boy is older he might like it. It's the sort of thing that a boy would like.'

'Money now, that would be different,' continued Mrs Reid. 'I suppose there wasn't any money?'

Miss Ranskill had meant to keep the story of the money a secret, but, either because her responsibilities as a trustee began to weigh upon her or because she could not resist watching the effect on Mrs Reid, she answered casually, 'There was just a little money, but we had to use it.'

'*Use* it! On a desert island? You said it was a desert island.'

'We used it to keep the fire going one very wild night about two years ago.'

'To keep the fire going! Of all the –'

In the pause that followed, while Mrs Reid tried to find words to express her contempt of such wantonness, Miss Ranskill's mind slipped overseas.

It had been a very wild night. Over and over again, the Carpenter had gone out of his shelter to guide, with the few dry twigs that remained, the spluttering flames from one part of the bonfire to another. He had fanned and protected them as they took their feeble hold.

It's no good, Miss Ranskill, I'm beat without a bit of paper or something dry. I'm beat, and it's how we'll get it going again once it goes out that baffles me. There's only one thing for it, my pocket-book or the notes. Which shall it be, Miss Ranskill, eh?

It was she who had urged the sacrifice of the notes, because she knew that to him the destruction of his pocket-book would have been the burning of all the slender craft that carried his thoughts to harbour. He was a man of few words, and fewer still when they were written. His pocket-book was a patchy record of measurements, expenditure and payments. He would flick over the pages in the evening and make comments on the entries.

Cabbage, beet, carrot, parsnip, spring onions, lettuce, two-and-eight. We could do with some of those seeds now, eh, Miss Ranskill? And to think how I wasted them. I never could grow the carrots thin enough nor the lettuce neither. And now I've got so mean I'll have a job to sow 'em thick enough if ever I get home again. It'll not be easy for us to waste anything after all this, Miss Ranskill. I sometimes think I'll never be able to throw away a bent nail after this without thinking that maybe there's some poor fellow on a desert island that'd give the next best year of his life for it. Not that my saving'd help him, but you never know – there's things we don't understand.

There were family entries too, for the Carpenter was no

diarist. He had had, during the whole of his manhood, one thick bulging pocket-book and that had sufficed.

Paid Doctor Laine four pounds fifteen. That was when my little lad died. We'll give that page a miss. Ordered teak from Stiggins. That was for the best door ever I made in my life, Miss Ranskill, a good job that, if ever there was one. What's this now? Finished floor in vicarage kitchen. There's a story about that, Miss Ranskill. Let me get it right now.

No, the pocket-book could not go: it was their library. Despair might rise like a bad phœnix from its ashes, so Miss Ranskill had said, 'Use the notes. We're well known on the island now: they'll all give us credit at the shops.'

That's a good one, Miss Ranskill, that's a good one right enough. I believe you'd make me die laughing if you was dying yourself.

But there was no time for laughter then if the fire were to be saved. In another minute the dull crackle of notes had been replaced by the gayer crackling of twigs, and a flame had been guided again, this time to take certain hold of the last dry twigs that would dry others before their death.

As the firelight grew stronger the Carpenter had straightened himself and laughed.

I felt fine then, Miss Ranskill. Queer, it should take a desert island to make a man feel grand. There was a picture I saw once and a bit in it where a man lights a cigarette with a five-pound note. It nagged me at the time to know what it felt like. I feel grand now, sort of rich.

Miss Ranskill had felt grand too, because they had maintained their values and not squandered the red gold of the fire. If a ship should pass that night, their beacon would be seen. Tomorrow could be spent in boat-building and not niggling savagely with dry twigs to start a story-book flame.

Reckless, that's what we are, Miss Ranskill, but we've kept the lending library. Wait till we see their faces at home when we get back and brag about our patent fire-lighters.

Now she was back, and the sight of one of the faces was an ugly thing. Its expression softened the Carpenter's death to her because, if he had seen it, it would have killed his laughter.

'How much money was there?' asked Mrs Reid.

'Three pounds ten, in ten-shilling notes. The rest of his money was in the ship.'

'They sent me that,' said Mrs Reid reluctantly, 'but I thought there'd have been more. You ought to have stopped him. To think of him lighting fires with his money and Colin outgrowing his boots.'

It was strange that values should make such a flashing change. In one world the thought of citizens wasting matches could be dementing: in another the idea of islanders feeding a flame with the price of boots could rouse rage. There was not one truth but many. Was it possible for anyone to be innocent of the death of one just man?

Miss Ranskill answered humbly.

'But, of course, I will give you the money: it was my fire too. And look.' She dragged the wallet containing the note-book from one pocket and the big silver watch from the other. 'These were his, I brought them back for you.'

Mrs Reid stretched out a plump hand and picked up the watch. The rims of her nails were edged with dirt though their surfaces were blood-red with varnish. She smoothed the silver with her finger-tips and Miss Ranskill, remembering how the watch had mirrored the reflection of other fingers, whose nails were blunted and broken by rocks, felt the tears pricking against her eyelids. And now Mrs Reid was crying too, and the tears were making runnels down the powder on her cheeks.

'There's nobody can say I didn't miss him,' she said. 'And now, seeing this – the times I've seen him pull it out of his pocket. I'd best put it away now before Colin comes in. What's this?' Her fingers were on the wallet.

'His note-book,' answered Miss Ranskill. 'We used the blank pages, but the written ones are all there, though some of them are loose.'

'All these pages to spare and yet you used notes for fire-lighting.' The indignant jerk of Mrs Reid's head shook a couple of tears to raise blobs on the sea-stained leather and add their salt to it. 'The very idea! What next I wonder!'

'What, indeed!' thought Miss Ranskill.

Then the door opened and Colin came in.

He walked straight over to the table. And now the fingers of his right hand were curving round the watch while the fingers of his left smoothed the sea-salt leather of the wallet, stroked and pressed it, as though through them he could learn its story.

'What's these, Mum?'

'Never you mind. They've nothing to do with you, anyway.'

His fingers, so it seemed to Miss Ranskill, still urged the question.

'Leave them alone, can't you, and give over fidgeting.'

The boy's right hand moved reluctantly, but he raised his left one to his mouth and licked his forefinger.

'It tastes salt,' he observed.

'And why shouldn't it be salt? Have you fed the chickens?'

'Yes, I've done that.'

'Then give me hold of those.'

Mrs Reid snatched the watch and the wallet. The former was put to join a débris of pepper-dust, soup-square wrappers, greasy bills, string, cloves and a three-penny magazine in the drawer of the kitchen table. With the wallet in her hand she hesitated, flicked over a page or two, and then walked towards the stove.

'There!' she said. 'That's what it should've done a long time ago – helped to make a fire burn better.'

The salt of the note-book quickened the flames to a blue burning: they licked upwards as though relishing the flavour.

Miss Ranskill sat very still. She scarcely dared to blink lest the movement of her lids should disturb the tears in her eyes so that the boy would see them. His presence tied her tongue as he looked questioningly from her to his mother, and then at the blue-spattered flames.

'What was it, Mum?' he asked.

'Nothing but a bit of old rubbish that should have been burned before.'

'We could have saved it for salvage, couldn't we?'

His lips made the question to his mother, but his eyes asked Miss Ranskill, before he moved quickly over to the fireplace. For a moment she was wondering if he were going to attempt a rescue, but he reached up for a big shell that lay on the mantelpiece beside the clock.

'*Now* what are you after?' asked Mrs Reid. 'Oh! *that*!'

The last words were spoken irritably, but only Miss Ranskill heard them. The boy was listening to something else. His right hand cupped one ear, his left pressed the big shell to the other.

'He never gets tired of that game,' said Mrs Reid as she tipped more sugar into Miss Ranskill's tea. 'I've known the baker knock three times before he'd heard.' All the same she lowered her voice as she added, 'It was best not to let him see the note-book. It would never do to upset him now and start him asking questions.'

The words meant nothing to Miss Ranskill, who was watching the death of the note-book – a death that reduced all the Carpenter's loyalty and all patient stoking of a fire to the level of child's play. There was only a small black fluting of paper left, a fluffing of ash and a red glow, and now the powder of the rest settled with a little sigh into the heart of the fire.

'Will you take another cup of tea?' asked Mrs Reid affably.

Miss Ranskill shook her head. She was looking at the boy now, noticing how the pupils of his eyes responded to the intensity of his listening, and how the pink curving of the shell lay closely against the dark hair that grew, as his father's had done, from the undisciplined crown at the back of the parting to a thick smooth sweep in front.

They say you can hear the sea in a shell, Miss Ranskill, would you like to try?

Surrounded as she was by the sea then, she had not bothered to make the experiment.

The boy smiled suddenly, as though enchanted by the song of a siren. He took the shell from his ear and held it out to the visitor.

'You can hear the sea,' he said gravely. 'Would you like to try?'

It was very nearly his father's gesture, and they were his father's words.

'Thank you,' said Miss Ranskill, wondering if he had guessed she was in need of comfort, whether the ashes in the fire meant anything to him and whether it was habit, or some sixth sense that had made him want to listen to the sea just then, and to let her share his listening.

And now the shell, warm from his ear, lay against her own. The boy and his mother moved silently about the room as the surge of waters deafened her to everything else. They were roaring and the wind was whining and the breakers were crashing inshore. Surely the others must hear too. She released the pressure of the shell. Instantly the crashing eased to a tender shuffling. It was the morning after a tempest and the little waves were tumbling up the beach. She closed her eyes and now she could see the long shifting lines with their silver edges. She was back on the island again: the Carpenter was fishing from the low rocks to the west of the bay while the pebbles frolicked underneath the water before being sucked back with a hushing swish as the waves receded.

By pressing hard on the shell she could raise a tempest. What an instrument to play! By flexing or unflexing her fingers she could bring any sea-weather to her ears, and be at home on the island again.

She opened her eyes to see that a stranger had come into the kitchen. Of course she had not heard the door open. He was a man with a facetious and rather gross face; and he was wearing a blue-serge suit. From his expression, she guessed he was arguing, and, though she was reluctant to interrupt the singing of the water, she took the shell from her ear.

Mrs Reid was talking.

'I shan't be more than a few minutes more. Somehow I got all behindhand today, and then –'

'Well, we don't want to miss the big picture, ducks. Sorry; I didn't see you'd got a visitor.'

Mrs Reid glanced anxiously at Miss Ranskill, who rose and put the shell back on the mantelpiece.

'I mustn't keep you any longer, and anyway, I oughtn't to stay now. Goodbye, Mrs Reid, and thank you. Goodbye, Colin, thank you for lending me the shell.'

The presence of the cheap-looking stranger made it easier to say goodbye lightly. The hour spent in the Carpenter's home had had its high and its low moments, and not one of them had been in the least what she had expected. It was easy to go too, because the music of the shell had lifted her to a curious state of ecstasy. The shell was important and the boy was important: nothing else really mattered in that exalted moment. She took three hands, one after the other, into her own. The first was plump and ploppy, the second a little greasy, and the third (Colin's) was hard and dry and vibrant.

She said goodbye again from the gate and turned her back on the bright geraniums in the flower-beds.

CHAPTER SIXTEEN

I

Edith, when Miss Ranskill returned, was not particularly interested in Mrs Reid or her boy.

'Well,' she remarked, 'that's *one* thing over, and now you can set your mind at rest. I had been rather *dreading* the visit for you, but evidently these people are in *comfortable* circumstances so the best thing you can do now is to put them *right* out of your mind and try not to think about that *dreadful* island any more.'

'It wasn't so very dreadful, looking back on it.' Miss Ranskill glanced towards the mantelpiece where a line of blackwood elephants were invading her sister's territory and pressing close (not unnaturally looking down their trunks, poor things) to another and still more ferocious photograph of the late Major Phillips, this time standing by while some natives packed the paraphernalia necessary to shikari.

'Looking back on it *now*, it doesn't seem to have been so very bad after all. At night, when I can't sleep, I go over all the –'

'Then you'd better ask Doctor Fenton to give you something to *take*. There *are* quite a lot of non habit-forming drugs that are perfectly harmless.'

'I don't know that I want to get out of the habit of thinking about the island though. I'd been wondering –'

Edith's face was not encouraging, and her sister knew that the plan she had in mind would not be approved. 'I'd been wondering if we couldn't ask the little boy to stay for a few days.'

'To *stay*? My dear Nona! Whatever for? Besides, where would he *sleep*? What would Philippa say? Think of the *rations* and a great boy eating his head off and bringing in mud and *banging* about all over the place. Besides –'

Miss Ranskill interrupted before the spate of objections confused her.

'He could sleep in the summer-house in the hammock: it's lovely weather. And he would bring his ration book: it couldn't cost much. It isn't muddy weather. He wouldn't bang about. If Mrs Phillips objected I might be able to borrow a tent and let him camp in one of the fields. I could camp with him for that matter.'

There followed a silence so long and so ominous that she broke it tremulously, 'I don't see why not!'

'If you *knew* these children as I do,' Edith put down the half-finished seaman's sock, 'you would know that the idea is absolutely impossible. The village is only just clear of evacuees. *I* know, if you *don't*, that it is perfectly *senseless* to try to take these children out of their proper places.'

A line from Blake frisked through Miss Ranskill's mind – 'White as an angel is the English child.' But only the child of the upper middle classes, not the little gutter boy, whose kind had disturbed but not, alas, shattered the complacency of householders when they had stormed the English castles. Not the Carpenter's son either, not even the son of the Carpenter of Bethlehem.

'From what you've told me,' pursued Edith, 'this boy had a perfectly good home, even if you didn't like the mother particularly.'

'He's not happy.'

'Did he say so?'

'Children *don't* say, Edith: they don't even *know*. But we know, or ought to, that peevishness is bad for them –'

'A good dose of medicine is the best thing for *that*.'

'Oh!' Miss Ranskill's voice rose irritably. 'If only you wouldn't be so reasonable always! I was talking about the mother's peevishness, not the boy's: he is too patient, and it's all wrong.'

'So,' said Edith, 'you want to ask him to stay here so that you can tell him how unhappy he is at home and how peevish his mother is. You want to spoil him for a week-end and then send him back to be dissatisfied with his own home; very mistaken sort of kindness, *I* should think.'

'I want to talk to him about his father, and –'

'Surely his mother is the person to do that. I don't want to damp your *enthusiasm*, Nona. You ought to know that nobody would be readier to help than I if it were a case of real *necessity*, if he needed warm *woollens* or anything of that sort, but you always have had such *wild* ideas.'

'I suppose so.' Miss Ranskill answered conversationally, but her mind was groping for an answer that could be made in words that would not shock.

She knew now how much she had loved the Carpenter, though not in the way that is usually described as 'being in love'. Slowly and steadily affection had grown between them, with such firmness that she, who had never known wifehood had yet felt herself widowed by his death. Her celibacy had been no bar to the true marriage of their minds; and the attunement between them had been absolute; so that they had become unwitting partners in the third, but not least blessed, state for which matrimony was also ordained – *The mutual society, help and comfort, that the one ought to have of the other, both in prosperity and adversity.*

Prosperity had meant food and the easy blazing of the beacon fire, a well-balanced fish-hook and the co-operation of wind and tide; adversity had been the snapping of a plank, the escape of a fish and squalling gusts that soaked the kindling. The mutual help had not only been expended on easing the daily struggle for existence, it had lent hope to the fight and eased and released the mind.

The moment she had been left alone on the island, she had known herself inheritor, not only of the boat and the jack-knife and the Carpenter's ragged clothing, but of his purpose also. The purpose was the restoring of a father to a son. She, to a certain extent, could do that restoring because, for four years, she had shared the mind of the father. She had power to raise the dead, and to foster that part of the Carpenter's immortality that had been bestowed on the boy at the time of his begetting.

Seems to me, Miss Ranskill, you never die properly, not if you're a father. Soon as you hear the first squall of the baby, you thinks to yourself, I've finished with sleep for a bit. Later on when the boy's running about you thinks, 'And I've done with death too.' It's like watching yourself grow young.

She had seen him grow young in the face of Colin and now, if she were allowed, she could add truth to the story held in the sea-shell.

'I expect you will soon be able to take up some war-work,' said Edith, dismissing the Carpenter's son.

'Yes, soon, I should think.' Miss Ranskill's words gave an impatient push to her dreams. 'I'm fit enough now.'

'By the way, Miss Hoskins asked me if I thought you'd be well enough to give a talk to the Women's Institute. I said I'd ask.'

'But what can I talk *about* – fish-drying or boat-building, or "How I Wore the Same Clothes for Four Years and Just Kept Decent"?'

'You could touch on that, perhaps,' said Edith, 'not the boat-building though, except *lightly*. Miss Hoskins suggested "My Life on a Desert Island" would be a good subject. Do *try*, Nona: it would be good for *you* and most interesting to *them*.'

Good for her? To parade the torments and hardships of the past four years on the platform of a village hall? Interesting for them to rub the bloom off the frail remembered happiness with questions?

'It would be a change from all the cake-making and bottling,' urged Edith. 'And it would save all the bother and expense of arranging for a lecturer from a distance and providing transport.'

When we get home, Miss Ranskill, we'll have some tales to tell that'll make 'em all sit up.

'Very well,' she agreed.

She *would* make them sit up. She would harden her heart against hurt, as once she had been forced to harden her body, before her hands had learned resistance to blisters, and her feet to withstand the biting of shale. She would tell them things that would make them forget the kitchen sinks and the rationing, the shortage of milk and the shortage of fat. In doing this, she would shake her own mind free of clutter and homesickness; and stop nursing her dreams in the way that demented young women of fiction hug dead babies to their breasts instead of getting supper for the older children.

II

Below the platform and to the left of Miss Ranskill, one of the Institute members was hammering our Parry's 'Jerusalem' on a piano that needed tuning: the others were singing Blake's miraculous words and showing no hint of zest or humour.

> Bring me my bow of burning gold!
> Bring me my arrows of desire!

wavered little Miss King, who could not even manage her knitting-needles, and who had said only that morning to Edith Ranskill that an extra two ounces on the fat ration would make *all* the difference.

'Bring me my chariot of fire,' shouted Miss Bridge, whose nervousness on a bicycle was a joy to all the village boys.

Then all of them, including Miss Moffat (a most ardent persecutor of some little Jewish children, members of a Polish-Jew refugee family who lived in the cottage next door), the rather feebleminded Miss Lindsay, and Miss Staples, who would not let her evacuees play with toy soldiers, added:

I will not cease from mental fight,
Nor shall my sword sleep in my hand,
Till we have built Jerusalem,
In England's green and pleasant land.

The last note quivered, the last chord was thumped but no rain of arrows descended on little Miss King, who would, doubtless, have used them as hatpins if they had. Miss Staples showed no sign of minding that her shout for a fiery chariot had not been answered, and Miss Moffat turned to whisper the latest Jewish iniquity to her neighbour.

Miss Hoskins, the President, rose and addressed the Meeting, but Miss Ranskill did not hear a word she said because she was busy making little parodies of her own forth-coming speech:

'It makes me feel very proud to see that so many of my busy co-workers have found time to spare to listen to the few dress-hints that our President thinks I may be able to give you.' (Pause for applause.) 'I am sure every one of you knows much more about this difficult problem of clothing in war-time than I do.' (Pause for denial.) 'The only excuse I have for being here is that for four years and more I have had to make do with a very insufficient wardrobe, only one suit, one pair of stockings, one pair of shoes, and one set of underclothes. There are no gentlemen present, are there?' (Pause for laughter.) 'You can guess, when I tell you that my one needle was made from a pierced fish-bone, my darning thread was hair, filched from my own head, and my patches were cut from the skins of wild birds, that I had to use considerable ingenuity at my little private make-and-mend classes.' (Pause for incredulity.)

'Yes, somehow or other, I contrived to ring the changes in my wardrobe, although I am afraid I never achieved smartness. I know you will all agree with me that variety of clothing is not a luxury but a necessity, if we women are to keep up our morale in these terrible war days. I admit, and I am ashamed to admit, that while I was on my island I did not realise there *was* a war.' (Pause for sensation.) 'So this dress problem is even more important to you than it was to me. Still we are all women together, aren't we? My problems *then* are our problems *now*, so that is why I am going to tell you how I managed. Well, I seldom wore more than two garments at once. It is marvellous how you can ring the changes with two garments. On Sunday the suit, on Monday the jacket and knickers, on Tuesday the skirt and vest, on Wednesday (if it happened to be warm and sunny) the brassière and knickers, on Thursday (another sunny day) the slip, on Friday (cooler, perhaps) the jacket and slip. On Saturday (becoming just a *little* more formal) the jumper and skirt. Really, that little dress scheme worked admirably. If any of you feel doubtful, I beg you to give it a trial. I see no reason why we should not all start together on the same day. I did not happen to have a hat, but there is no reason why we should not all wear our prettiest hats with the new war-time ensembles I have suggested to you.'

Miss Penrose had nearly finished reading the Minutes by now, and Miss Ranskill was giving another imaginary talk on Desert Island Recipes:

'When you have caught your fish (personally I had no net, but I contrived an excellent substitute for one out of my vest. By the way, if any of you ladies wish to go fishing in your vests, I must remind you that it really *is* important to stitch up the neck and the armholes before beginning, unless, of course, you are only fishing for *sport*) when, as I say, you have caught your fish, the next thing is – Oh! no, no, no, not to *cook* it – to clean it. Take a jack-knife or piece of sharp shell –'

Miss Ranskill, interrupted by the sound of her own name, glanced at the President, who was smiling down at her.

'And now I will call upon the lady, who knows more about Desert Islands than anyone in this village, to give us the promised account of her experiences. Miss Ranskill!'

The President sat down and the travelled speaker stood up. There followed the usual shuffling, throat-clearing, chair-scraping and coughing. Somebody said 'Hush!' But there was no need.

Miss Ranskill stared at the faces before her, at Edith's, plaintive and tense, at Mrs Phillips', hostile and disapproving, at Miss Moffat's, like a sea-gull, at Miss Bridge's like another sea-gull, at Miss Lindsay (surely she was more like a sea-gull than either of the others!) Miss King was more like a sea-gull than any bird could be.

'It – it was quite a small island.'

Miss Ranskill's voice sounded so loud in her own ears that it startled her. It should have been loud enough to scare any sea-gulls.

'It was really quite small. It was not much bigger than – well, smaller, of course, than the Isle of Wight, but not so big as – as –'

As what? She didn't know. She only knew that she couldn't tell them anything, wouldn't tell them anything, couldn't remember –

Still they sat on in their long straight rows. They were sorry for her, but she mistook their sympathy for inquisitiveness, their tenseness for malevolence. Why couldn't they have the decency to go away?

'It was, it was –' (a phrase from her first geography book shot into her numbed mind) 'it was a piece of land entirely surrounded by water.'

They shouldn't hear anything about the Carpenter, or anything about feelings at all. She was here to talk about the island. Very well, then, she would talk about the island. Where had she got to?

'It was a piece of land entirely surrounded by water.'

Miss King gave a little titter, the titter of one determined to appreciate jokes, even if she didn't quite understand them.

'There was a beach all round it. There – there was a stream of fresh water – We – I drank from it. It was nice clear water.'

The picture of the island was clearing in her brain. She saw the pretty stream, the shelf where the Carpenter had set the drinking shell as a surprise, the gleam of the sun on rock, the glint of water, and the perpetual gulls, watching sardonically, waiting for the slip that could turn man or woman into carrion.

She was being watched again now. She was also watching herself.

We'll have to watch ourselves when we get home, Miss Ranskill. We'll have to watch our table-manners and watch out what we say or they'll not believe half of it.

She continued:

'We lived mostly on fish and there was a sort of seaweed that was quite good to eat. We – I –'

Once more Miss King giggled encouragingly, and Miss Ranskill looked down at the rows of faces. She couldn't distinguish one from another. They were all exactly the same: they were all gull-like and watching.

'The island was – the island was – I can't go on.' Her voice rose. 'There are too *many* of you. There isn't anything to *say*.'

Someone began to clap politely. Others followed the example. The clapping was subdued because they were sorry and embarrassed. To Miss Ranskill it sounded like the mocking of wings. The birds would rise soon, scatter and come wheeling round her head. She put up her hands to guard her face. There was something else she must say, but what was it?

'Nothing but a pack of cards!' she remarked quite loudly and clearly.

Now she was sitting in her chair again and the President was holding a glass of water to her lips. Voices were whirling round her. 'It's the heat of the room.' . . . 'It's the reaction.' . . . 'Perfectly natural after all those dreadful experiences.' . . .

'I always think just two aspirin and then a glass of *very* hot milk.' . . . 'When my sister had *her* nervous breakdown.' . . . 'Of course, it *is* very hot in this room.'

'I feel so ashamed.'

Miss Ranskill looked appealingly at the President.

'Not at all. Why, I could tell you of one quite well-known broadcaster who *always* breaks down if he has to speak in a public meeting.'

But she wasn't a broadcaster.

So she had broken down, had she? She had hoped the speech had not been quite so bad as that. She had thought a lot about the island, but evidently she had not expressed the thoughts even coherently.

'A good night's rest and then a good day's gardening,' recommended Mrs Phillips savagely, 'I've always heard that work is the best cure for nerves, so I suppose that's why I've never suffered from them.'

'You had better come home now, my dear,' said Edith gently, much, much too gently. The tenderness in her sister's voice made Miss Ranskill afraid.

'Thank you so much for coming,' said the President. 'We shall look forward to a talk from you another day when you are feeling stronger.'

Kind little Miss King (too, too kind Miss King) came forward and spoke in a chirruping voice.

'I was enjoying the talk immensely. I only wish it had been *longer*. The island sounded most interesting. Now don't forget – two aspirin and a glass of *very* hot milk.'

CHAPTER SEVENTEEN

I

Summer in England had softened to harvest time. The downs were a shimmer of gold and blue. Men and boys, women and children laboured in the blazing sunshine to harvest the best crops of any war and Miss Ranskill, recovered now, worked with them; her ankles ragged by stubble and her forearms sore from the rubbing of stooks. Summer, a most glorious summer, was passing and she, like all the other women in the village, had scarcely had time to notice it. In some couple of dozen cottages middle-aged ladies, without domestic help, had somehow or other done all their own housework as well as keeping their gardens gay and profitable. The deck-chairs in summer-houses were bound by cobwebs, for there was no time to sit in them. It had become a sin to idle, and the fear of that sin was rife in the land. Yet never before, in all the long histories of villages, had houses been better kept, furniture more beautifully polished or cooking more exquisitely done.

If a word in common could have been inscribed on every female heart in the village it would have been 'bottling'. The spinsters became savage in their quest for bottles and jars, snap-closures and every variety of airtight cover. Never were women so determined and indomitable, in their lust to avoid waste, and in their haste to fill store-cupboards. They had an uphill fight too. At the time when sugar was scarcest because stewed fruit was eaten at every meal, a glut of plums followed a glut of soft fruits. No sooner were two-pound jars collected than two-pound snap-closures went off the market.

'But, Edith,' protested Miss Ranskill, 'in peace-time we never had so much bottled fruit.'

'In peace-time we could buy all the tinned fruit we wanted.'

'But we scarcely ever *did* buy any.'

'There was suet in peace-time.' The remark seemed irrational to Miss Ranskill, who had been a desert island housewife, unaware of war or peace, and without suet or bottled fruit. She felt disloyal in her conviction that the old way of eating apples till apples came again (or very nearly) was quite as healthy and a great deal less complicated than this new turmoil.

However, the Ministry of Food fed the prevailing passion by printing instructions for bottling in every newspaper nearly every day. The bookshops and bookstalls pandered too. Nearly all the literature on the bookstalls was devoted to new ways of growing food; and the other half to ways of cooking and preserving it.

'I must,' said Edith, 'I must save two pounds of sugar somehow from now until the rose-hips are ripe.'

'Whatever for?'

'Rose-hip syrup, of course, for the children.'

'Whose children?'

'My dear Nona, don't be ridiculous, *all* the children, of course. Now that they can't get oranges they *must* have *rose*-hip syrup and black-currant *juice* to make up for the vitamins they *don't* get in orange juice.'

'But I thought they *did* get orange juice through the children's ration books.'

For by now Miss Ranskill understood all about ration books and points and the 'zoning of certain commodities' as well as clothing coupons; and she thought that a most unnecessary fuss was made about the whole lot.

'They don't get nearly *enough*. It's most important that we should do *all* we can for the children. *They* are the future generation; they are a sacred *trust*.'

'We didn't even have orange juice and we grew up all right. Don't you remember Mother wouldn't let us eat oranges within two hours of drinking milk because she said the juice would curdle it?'

Edith Ranskill sighed.

'Really, Nona, you are *difficult*. I suppose things were *different* then. Times *change*. Anyway, we're *told* to collect rose-hips, and it *is* so important that the children should have the *best* of everything.'

Miss Ranskill, aware that she was being difficult and now being so deliberately, hurled another dart.

'You did tell me you'd tried not to have evacuees. And when you had to have them, you got rid of them as soon as possible.'

'They were *different:* they were absolute *savages* – not even *house*-trained.'

'The future generation all the same,' quoted Miss Ranskill as she pushed another plum into her nearly-full jar, 'and a sacred trust, Edith.'

Her sister shook herself, remarked that she must collect sticks for the boiler because it was bath-night and strode out of ear-shot.

Baths were another great mystery to Miss Ranskill. The boiler was lit only two or three times a week and a broad red line had been enamelled at a height of five inches all round the inside of the bath. It had been indicated to Miss Ranskill by Mrs Phillips that in the interest of national economy she must not fill the bath above that level and she had replied loyally that if it would be any help to the country she would give up baths altogether.

Mrs Phillips had replied disapprovingly that two were allowed each week.

One morning at breakfast she announced archly that someone, she wouldn't say who, but certainly *someone* had taken a bath at least ten inches deep.

'I did,' said Miss Ranskill, 'I had the last bath and there was lots of hot water that would have been cold by the morning, so I didn't see the point of not using it.'

The remark was not received pleasantly by Mrs Phillips.

'Nona's so difficult,' was becoming Edith's favourite remark. 'If only that man on the *island* had been someone of her own *class*, things might have been very *different*. As it *is*, she doesn't seem to fit in *any*where.'

Certainly, Miss Ranskill was finding life in the village difficult. Her only pleasure (a strange one) was the fact that she had been made an ARP Warden and was occasionally summoned to patrol her 'beat' by night. Others might grumble, but she was perfectly happy and bore the discomfort of the tin helmet for the sake of free feet. No orders had been issued about shoes, so, though she wore the official blue overcoat and respirator, she carried her shoes and stuffed her stockings into her pockets.

The 1943 moons matched that year's harvest in their generosity, and, on one memorable night, she saw sunflowers, golden as at noonday, against the wall of a cottage and below them a row of tobacco plants, silver as the moon itself.

In some ways, the moonless nights were even better. Then the tiny illegal strips of light, chinking down the sides of cottage windows, gave her excuse to knock. Sometimes she would be given a cup of tea or an apple: and a slow easy friendship would be made in that friendly hour between today and tomorrow, when evening has slipped away and morning is still far off.

Sometimes there would be an encounter on the road with a soldier, who had snatched the last hour of his embarkation leave and was walking to the town to catch the midnight train. The soldiers were mostly local lads, a little sad after their recent goodbyes, a little solemn at the thought of what might be coming; but glad to meet a middle-aged woman to whom, just for a moment or two, and because she was almost a stranger, they could stop pretending to be real soldiers and show what was in their minds before they turned the corner that ended her beat.

Other wayfarers went overhead – the great night bombers

on their flights to France or Germany or the Low Countries. Their lights helped her to conjure up their shapes – the long bodies and the great stiff wings. Her own thoughts soared with them as she tried to understand the feelings of the men in the machines. Were their minds exalted as their bodies? Were they excited? Did they think of the return or only of the setting forth? Were they afraid, or numbed to a sense of fatality? Were they squandering their thoughts, fussing perhaps over a mounting mess-bill, feeling irritable or nagged by the difficulty of finding lodging for their wives in the crowded villages near the aerodrome? Or were they, perhaps, concentrating on the beauty of the moonlight, looking their last on all things lovely, so that they could store it up as spiritual armament against what might befall, if ever they needed to turn their inward eyes towards an English moonscape at the moment when the foreign ground roared up to meet them?

It was easier to hear them go when she was helping (or trying to help) to safeguard the land they were leaving than when, lying in her bed, she listened to the pulsing of the machines overhead, beating like heavy hearts in rhythm one with another. Then it seemed betrayal to feel sleepy, to turn between the sheets while the engines beat out their reproach – *Could ye not watch with me one hour, one hour, one hour? Could ye not watch with me one hour?*

Often, towards the end of a night-patrol, she watched the machines coming back. One safe, another and another and another. Surely there was a gap in that formation? No, another lonely one was coming in. Soon the men would be breakfasting in the mess; they would have made their reports, and, later in the day, she might see some of them in the village, unchanged outwardly, carrying their wounds and scars within.

She knew now what happened when a bomber crashed.

One day when she was harvesting, alone with an old farmer in an upland field, a low-flying bomber had swooped towards them, tilting its wings while the shadow it threw rocked in blackness across the golden stubble, then turned and flew away.

'Like a great bird!' said the farmer.

They watched it fly low into the valley, swoop towards a hedge, rise, clear it, and go winging its way towards a belt of trees that fringed the village.

'Queer!' said the farmer. 'I've never seen a bomber stunt like that.' He turned to his stook, but Miss Ranskill stood watching. Even in that moment, she felt a little guilty. She was used to aeroplanes by now and should have learned better than to stand, like a lazy child, gazing at something that would relieve the monotony of stooking.

The bomber couldn't possibly be so near the ground as it looked. It couldn't surely be going to land in front of those trees. Suddenly it rose on its tail, its wings outstretched like giant arms in the position of crucifixion – up, up – and, with what seemed no more to spare than when a Grand National horse clears Beecher's Brook – over. Then, a crash (a memorable horror of sound so impressing itself on Miss Ranskill's mind that she recognised it again on nights when others said bombs had fallen) and a pillar of smoke rising black against the sky.

The aeroplane had managed to fly just clear of the village. The young men had saved the old ladies, but three of the crew were killed.

II

One morning, when Miss Ranskill had entered a field of corn that had been cut the day before, she saw that a girl was sitting by the side of the hedge. Her dark hair was tumbled across her cheek and her head was bent over something she was making a lap for. The sight of her roused memory, and, as Miss Ranskill walked nearer and saw what she was holding, she realised it was significant that a girl, who looked as this one did, should be nursing a rabbit so tenderly. A girl and a baby rabbit, where had she seen the two together before?

She turned a stook with her pitchfork, seeing dew-silvered cobwebs against the gold of the straw, seeing the amazing red and blue brilliance of the trespassing flowers that always seemed to draw more colour from a wheat-field than from any other soil. But she was watching another scene as well, a scene in a cellar where a bare-legged girl, looking at her young man, had somehow reminded her of a young and very frightened rabbit newly aware of horror in the world.

'Does it matter my being here?' The girl was looking at her. She was also soothing the rabbit with her fingers.

'No, of course it doesn't. We've met before, haven't we?'

The girl furrowed her forehead.

'It's all *right*, my pet: don't wriggle so. Sorry! I wasn't speaking to you. Yes, I think we did meet, but I can't remember quite where –'

'In Marjorie Mallison's cellar.'

'Oh! yes, of course. It was the night our house was bombed out and Mummy and I and you and Rex – and you were kind. It's awful of me, but I can't quite remember your name?'

'Ranskill, Nona Ranskill. And you're Mrs Mallison now.'

The gold of a slim wedding-ring was half buried in rabbit's fur until the girl lifted her left hand a little.

'To strangers I am. I'd rather be Lucy to you, though. Don't you remember how we talked that night, and how I hadn't any wedding-clothes or anything?'

'And now?'

Miss Ranskill dropped her coat by the hedgeside and sat down.

'Same clothes.' Young Mrs Mallison patted her brown tweed skirt. 'And they gave me some extra coupons.'

That wasn't what Miss Ranskill wanted to learn.

'Look at this *poor* little rabbit. It's sopping and frightened. It must have been out all night. It doesn't seem damaged though. I wonder if it got a wump on the head from one of those beastly harvesters and hid and then sort of fainted. It's coming round now.'

'Probably it did.'

Miss Ranskill fingered the soft fur, grey like matted cob-webs where it was not darkened by dew. She remembered the last strip of corn and the gang of children surrounding it. Their knuckles had whitened as they gripped their sticks tightly, and, as the terrified rabbits darted towards the cover

278

of the fallen stooks, shrilled an age-old cry of persecution –
'Yi-yi-yi. Yi-yi-yi.'

'Sorry, I suppose you are a harvester too.' The girl glanced towards Miss Ranskill's pitchfork.

'Yes, but not that sort. It's the one thing I hate about harvesting, especially when the little girls join in.'

'It seems so frightful somehow, just as though there weren't enough ghastly things going on.'

Miss Ranskill looked at her anxiously for a moment and then her anxiety slipped away. For the girl had that undefinable bloom on her that flourishes through love and cherishment. There was serenity on her forehead and aware-ness in her goldeny eyes. Possession shone in her. She had her armour now against bewilderment and fear and loneliness, if these things should assail her.

The rabbit quivered, its ears flicked backwards. For a moment it crouched in the girl's lap, and then, it seemed only in another moment, its white scut was disappearing under the cover of a stook two yards away.

'It *is* all right then – for today, anyway.'

'*For today, anyway.*' Miss Ranskill wondered how often the young wife had used that same phrase in her heart after the night bombers had returned. She shook the thought away, and asked a question.

'Are you staying here?'

'Yes, at a guest house. Rex is on leave, and I managed to get my holiday at the same time. He's stationed near here now. We would have gone right away, but we've been looking for rooms for later on. There isn't *any* inch *anywhere*. We can't afford hotels, and anyway they're crammed, besides – it wouldn't do. We thought perhaps two rooms in a friendly house. I'd help with the cooking and everything as soon as I could, of course. But people seem so frightened of babies.'

She continued to talk in jerky sentences while her hands moved restlessly in her lap, as though she were still caressing the rabbit.

'One's got to look ahead – even if it's going to be a quite different "ahead" from the one we had planned. It wouldn't be yet, of course. But presently they'll release me from my job, and then I shall have to go steady for a bit. I could go into a nursing-home to have the baby. It's *afterwards* that's going to be so difficult. Mummy's been living in hotels ever since our house was bombed. There is Rex's mother, but – I ask you!'

Miss Ranskill had no need to be asked. Her mind, busy home-hunting, had already rejected Marjorie's battle-eager establishment.

'No, not unless you have triplets who could be made to form threes when they're learning to walk.'

'Poor tinies! They'd have to be boys too, one for the Navy, one for the Army, and one for the Air Force!'

She laughed suddenly, and Miss Ranskill remembered Rex's description of her – 'She laughs a lot and she's comforting.'

As though the word had carried from one mind to another, the girl used it again in her next sentence.

'Mother-in-law's such a silly name, isn't it? It ought to be mother-in-love or – or something *comforting*. It's so *stupid* too.

Fancy being a *wife*-in-law; there'd be legal disputes at once! I say, I'm keeping you from your harvesting.'

'No, it's very wet still; anyway, this is important.'

Without the young green corn there could have been no harvest; without the young generation, bred in war-time and nurtured through danger, there would be no meaning in the golden fields. The sun would shine in vain.

'The mater (I've got to call her that) is against the baby. I mean she thinks we ought to wait till after the war. She thinks it will distract – that's what she said – *distract* Rex from his job, bothering about me and it. As if, as if he oughtn't to be distracted in that way. What's the *use* of killing if you aren't giving anything back? I mean, well, I mean, a gardener spends a lot of time weeding, doesn't he? But what's the use if he's just going to leave bare beds and not plant better things instead of the weeds? It wouldn't make sense; it wouldn't be worth while.'

Truth was throbbing in Miss Ranskill's mind. She, in her confusion, had been irritated by all the little affairs and incessant pin-pricks of war-time, had made too many lazy journeys back to the island to rest in the comforting shadow of the Carpenter's memory. This girl had a clearer view.

'You see, it isn't as if they like killing. Rex says it's only the old women who think they do. Even when they hate, as most of them do, because of things that have happened to their friends in the Forces and relations at home, it's all too sort of impersonal to be satisfactory. It's all sort of – oh! I can't explain, deadening in a way, except to the few. It's different in Fighters, of course, their fighting is closer. But if you've got to kill, well then, you've got to, well, *birth* as well. I can't think of another word. It's *compensating*. Rex is clever. He understands better than I do. He can explain things, but I *know*.'

Yes, she knew now: she was a woman. Reason made way for wisdom in her. For the next months, anyway, she would be guided by instinct. Her body would obey the tiny indomitable unreasoning will within her, would give way to its slow growth with perfect timing, and make ready for its later needs.

The corn-stook was rustling now and she smiled as she looked towards it.

'It's easier for rabbit mothers, isn't it? I don't mean in the silly way people talk about having babies as easily as rabbits do. I mean there's plenty of room in a burrow, and there doesn't seem to be any room in houses. That's another thing the mater said. She said it was selfish to bring babies into the world just now, when everyone ought to be doing war-jobs and not thinking about milk-bottles. The only thing she *will* like, will be being a grandmother in ARP uniform. She'll get a sort of kick out of that; because everyone will tell her how splendid she is, and what an example to people like me – young mothers.'

She gave a fair imitation of Marjorie's voice.

'"Young mothers who have nothing better to do than to idle along the roads pushing perambulators." That's one of the things she said, and she sort of hinted that I was only having the baby so that I could leave my job. Just as though it isn't my job.'

A small quivering nose thrust out between the corn-stalks, and then the whole of the rabbit emerged, glanced in horror at the humans, and went bobbing across the field.

'It's quite all right again, look!' The girl pointed. 'Perhaps it's a sort of omen against all the things they say about not having babies in war-time, not bringing them into such a dangerous world. The rabbit had a bad time, but it's all right now.'

'It's all right now,' echoed Miss Ranskill. 'So are the kittens that were born in the cellar. Do you remember? They've all gone to different homes.'

The smooth forehead wrinkled again.

'Oh *yes!* And you told me you'd promised the cat they shouldn't be drowned *because* they'd been born in a cellar and in spite of Germany. I must have been remembering without knowing it all the time I've been talking to you. That's why I've said so much. And of course you know the real reason.'

'What reason, about *what?*' asked Miss Ranskill.

'The real reason why I must have the baby. In case there wasn't any – any Rex after the war; there'd still be a Rex in a way, wouldn't there?'

'Yes.'

One couldn't deny in the face of truth. One couldn't say that everything was bound to be all right. Miss Ranskill groped in her mind for the quotation she needed and found it.

'You mean – "And those who would have been, their sons, they gave, their immortality."'

'Yes, I suppose so. He mustn't give *that* as well if he's got to give –'

She jerked up the cuff of her white sweater and looked at her watch.

'I must go. Rex was writing letters, but he'll have finished now. We're going to look at another lot of rooms, but I don't suppose they'll be any use. Thanks most awfully for bothering to stop to talk –'

Miss Ranskill smiled as she remembered how very little she had spoken at all. The young and the old, she remembered, were always in the greatest need of listeners.

'I say, if by any chance you should hear of anything near here, could you let me know? Rex's mother would always forward a letter. It mustn't be grand or expensive. We wouldn't be any bother in the house. *Anywhere*, where the people wouldn't hate a baby. And about Christmas time. Goodbye.'

Miss Ranskill picked up her pitchfork.

'I wish my sister – but it's not her house and there's only one spare room.'

'No, I didn't mean that, of course. Goodbye.'

'Goodbye. And –'

'I wish you could have come to see us this evening, but it's the very last day. Rex goes back this afternoon, and I go back to London. I'll ask him to look you up. Goodbye, thank you so much.'

For what? thought Miss Ranskill, as she watched the girl out of sight. For not being able to say, 'Come to my house and I'll look after you.'

She stooped down and picked up a couple of stooks, tucked one under each arm, plumped them down into place and brought their heads together. A plan was struggling for birth. The rhythm of her work might help it to be born.

'About Christmas time.'

Her last Christmas Day had been spent on the island. She remembered the little presents. She had polished a new set of shells for plates. The Carpenter had wrapped the powder-bowl he had made her in a packet of dried seaweed.

Next Christmas we might be home, Miss Ranskill, you never know. Filling stockings and singing carols. It's the grandest day in the year, but you need to have children about you. Not that there's anything to stop us singing a carol now. Maybe cheer us up a bit. Now then, Miss Ranskill – Hark the Herald –

They had sung to grey sea and to grey mist and to seagulls, whose white wings flickering up and down between sea and sky heralded the approach towards shore of the fish they needed.

It was difficult to think of Christmas time in this field under the blazing, burning sun that was also beating down on the Sicilian vineyards, on the tanks and the men and the menacing slopes of Etna.

III

The letter to Edith came during an epidemic of influenza.

Mrs Phillips, just recovered, was striding from Committee to Committee. Her illness had been unnecessarily long because she had insisted on answering her country's rallying cries by trumpeting through her handkerchief on platforms in draughty halls until her bark had become a very great deal worse than her bite. She had refused to let up or let down, until speechlessness made her work in lecture halls a sinecure. The household had suffered; so, too, had many of the loyal listeners who had received largesse of germs from her cornucopia of a nose.

Edith's temperature was at its height when the letter came. She summoned her sister plaintively.

'The tenants have given notice. The ban is being lifted and Lynchurch isn't in a prohibited area any more. Mrs Staples says the people they sub-let to have gone already, and so have most of the troops. It *would* happen just now, wouldn't it? No,' Edith picked up the letter again, 'they go tomorrow. . . . What are we to do, Nona?'

'I don't see that we can *do* anything, can we? I suppose the Wilsons, poor things, will have to go on paying the rent till Christmas time. I wish you'd keep your arms under the bed-clothes.'

Edith obeyed petulantly.

'I know, but Mrs Wilson says if we could re-let the house, it would make things much easier for them. I don't think there's anything but his *pay*. I'd hate to take money when they aren't using the house, but if all the soldiers are going I don't suppose we'll have a chance of re-letting. And it's so *bad* for a house to be left empty *now* with winter coming *on* and *everything*.'

Edith produced her next sentence between coughs and chokes, 'I suppose . . . old Emma . . . can see to fires and . . . things.' (Old Emma had once been the Ranskills' housemaid. She was married now, but still in the village.)

'You oughtn't to talk so much.'

'I must talk.'

'You needn't talk now. I'll write to Emma.'

'But there's the *inventory*. Nona, I wonder if *you* could go down tomorrow?'

Miss Ranskill's heart gave an excited little jump. Of course she could go down. It would be lovely to be alone again and in the old house and among remembered villagers, and the friends who had known her since girlhood.

'I simply don't think I *can* go myself.'

Edith's voice was reproachful and she sneezed pathetically. 'I know it isn't in your *line*' (the reproachfulness increased), 'but old Emma would help. She's quite methodical even if she is *slow*. I'll send her a telegram if you think you can go.'

'Of course I can go.'

'Very well then, I'll send her a telegram, or you might, and ask her to spare what time she can. Then you and she and the man from the agents can go over the inventory together. And do try to *remember* that it *does* matter if the right number of sheets isn't returned. You can't get *teacloths* now without coupons. . . . The *inventory* should be comparatively simple if the Wilsons are as careful as they sound. They've always written very *nice* letters. . . . Oh! how my poor head aches!'

'Shall I get you an aspirin and a cup of hot tea?'

'Oh, Nona, not *now*, when there's so much to think about. We've *got* to make arrangements.'

'It's no use thinking at a distance. I'll do all the thinking when I get down there.'

'The house isn't the only thing we've got to think about. There's the nephew too.'

'The Wilsons' nephew?'

'No, Philippa's nephew, Martin, the taller of the twins. He wants to come down next week on indefinite sick-leave.'

'I see.'

Miss Ranskill's thoughts skipped to the small spare room. At other times, when the nephews had come home for their short leaves, she had occupied a room in Miss Banks' house at the other end of the village. She wouldn't be able to do it again though, because Miss Banks had let the room to a government official, who was employed in the neighbourhood.

'I'd meant to tell you last night, but I felt so ill. My head was going round and round and I couldn't *think*.'

'Something will turn up.'

'You don't *understand*, and my head's simply *racking*.'

Edith was always angry when she was ill. Her mental dominance increased with her body's powerlessness.

'Much better let me make you some tea, and then, if you must think, we can both think quietly.'

Miss Ranskill longed to escape from the room and collect her whirling thoughts. These were not concerned with tea-cloths and bed-linen, but with the waiting garden and the empty rooms.

'Think *quietly*!' repeated Edith. 'You could scarcely call me noisy just now except when I have one of my *sneezing* bouts and they simply *rack* me. No, it isn't the inventory that worries me so much, it's the wear and tear and what's *fair* and what isn't. We can't expect them to do too much in war-time: there isn't the labour and one can't get the *things*. But they *must* replace burned-out saucepans and badly *cracked* crockery as well as the things that are actually *broken*. And if they've spilled things on the carpets. Are you listening, Nona?'

Miss Ranskill returned from her vision of welcoming fires, clothes drying before a fender and happily-lived-in rooms and looked at her sister.

'Stained carpets,' she repeated dutifully.

'Yes, but now I've forgotten what I was going to say next. Hadn't you better get a pencil and make a *list*, Nona. After all, it *is* your house as well as mine.'

So it was. Miss Ranskill had forgotten that. She wasn't even quite a pauper any more. The Death Duty had been returned, and though she had refused, so far, to touch her share of the joint income, she had earned money in the harvest-field and did Mrs Phillips' garden now in exchange for her keep. The plan in her mind began to prosper.

'I don't know,' continued Edith. 'I don't know if we *could* let the house again. You'd better talk to the agent about that. The first thing to do is to see that everything's all *right* –'

'Couldn't we go back and live there?' asked Miss Ranskill.

'It's too big, and it's too expensive to run, as things are just now. Besides, I couldn't suddenly throw over all my work in this village even if I could break my agreement with Phillipa. Do get a pencil, Nona.'

Miss Ranskill got a pencil.

For a quarter of an hour she used it dutifully, writing down details about sheets and blankets, china and kitchen utensils.

Ordinarily, she would have been bored, but now her mind was absorbed by household matters. It was important, of course it was, to make sure that the linen for all the beds was in order. She did not speak of what was in her mind until quite late in the afternoon, until the telegram had been sent and answered, trains looked up, and a woman from the village bribed to 'oblige' for two or three hours for the next few mornings, so as 'to do for' the elder Miss Ranskill.

Then, when Edith, who was feeling a shade better, was sipping Bovril, her sister made an announcement.

'I've been thinking.'

'So have I, all the afternoon.'

'I've been thinking there isn't room for me *here* and there is room *there*. I could look after that garden, *our* garden, instead of this one. You know I believe the kitchen garden could be made quite profitable. I could grow vegetables.'

'But you couldn't do the house *and* garden. And think of the expense of heating and lighting just for one.'

'I didn't mean just for one. I thought I could take in lodgers.'

'*Lodgers!*' The horror in Edith's voice was ended by a sneeze.

'Lodgers!'

'Babies,' said Miss Ranskill. If Edith wished the conversation to be a series of single words she could play the same game.

'Babies?'

'Mothers.'

'Nona! But think of the house overrun with babies. And *whose* babies? You don't know any babies.'

Miss Ranskill took the questions and objections in turn, beginning with the last one.

'I could know some babies quite easily. They'd be officers' wives' babies. And babies don't run at first: they couldn't overrun the house. Besides, some of the lodgers –'

'I do wish you wouldn't keep on using that word.'

'Well, then some of my guests wouldn't even be born. Even

you can't think that unborn babies could damage a house: they're completely self-contained.'

'Nona!'

'Well, aren't they?'

'I don't understand. Officers' wives' babies?'

But Edith's voice, so her sister noticed, was not quite so horror-stricken as it had been. The word officer overpowered *lodger*.

Miss Ranskill repeated some of the conversation in the harvest-field on the day when she had met Lucy Mallison for the second time.

She concluded, 'You've only to look at the advertisements in the agony columns to see how many mothers are homeless. They're taking any sort of jobs – going out as cooks and matrons and helps so that they can keep their children with them.'

'But think of the *work?*'

'There wouldn't be much work if they did their own rooms and took it in turns to do the cooking. They'd pay a reasonable amount. I could have three mothers and the husbands could come down for leaves. I don't see why not.'

'Well,' Edith was weakening. 'I suppose you could *try*. It would be better than having the house empty, I suppose. And now that Martin's coming down on this indefinite sick-leave – you could try it till Doctor Fenton lets you do some proper war-work.'

'Isn't it war-work,' said Miss Ranskill, 'isn't it war-work to make it possible for the next generation to be born and to have somewhere to go when they are born?'

CHAPTER EIGHTEEN

I

The walnut tree had finished work for the year, and now its sap was seeping downwards. The last of the leaves, their life-current withdrawn, clung listlessly to the branches or allowed the air to drift them down to settle and whisper among their more impetuous fellows.

'That's that! That's that!' remarked the very last of the nuts as their shells rapped the gravel, and wakened Miss Ranskill.

The air of her bedroom was moist with the heavy breath of autumn: it carried little whiffs of damp leaves, the scent of late violets, the stable smell of chrysanthemums and little hints from roses that had almost outworn their fragrance. The air also carried excitement with it, and, for a moment or two, she lay with closed eyes, postponing the moment of actual parting from sleep and return, by morning light, to the house she had left all those years ago.

There was still a little hump in that part of the mattress that met her right shoulder-blade. The bed creaked as she stretched out her legs – that was because the worn hollow in the floor-board had never been repaired.

She turned her head. Should she open her eyes now and let the mirror on the gate-legged dressing-table be her first welcomer or should she turn to the open window and the walnut tree where a robin (surely the descendant of cheekier and Ranskill-tamed robins) was singing?

The mirror had held all her changing portraits from childhood to middle-age. From its breath-smudged surface another blue-overalled child had grimaced back, in perfect timing, as Nona Ranskill had contorted her own features. Its little girl had grown smaller and had also backed towards the door – the door that led to goodness-knew-where, step by step as Nona had backed towards the door that only opened on to the familiar landing. She had never been able to catch out the mirror's child who mocked each movement, slow or fast, jerky or surreptitious, whose features followed hers (she knew by the feel) making simpering or hideous or pathetic 'faces'.

She had worked very hard, after reading *Through the Looking-Glass*, to make friends with the other child who, at times, looked wistfully back, as though she too wanted to play and to take Nona through that other door that led into the enchanted house where the dear feckless White Queen fiddled with her rakish crown, the Red Queen bossed, and the Sheep used fourteen pairs of knitting-needles at once.

She had tried every method. She had even held up the black kitten, but the other child had produced a Dinah's daughter too; and each little creature had patted the mirror, prettily, but in vain.

There was a red-brown mark on the right-hand corner of the mirror. It stood as perpetual memorial to the day when

Nona Ranskill had used scissors and pliers to remove the wooden backing, and had then scraped at the paint in order to discover if any magic lay between it and the glass.

She had been sent to bed for what the governess described as a 'piece of wanton destruction that a big girl ought to be ashamed of.' What had that mattered? The other little girl had been sent to bed too, and the pliers and scissors lying on her carpet had proved that she had wanted to break through from Looking Glass Land in order to play with Nona.

Yes, the mirror was a very old friend and had been quite kind at times when the light was rather dim, though it had been more brutally frank even than her sister Edith, during the half hours she had prepared herself for parties.

So Miss Ranskill turned towards the window and opened her eyes to the tree, whose branches had thickened since last she had looked at them.

She was back in her old home, alone in it, free to love its blemishes – the kicked white paint, the protests of the stairs, the doorstep that must surely hold an even deeper puddle in wet weather now that more footfalls had left memorial on it.

Presently she would get up and make some tea. At nine o'clock Emma, one-time housemaid and now the mother of a growing family, would 'slip in' and help 'Miss Nona' put things straight after the tenants.

II

Three weeks later, Miss Ranskill awoke suddenly in the dark hours of the morning.

Recently, she had always wakened happily, assured (as when she was a child on Christmas morning) that something lovely had happened, secure in the knowledge that she was home again.

For everything had been going smoothly, and even the inventory had been correct. Lucy Mallison would be coming in a few weeks. Later a friend of hers, who had one small child and was expecting another, would join the party. Miss Ranskill had answered a third advertisement and the reply might come any time.

There would be a Christmas tree in December. There would be socks hung on the ends of cots. The old house, accustomed to children since the days of Queen Anne, would be contented again. Its stairs would respond with little excited creakings to the sound of small footsteps and its echoes would be happy.

The war news was better too. The Allies were heading towards Rome. The triumphant salvoes from the big guns in Russia sounded more frequently now.

There seemed just a hope that the unborn children, soon to be lying in their cradles in the friendly house, might make their first staggering footsteps into the way of peace.

Yet, this morning's awakening was alarming. She had been dreaming of the island and something had startled her. This time it was not the cry of a gull, winging to the very edge of sleep and hovering on the horizon where dreams merge into wakefulness.

There was something wrong this time. There was a surge of water in her ears. Waves were hurrying towards her, summoning restlessly – 'Hush! Hush! Hush!' Those were the little ones shuffling up the shingle. 'Cr-ash! Cr-ash! Crash!' She could almost hear the big ones curling before they deafened. 'Hush! Hush! Hush!'

If only they *would* hush and give her the chance to listen to whatever it was she ought to hear.

Yet she was awake and she was in bed. Her feet felt the sheets and her ribs were conscious of her right elbow's pressure. She raised her head from the pillow and the surging died away.

After all, she had only been cupping her ear with her hand. That was all. Her hand had been curved like a sea-shell and she had heard the sea again, as once she had heard it through the shell from the mantelpiece in the Carpenter's kitchen.

She repeated the experiment. Once more the swirl of waters overpowered her thoughts and again she heard the insistent – 'Hush! Hush! Hush!'

She closed her eyes, but sleep had been sent away by the water-music.

She thought of Colin, the Carpenter's son, and wondered if he were in distress. She pictured him standing, barefooted in the little kitchen, pressing the shell to his ear, listening (Hush! Hush! Hush!) for the comfort that only she could bring.

That was nonsense, of course, a silly sentimental idea. The boy would be in bed now and asleep.

If there were such a thing as telepathy, it would not need the invocation of a sea-shell and the hand of a middle-aged woman cupped against her ear.

She switched on the lamp beside her and the clock on the table told her that it was three o'clock.

Could ye not watch with me one hour?

But an hour of watchfulness had nothing to do with *Colin*. That was the sentence she recalled when the night bombers flew across the house and she remembered the cry of another Carpenter's son in a dark garden. There were no bombers overhead tonight.

She could hear the rain slushing from the walnut tree, but she had no sense of comfort. As a rule, wild or wet weather added to her happiness, making her realise her bed and the security of walls.

She turned out the light and lay for some time in that state of restless confusement that is not quite sleep and not quite consciousness. Presently, the squalling of a cat drifted her into dreaming.

Colin was running down the village street. A tin-can was tied to his pyjama coat and children with rat-like faces pelted him with sea-shells, crowding and scrabbling, making a Pied Piper of a nightmare.

Now he was in a boat, the boat his father had made. He was baling out water with a sea-shell, but the water was gaining. Waves were rushing over the bows and every wave had a rat's face. The water was snapping. White teeth and white spray were indistinguishable.

Miss Ranskill shrieked, and this time her own voice awakened her.

Memories of the boy dominated her all the time she was dressing. Certainty of his need took possession of her. She scarcely realised, even, that she had put on her only tidy coat and skirt instead of her gardening clothes.

She was lacing her best shoes when Emma arrived, and she answered the enquiring glance automatically.

'I've just heard I must go away for the day. I shall be back this evening, I expect. Could you lay the fire in the sitting-room, please, Emma.'

'Yes, Miss. And shall I put the egg ready by the saucepan. That would be as nice as anything for your supper, wouldn't it?'

'Yes, two eggs, please. We'll want something else though when we come in. Don't let's bother to arrange now. I can make something. I didn't know until this morning that I should have to go away.'

A knock sounded on the front door.

'Postman,' said Emma, 'I passed him in the lane. He's late this morning.'

She went out of the kitchen and returned with an envelope: it was penny-stamped, an unmistakable bill.

'It's for Mrs Wilson, Miss. We'll have to forward it.'

'Yes.' Mrs Wilson seemed very far away, as far as the Carpenter's boy was near. 'Emma, if you've got time, you might make up the bed in the little south room, just in case – I don't really know yet.'

'In the little *south* room?'

'Yes, please.'

'Miss Edith never did care much for that little room.'

'Miss Edith?'

'It wouldn't take me long to get her own room ready. We could leave beating the carpet till later if I just gave it a good sweep and washed round the skirting boards. It wouldn't take all that time –'

The sound of a tinkle interrupted her. The noise was repeated.

'Didn't the men come then, Miss?'

'What men?'

'The Telephone men. You said they'd promised to come yesterday afternoon to set the wires to rights?'

For all through the wind and rain of yesterday, the telephone bell had kept up a ceaseless tinkling. It was a thing that sometimes happened, so Emma had told Miss Ranskill, when the telephone lines became entangled in the walnut tree. Until they could be disengaged the telephone was useless. It had been useless all yesterday.

'No,' said Miss Ranskill slowly, 'they didn't come after all.'

She noticed Emma's bewildered expression, saw how the elderly woman glanced again at the single letter on the table. She had been too well trained by Edith to ask questions, but Miss Ranskill felt sorry that she could not satisfy a curiosity that was born only out of the friendliness that had gathered through long years of service.

But how could she explain the inexplicable and say that what she had heard in the morning had not been learned by written word or over the telephone?

'I must go now or I'll miss the train. I'll leave everything to you, Emma. If you'll just leave the key in the usual place.'

'And which room shall I get ready?'

There was just a hint of hurt disapproval in the voice.

'Oh! the little south room, *please*. It isn't for Miss Edith. I must go now. I – I'll explain when I come back.'

She must go now, even though she might have to wait for the train. She must go before the matter-of-factness of every-day things smothered the sense of power within her, before the mockery of reason killed the compelling instinct; and made her slave to what Emma might think if she chanced to return alone in the evening.

'Don't forget your mackintosh, Miss.'

III

She had not, until she stood for the second time in her life outside the Carpenter's cottage, thought what she must say or how she could explain her anxiety over the boy.

There was nothing about the cottage to hint at any tragedy. Indeed, it was more like the cottage she had seen as the Carpenter talked, than the one she had entered a few months ago.

White curtains hung crisply between frames of glossy green paint. The doorstep was whitened; the knocker gleamed so that it showed a little contorted reflection of her face.

She thought, as she waited for the knock to be answered, that perhaps she had misjudged the Carpenter's wife. Women, like houses, have their off days. There was nothing slovenly now about the house or about the diamond-shaped beds on either side of the door. They had been freshly forked and the edging of little green plants lay in tranquillity, waiting for spring.

Footsteps sounded along the passage within and Miss Ranskill strained her ears. The footsteps were quick and light, but they did not suggest a boy's movements – a boy would walk more stumpily.

The door opened and she looked into the face of a stranger – a pleasant, well-washed face.

'Is Mrs Reid in?'

'Mrs Reid doesn't live here now.'

'Oh!' Miss Ranskill's voice was flat. 'Do you mean she's left the village?'

'No, she and her husband have taken one of the new bungalows in Westley Road.'

'Her husband?'

'She's married again. Let me see now, she married about six weeks ago. I doubt if you'd find her in this morning, though, but you might try.'

Married again? Miss Ranskill wondered if Mrs Reid had married the gross-faced man who had interrupted the song heard in the sea-shell. She understood now why the cottage was so transformed.

'The name's Amery now. Amery, Woodway, Westley Road. You can't mistake the bungalow. It's right at the end, and it's got yellow railings. Do you know Westley Road?'

'No, I'm afraid I don't.'

Miss Ranskill felt dazed as she listened to the directions, and that was not because they were complicated. She felt that the Carpenter had suffered yet another death. There was so little of his pride left.

Then the voices of boys, shouting to one another on the other side of the road, reminded her that it was Saturday morning.

'First right, then left, and it's on the right-hand side at the far end of the road. As I say, I shouldn't think she'd be in this morning, but there's no telling with her.'

The face of the speaker was not quite so pleasant now and the last words were spoken rather viciously.

'Perhaps the boy, Colin, perhaps he'll be in.'

'He won't be in – not this *morning*. If it's the boy you want, you can save yourself the trouble.'

'He isn't ill, is he?'

'No, he's not *ill*, wasn't yesterday, anyway.'

The new owner of the house stepped back a pace, but there was reluctance in her tread. Her lips were pursed and she shook her head knowingly.

'If you want to know about Colin you'd best ask his mother. I've had trouble enough with the lot of them. I'd sooner not say anything than have her throwing it up at me that I've been talking. If you ask me, though, she's nobody to blame but herself. I wash my hands of the lot of them.'

'Well,' Miss Ranskill turned to go, 'I'm sorry to have bothered you. I hope –'

'I'd sooner not *say*. Good morning.'

Miss Ranskill was left alone in the narrow strip of garden. First to the right. Her feet rustled through dead leaves as the wind whistled up the broad street of the village.

She passed a group of boys playing 'conkers' and thought she heard the name Colin.

He wasn't ill, but he wouldn't be in this morning. That ought to be natural enough. The wind had blown the rain away and other boys were out at play. She came on another group of them as she turned the corner, but the stocky figure of the Carpenter's son was not among them.

A red-haired boy was twirling his conker on a string and shouting:

'Anyone else want his block knocked off? I've beat you all same as I always does.'

'No, you don't.' A shrill-voiced child with greyish-golden hair was piercing another chestnut. 'You've not beat Colin yet!'

'Yes, I have.'

'No, you've not.'

Another child shouted.

'Bet you Colin'd like to be playing "conkers" this morning.'

'Not half he wouldn't.' The fair boy swung his chestnut and rapped his neighbour on the head. 'My Dad says Colin'll never come back.'

'Go on!'

'Go on yourself!'

Miss Ranskill, shuffling through the wayside leaves, felt as though she were walking in a nightmare. She must hurry, but it seemed to her that her legs were moving ridiculously slowly. They would not stretch far enough. Her feet, cramped by shoes, were inelastic. She began to run at a jog-trot.

At last she reached the bungalow with the yellow railings. The gate was open. She forced herself to walk slowly up the cinder path. It would be silly to be breathless when she arrived and unable to speak except in gasps, but she was still gasping a little when she pressed the bell.

For a long time there was silence, or rather a series of silences, punctuated by Miss Ranskill's frequent ringing of the bell. Yet, although there was neither response nor promise of it, she felt certain that someone was inside. It was almost as though the house were breathing and asserting its habitation. She looked at the lace-hung window to the right of the door and saw that the curtain was moving. It was being more closely drawn from inside. She caught a glimpse of reddened finger-nails. Then she turned to the door again. This time she hammered as well as ringing.

At last her insistence won, and she heard shuffling reluctant footsteps. The door opened chink by chink and the Carpenter's wife; no, Mr Amery's wife looked out furtively. Her face, under its thick coating of powder, was puffy and the eyelids were reddened.

'What is it now?' The voice was weary and petulant.

'Don't you remember me? I'm Miss Ranskill. I called to see you a few months ago.'

'I remember all right.'

'I came because I wondered –' And then because the face looked so dreadfully unhappy and lifeless, Miss Ranskill ended impulsively. 'Is there anything I can do to help?'

'It's all right, thank you.'

Voices sounded in the road behind – the shrill lively voices of boys, heartless in their exuberance.

Mrs Amery opened the door a little wider and spoke reluctantly.

'You'd best come in for a minute, if you don't want to go. I don't want all that lot standing around and gaping. We've had about enough of them.'

A cat-call shrilled from the road. It was followed by another one, and Miss Ranskill went into the house.

She followed her hostess into a small pretentious sitting-room. Coloured crinkled paper filled the grate. A vase of artificial roses stood beside a biscuit-barrel on a fumed oak dresser. The chairs were upholstered in green plush. Nothing was familiar except the clock in the centre of the mantelpiece and the great sea-shell that lay beside it.

'Will you sit down a minute?' Mrs Amery jerked a chair out of place and sat down on another one. She stared at the fire-place and did not even look at Miss Ranskill as she asked, 'I suppose you've heard something?'

'I went to the house where – where you used to live, and I was told –'

'Trust *her* to talk,' interrupted Mrs Amery bitterly. 'All said and done, it *was* his father's work-shed, and if he did think he'd a right –'

'How *is* Colin?' asked Miss Ranskill, dreading the answer to direct question less than information given in the belief that she had been listening to gossip.

'You wouldn't know him for the same boy since all this. Nobody would.'

'Is he at home?'

'No.' Mrs Amery gave a furtive glance, and said no more.

'I should have liked to see him again.'

'He'll not be in till late – if he's back at all. I ought to have gone with him, but the doctor said "no". He wouldn't hear of it. "Best stay at home, Mrs Amery," that's what he said, "best stay at home and let your husband get on with it." Yes, the doctor knows how I suffer from my nerves.'

'Then Colin *is* ill?'

'It's me that's ill. All gone to pieces my nerves are. No

wonder neither, after all that I've been through. And what his poor Dad would have said.'

'Where *is* Colin?'

'If you *must* know,' Mrs Amery dabbed at her eyes, 'if you must know they've taken him to Court.'

For a moment the words conveyed nothing but grandeur to Miss Ranskill, glittering grandeur, soft with feathers, shining with the glint of orders and jewels and swords. Mrs Amery's next words banished romance.

'The Juvenile Court at Mallingford.'

'Oh! *poor* little boy!'

'He done it all right,' said Mrs Amery, and not, perhaps, without a touch of pride. 'Five charges, petty larceny mostly.'

If Colin was to turn out bad, Miss Ranskill, it would break my heart.

'He was all right till after the wedding,' continued Mrs Amery. 'You couldn't have found a better boy anywhere – not if you'd *looked.* . . . Yes, he was all right till then, but he and his stepfather never did hit it off and it got worse. I suppose I might have taken a bit more notice, but you know what it is when you're just married. Mr Amery got sick of him mooning about in the evenings and always fiddling with his bits of carpentering. It isn't as though we'd a shed here. I don't say Mr Amery wasn't a bit sharp. Pushing him out of the house and that. I ought to have noticed what was going on, but then, you see, he never brought his friends back home, so how was I to know? I did have one or two complaints, but I didn't take much notice of them. You know what boys are, you can't expect them to be angels all the time.'

There followed a long description of Mrs Amery's nerves, but the visions in Miss Ranskill's mind spared her from noticing those details. She was looking at the boy's face and his father's face: she was looking into the future. Six weeks couldn't be long enough to make a criminal surely?

'It's what's going to happen next that's worrying me,' said Mrs Amery. 'It's the idea of the probation officer or the police nosing round that gets me down. Mr Amery says he won't have it, and you can't really blame him. They might send him to an approved school, but Mr Amery says that's not likely; it's not as though he'd a bad record up to now. He says he'll not have him back in the house at any price. It is an upset and no mistake.'

'Would, could –' Miss Ranskill had made up her mind, and the words came tumbling out. 'If the magistrates will allow it, will you let the boy come and stay with me for as long – as long as he likes?'

'I'm sure it's ever so good of you,' declared Mrs Amery.

'I owe his father a debt,' Miss Ranskill told her, adding hastily as the expression of distress on Mrs Amery's face turned to one of suspicion, 'I don't mean a money debt: he taught me things I shall never forget.'

'It's ever so good of you. I don't see that there's anywhere else he could go, seeing Mr Amery's determined he shan't come back here.'

And now Miss Ranskill was in a hurry to be gone. She asked a few more questions, and learned that it was unlikely that Colin's case would be heard until after lunch.

'There are so many cases just now. It's this dreadful war

and the fathers all being away. The boys go about in gangs. One's as bad as another. The policeman told me that when he said they'd got to make an example of Colin seeing as how he was a leader. Yes, there'll be a lot of cases on today. There's young Pyecroft, for instance – now he's a bad boy if ever there was one – a real bad-hearted boy.'

But Miss Ranskill had not time to listen to the iniquities of young Pyecroft. She asked a few questions, discovered that the coal merchant had a taxi and might be persuaded to drive her into Mallingford, since it was within the nine-mile limit for taxis, said goodbye and let herself out of the front door. The little gang of boys was still lurking and cat-calling by the gate.

The sea-shell was in her pocket. She had taken it as a talisman. His clothes would be sent on.

CHAPTER NINETEEN

The little boy sat hunched up in the corner of the third-class carriage. He had scarcely spoken a word through the journey that was very nearly at an end.

The distressing blue light that made war-time travel so melancholy showed Miss Ranskill that his eyes were closed. She did not believe that he was asleep; his eyelids were pressed down too tightly and his lips were too firm. He was defending himself from question and scrutiny; and containing within himself all the horrors of the courtroom – the looming police, the inquisition of the prosecution, the publicity and the inner loneliness.

Miss Ranskill had not witnessed his humiliation but she had seen his face, dour and defiant, before he went into the court; tear-blotched and glum when he came out. She had seen him shrug away when his stepfather had laid hand on his arm, had seen his contemptuous eyes as he listened to the half-jocular, half-bullying words, spoken more for the benefit of the ghoulish onlookers than for the boy himself.

'Let this be a lesson to you, my lad. I can tell you, you'd have copped it proper if I'd been the Magistrate. You will next time, make no mistake about that. Don't you look at me in that saucy way neither, as though you fancied yourself a hero, you dirty little sneak-thief, you.'

She had seen him duck his head and look into all the corners of the outer room as though searching for cover.

She, herself, had had an exhausting day. There had been interviews with the Magistrate, another with the Probation Officer, a third with the stepfather, besides formalities that seemed endless. Her own credentials, as a suitable and responsible guardian of the boy, had had to be established. There had been telephone conversations with the doctor in her own village and with old Mr Jelks, the local Magistrate, who had known her since girlhood.

The Probation Officer had been kindly and helpful.

'We get so many cases like this. From our point of view it is always more difficult when the child does not come from a really bad home. We have more power, when we can prove neglect and can make use of an Approved School. There *was* neglect in this case, of course, but not *physical* neglect. The boy is well-nourished and well-clothed. His sort of case is more puzzling to the outsider than it is to us. Here we have a boy with a perfectly good previous record, a fairly quiet, well-mannered boy, who suddenly becomes a little villain, loses all sense of right and wrong, and, when he comes before the Magistrates refuses to say a word that might help him. What has happened? He may have been to too many gangster films. He may have come under the influence of older, more sophisticated boys. He may have had too much love or too little, or his pride may have been hurt so badly that he felt an urge to assert himself and become important to someone.

I think that is what happened here. This little boy became the leader of a gang of small hooligans.'

The Magistrate had been more general.

'This particular sort of case is being repeated day after day all over the country. It is one of the evils of war. These boys are too young to differentiate between crime and what I can only call legalised crime. Don't mistake me, Miss Ranskill, I am not a pacifist, *I* can see the difference between the public executioner and the common murderer: the one is the servant of the community, the other is a slave to himself. In these days, most of our young men are public executioners. It is difficult to explain that to children *and* stimulate their patriotism though. Train-busting would be a crime in peace-time, but in war it is a triumph. These boys read about successful Commando Raids and think it would be thrilling to be a Commando. They can't go to Germany, but they can break into empty houses and have some of the fun (the imagined fun) of being a Commando.

'Remember another thing, these boys are too young to remember peace conditions properly. Four years, more now, is a long time in a child's life. The best people in the country, the *disciplined* younger people are mostly out of the country. All their examples are gone and their fathers are away. Old fogies like myself can't do a great deal of good though we try our best. Yet these children must be saved or the war will be a mockery and we shall only have bred a race of hooligans who will menace peace as the Germans have menaced it.

'If you make yourself responsible for the boy, you may not have an easy time. Don't spoil him, don't sentimentalise over him, but show him the past and let him look at the future.'

Miss Ranskill remembered all this as she glanced across at the boy. His face was a little more relaxed than it had been when he shuffled beside her out of the Town Hall past the craning onlookers and into the chill of the Market Square.

The parting with his stepfather had been brief.

'You try and mend your ways, my lad, and be a credit to your Mum and me. She'll be sending your clothes along for you. Goodbye.'

The boy had stood looking down at the muddy pavement.

'Saucy, eh? Well, I'll give you another chance. Goodbye.'

The boy, prompted by a nudge from Miss Ranskill, had muttered 'Goodbye', but he had addressed a leaf in the gutter, and had continued to regard it until his stepfather joined some waiting acquaintances on the opposite pavement. His coarse laughter sounded across the square. He tilted his cap at an angle and remarked in a voice evidently meant to be heard:

'Surly little bastard! I wish the old fool joy of that one.'

'Come along,' said Miss Ranskill, 'let's go to the station. We can get something to eat there.'

The meal had not been a very great success. The boy drank a great deal, cup after cup of urn-tasting tea, but he only fiddled with the sausage rolls, crumbling the pastry into flakes and kneading the meat between finger and thumb. Miss Ranskill guessed that his hands were hungrier for occupation than was his body for food. Every movement of those hands reminded her of the Carpenter's, and she wished he would keep them still.

Conversation was difficult. One could not discuss the events of the afternoon, but she did make a little attempt to explain the future because the boy had followed her hopelessly as a lost dog, trailing a strange pair of heels, without question or interest.

'Colin.'

He had glanced up at her.

'You do understand, don't you, that you are coming to stay with me in Hampshire?'

He nodded.

'The house we're going to live in isn't far from the sea. You'll like that, won't you?'

'I don't mind.'

She went on to describe the house, and then told him about the little potting-shed that he could use as a workshop in the evenings and on holidays.

'Won't it be rather nice to have a workshop of your own?'

He flushed and bent his head still lower over his plate.

'Not if there's no wood.'

The flush deepened. Miss Ranskill remembered that one of the charges against him had been one of stealing wood, finely-grained wood for boat-building from the workshop of his father's successor. He had taken some tools too. He had also stolen a bicycle lamp from another house and a tin of varnish from the local shop. All these things had been found in an old chicken-house at the bottom of his mother's garden. He had been trying to equip the chicken-house as a workshop. The light shining through the window had given him away to the policeman. The boy had not remembered the need for black-out curtains.

Miss Ranskill waited until the flush had faded from his cheeks. Then she spoke again:

'But there will be wood this time. You can buy some if you work in the garden and earn money.'

'Can I?'

It was the first responsive thing he had said, and though he ducked his head again immediately, Miss Ranskill was satisfied.

Later on, she would tell him stories about his father, but not just now while his mind was closed and clutching on misery. One thing must make room for another.

There's one thing I reckon you can't do, Miss Ranskill, you can't hurry comfort. You can't give happiness while a misery's still there. I remember when I was a little lad and my pup had been run over, they wanted to give me a new one straight off. That didn't do. I'd got to get shut of a part of the misery first.

No, she must not hurry comfort.

That was why, so far, she had left him alone with his misery, allowed him to hunch himself up in the far corner of the carriage, to twiddle with the window-strap and swing his legs, now with seeming nonchalance and now listlessly. Even his knobbly and rather grubby knees looked forlorn. His face, travel-stained and white with misery though it was, still carried the likeness of his father's. His right hand lay relaxed on the seat of the carriage.

Miss Ranskill was not sure now whether he was asleep or not. His lips had parted a little.

She took the sea-shell from her pocket and laid it on the seat two inches from his fingers. Then she lifted his hand gently and laid it on the cool curved surface. He shrugged away from her resentfully, nuzzling his head into the corner between the upholstery of the seat and the window-blind with a movement suggesting that of a small wild animal, carried in from darkness to the publicity of a room.

But she noticed, when she had returned to her own seat, that his fingers were gripping the shell.

It was time now to close her eyes.

Presently she became conscious of small scuffling movements in the far corner of the carriage. She did not dare to look yet.

In her own mind, the island was taking possession of the railway carriage.

She would wait for two minutes and then she would open her eyes. She began to count sixty twice over and slowly.

One leg was crossed over the other, his elbow was pressed into his knee, the shell was against his ear and he was listening.

The water-music was pouring into his mind, sweeping it clear of trouble, lulling the nightmare thoughts and making peace. And, as the magic of the shell did its work, the boy's face changed. Surliness slipped away, the grey eyes lost their furtiveness and the lips smiled. He was enchanted back into himself again.

His fingers pressed harder against the shell, and Miss Ranskill, who remembered her own listening, knew that he was hearing a crescendo now – a tumult and surging of many-voiced waters.

Suddenly he dropped the shell. His face puckered and his right hand groped at emptiness until Miss Ranskill reached him. He was a little boy, haunted by ugliness, bewildered and softened by sudden beauty, crying into her shoulder, 'I didn't want to be bad.'

'Yesterday's over. Listen, Colin, today's finished too: it's tomorrow that counts.'

He began to quieten slowly as he nuzzled into her shoulder and choked, 'I didn't have anything – nothing at all.'

'Listen, and I'll tell you a story.' His fingers were gripping the lapel of her coat.

'Once upon a time there was a man on an island. He was a carpenter, like you're going to be, and he hadn't anything either except his clothes and a jack-knife. And he wanted to build a boat – a big one. There were trees on the island, but there was no felled timber. It took him more than four years, but he made his boat and he made it seaworthy, so that I could come across the sea to England to look after you because he wasn't able to come himself.'

Colin's head jerked up for a moment.

'Did you know him?'

'Yes, and so did you.'

'Not –' the boy's eyes pleaded queerly in the strange light, 'not – it wasn't my Dad?'

'Yes, it was.'

'But, my Dad's dead.'

'Yes,' said Miss Ranskill, 'yes, but he made the boat first.'

The boy's eyes were hazy with sleep and weeping. His hand groped for the shell. Miss Ranskill gave it to him and settled him into his corner. He gave a little whimpering sound and fell asleep, his fingers twitching on the shell. He handled it as his father would have handled it.

Nothing of him that doth fade, but doth suffer a sea-change into something rich and strange.

The engine took up the refrain *Into something rich and strange, rich and strange, rich and strange. Yesterday's over, yesterday's over, yesterday's over. A re-eed shaken with the wind, a re-eed shaken with the wind.*

Yesterday was over for Miss Ranskill too.

The island was still there, but she did not need it any longer. This other island needed her more. There was so much to be done, so much to be restored to compensate for what had been destroyed.

The Carpenter was not really dead: he was alive in his boy and she could share in that immortality.

Her mind was harking forward, away from the island and into a garden, forward to a spring morning, to a thrush whistling on a walnut tree and a boy whistling in a woodshed, to a liver-and-white spaniel, very fat and very kind, waddling beside a perambulator, to Lucy's voice repeating, 'What's the *use* of killing if you aren't giving anything back?'

The engine was hurrying now and Miss Ranskill's thoughts speeded with it.

The train stopped with a jerk, and Colin opened his eyes.

Then the carriage door was opened and a porter bawled 'Lynchurch! Lynchurch!'

'We're home now, Colin.'

He blinked sleepily and smiled at her as he tucked the sea-shell into his pocket.

Miss Ranskill had come to the end of her journey.

AFTERWORD

In the autumn of 1946, the novelist Rosamond Lehmann, then at the peak of her literary career, was commissioned to write fiction reviews for *The Listener*. Her judgments were perceptive: she gave high praise, for instance, to Albert Camus's *The Outsider*, which was not then recognised by other critics as the modern classic it has become. I came across these reviews while researching for my forthcoming book on Lehmann's own literary reception, and was intrigued by her warm commendation of a novel which I discovered to have been long out of print, and whose author, named as Barbara Bower, was unknown to me. *Miss Ranskill Comes Home*, Lehmann said, 'is a work of great originality, and delightfully readable, a blend of fantasy, satire and romantic comedy'. I was able to find a copy in the British Library, and having read and enjoyed it, I contacted Persephone, and this republication is the result.

Rosamond Lehmann was not alone in her appreciation of the novel, as I was to find out. J D Beresford, in the *Manchester Guardian*, congratulated Miss Bower on 'a witty first novel which besides being continuously entertaining displays a fine appreciation of life's values'. The book also received an enthusiastic reception in America, despite transatlantic readers' lack of experience of the wartime shortages, black-out and other restrictions, which are an integral feature of the plot. Sara Henderson Hay in the *Saturday Review of Literature* said that the novel was 'somber, satiric, often bitter, a mixture of realism and romanticism', and that it 'approaches a modern morality play; it is an idea, an allegory in a way in which fantasy is blended with fact for the purpose of the whole'. Anne Richards in the *New York Times* also praised the blend of 'reality and fantasy, irony and pity'.

The novel received an unprecedented accolade from one of America's most influential popular journals, the *Saturday Evening Post*. At that time that magazine's fiction section consisted of short stories, serialised (and almost always abridged) novels, and condensed novels, contained within one issue, and labelled 'Novelettes' but evidently not with any pejorative meaning. For instance, one such novelette was H E Bates's acclaimed *The Cruise of the Breadwinner*, rightly described by the Post as 'a distinguished war story'. In the case of *Miss Ranskill Comes Home*, however, they announced that, since they felt it to be 'one of the finest stories we have read in a long time', they would publish it neither in instalments nor as a Novelette, but in full 'in three long parts, each about three times the length of a typical *Post* serial installment'.

So who, I wondered, was Barbara Bower, and why, despite her book having been so well received, did she only seem to have written one novel? The answer partly lay in the fact that Bower was the author's married surname; her full maiden name was Barbara Euphan Todd, the name under which for some twenty years previously she had enjoyed considerable success as a children's writer, most famously as the creator of the talking scarecrow of Scatterbrook Farm, Worzel Gummidge, and his friends.

The only child of a country parson, Barbara Euphan Todd was educated, as she later put it, 'very slightly' by daily governesses until she was sent to boarding school at the age of 14. She appears to have been somewhat coy about her date of birth; reference books cite the year as being '1890 (?)'. During the First World War, she worked on the land, and as a VAD nurse. After the war, she returned to her parents' home, and began to write, first collaborating with various others on collections of fairy stories, and then writing her own realist adventure novels appealing to slightly older children. Her first attempt to combine the worlds of fantasy and real life adventure in the shape of Worzel Gummidge was however rejected by several publishers, and the manuscript was put away in a drawer for a number of years.

Later Barbara had poems and short fiction for adults published in *Cornhill Magazine*, and regularly reviewed books for *Punch*, which, even at the modest rate of £2. 12s. 6d. per contribution, provided a steady income. By strange coincidence, in 1936, she was among the critics who disliked Rosamond Lehmann's *The Weather in the Streets*. The heroine, Olivia, irritated her, and so, she continued, 'does her creator, who seems to show an almost old-fashioned determination to shock'. While admitting that the book was clever and interesting, she nonetheless wished that Lehmann, 'who can write so beautifully about beautiful things, would not bother to write so badly about ugly ones'. It should not be thought, however, that in praising *Miss Ranskill*, Lehmann was being remarkably forgiving ten years later: she was unlikely to have known the name of the reviewer, *Punch* reviews then being unsigned.

It is tempting to identify the Barbara Euphan Todd of the years before her somewhat late marriage with the middle-aged heroine of her first story published in *Cornhill*. Miss Blessop has unexpectedly inherited a large fortune, and sets out to relive her childhood as it might have been, had it not been blighted by the severe, unloving aunt, who had brought her up. Despite an empathy with childish desires, the narrator tells us, Miss Blessop 'was not a sentimentalist':

> She had no desire for little fingers to clutch at her heart-strings, for the sound of little feet to patter up and down her new corridors in Kensington. Never once since the days of her anæmic girlhood had she sighed for a family fireside and the love of a good man – the former would worry, and the latter embarrass her.

But at the age of 42 Barbara Euphan Todd did find a man to marry, who was unlikely to have embarrassed her. John Graham Bower was a family friend, formerly married, with two young children, a retired naval commander awarded the DSO in the First World War, who listed his recreations in *Who's Who* as 'shooting, hunting, and boxing'. A devout Christian all her life, it might have seemed uncharacteristic that Barbara should marry a divorcé, but throughout her writing there is an unconventional streak, and a dislike of authoritarianism in any form. This attitude is made clear in 'Sign-posts', the poem signed B E T, which is the foreword to *The Very Good Walkers* (1925), her first published novel for children, written in collaboration with Marjory Royce. The sign-posts 'along the hot and dusty roads where grown-up people go' are 'policemen tall and straight', declaring: '"There really isn't time to play."' But children and other free spirits, the poem continues, should follow the swallows who 'flash and flicker past':

> They point the way to Over There
> To Far Away and Anywhere,
> 'Beyond', they say, 'the hills are blue,
> Beyond, Beyond, the roads are few,
> We are the finger-posts for you!'

John Bower, the younger son of a baronet, had himself published adventure and travel books for adults, using the pseudonym, 'Klaxon'. His novel *Heather Mixture* (1922) seems to have autobiographical elements, his hero being a much-decorated Lieutenant-Commander, 'Dicky to intimates, Fawcett to others, and Lofty to the Lower Deck', who finds in 1918, in common with many of his fellow-officers, that the welcome home offered by the Admiralty amounts to relegation to six months' unemployed pay. Bower nevertheless stayed in the Royal Navy until the year before his marriage to Barbara. The couple pooled their interests, and collaborated, as 'Euphan' and 'Klaxon', on several educational but entertaining children's books. They lived in Blewbury, a picturesque village in Oxfordshire, inhabited by a number of writers and artists, with whom they became friends, including the painter William Nicholson and the novelist Marguerite Steen to whom Barbara later dedicated *Miss Ranskill Comes Home*.

John Bower died in 1940, so their marriage was to last only eight years, but it seems to have been very happy. The Bowers are remembered in the village even today for the big summer parties they used to give for the local children, whose mothers, however, were always apprehensive of the Commander's method of signalling the end of the party; he would fire one or both of two enormous guns usually hanging in their entrance hall. It became a village legend that he had been a big-game hunter, although there appears to have been no truth in this.

In 1936, Barbara's Worzel Gummidge stories finally found a publisher. Such was the success of the first book (it was chosen by Penguin to be the first of their children's series, Puffin Story Books, when the series was launched in 1941, and has been reprinted many times since) that it was followed by nine other Gummidge tales. The stories became still better known after the war when Barbara's friends, radio scriptwriters Mabel and Denis Constanduros, persuaded her to adapt them for the then enormously popular 'Children's Hour' programme with Uncle Mac. At the time of her death, negotiations for the television rights were underway, but no agreement had been reached. It is sad that she was never to see her favourite character immortalised by Jon Pertwee. She also wrote at least eighteen other children's books, but rarely returned to the same characters as she did with the Scatterbrook farm series.

Contributing a profile of the author to *Twentieth Century Children's Literature*, Norman Culpan maintains that:

> The fame of Barbara Euphan Todd will rest on the stories that feature Worzel Gummidge and his fellow-scarecrows. Typically, in *Worzel Gummidge, or the Scarecrow of Scatterbrook*, John and Susan, aged 10 and 12, spend holidays at Scatterbrook Farm, where they have hilarious and singularly credible adventures, protecting the nature and escapades of these walking, talking scarecrows from discovery by adults.

He praises 'the strongly individualised' characterisations of the scarecrows: 'Chief among these is Worzel Gummidge himself ... full of professional pride, unpredictable, and almost always irritatingly right.'

Gummidge's principal enemy is the officious Mrs Bloomsbury-Barton (a forerunner of Ambridge's Lynda Snell – no village event is safe from her interference), but he usually manages to get the better of her, putting her down notably on one occasion when she has mistaken him for a tramp, and addressed him as 'My good man'. Gummidge snaps back:

> 'That's where you're wrong . . . that shows that you don't understanding nothing about anything. I am not yours, I am my own. I am not good, I am just fair to middling, and I'm not a man – I'm a scarecrow.'

Elements of Mrs Bloomsbury-Barton (described by Barbara

Euphan Todd in the introduction to a later Gummidge story as being 'very good and proper, but very, very tiresome') are apparent in various female characters in *Miss Ranskill Comes Home*.

After Barbara Bower's death, her step-daughter, Ursula Betts, wrote very fondly about her; Barbara had been, she said, 'deeply and strongly emotional, although this was strictly controlled. She was warm and kind, and I personally owe her much. I think, however, I chiefly remember her for her dry – and sometimes wry – sense of humour.' These qualities permeate *Miss Ranskill Comes Home*.

When the novel opens we meet the heroine digging the grave of the man who has been her sole companion on a desert island for four years and two themes are immediately estab-lished. Firstly, the capitalisation of 'Carpenter' suggests a religious dimension, which perhaps unsurprisingly is most in evidence as Miss Ranskill is striving to call to mind the liturgy of the Burial Service in order to give her former com-panion a Christian, however unorthodox, interment. The second theme, contemporary class consciousness, is more widely explored. Miss Ranskill is wryly aware that her own sense of propriety had verged on the absurd. She reflects on the Carpenter's invariable form of address to her:

'Miss Ranskill', yes, she had always been Miss Ranskill to him since the time he had dragged her chilled water-heavy body out of the sea. The 'Miss' and her surname had made her armour against an assault that had never

325

been hinted at. She had called the Carpenter, Reid. His surname seemed to set the right distance between them.

In C S Forester's *The African Queen* (1935), a similarly disparate pair are thrown together in survival conditions, but Miss Sayer, the prim missionary's sister, so memorably portrayed by Katherine Hepburn in John Huston's 1951 film version, rapidly becomes Rose, Rosie, old girl, sweet'eart, to the Cockney engineer, Allnutt, who in turn becomes Charlie, dear, (and, following the consummation of their love, 'husband' in her thoughts) to Rose. But Miss Ranskill 'had cherished the flower of her virginity', which

> had remained the same all through the years on the island. She had always been proud of her integrity and of the Carpenter's too. They had made between them a greater story than the ones usually begotten on desert islands in books.

The *New York Times* reviewer, for one, did not however find this aspect of the novel unbelievable. Anne Richards' verdict was that:

> The relationship that develops between prim, virtuous, old-maidish Miss Ranskill and the gentle Reid, who is still intensely devoted to his home and family back in England, becomes with the author's fastidious and imaginative touch, a fragile, guileless experience, touchingly persuasive and real.

There is, however, a degree of wistfulness manifest in Miss Ranskill's recollections of the preservation of her honour, and also the recognition that her feelings about class differences have undergone a change which would be incomprehensible to her previous friends and family in England. Had they been rescued together, they had planned to visit each other's homes, and she imagined the perplexity of Edith, her elder sister, as to how he should be received:

> 'The man is neither fish, fowl nor good red *herring* now that you have made a *friend* of him, as it were. Yes, I *know* the circumstances are peculiar, but that makes it all the more *difficult*: people won't *understand*. We can't let him eat in the kitchen with Emma if he's a *visitor* – so unsettling for *her*, and he can't possibly feed with *us*.'

Nona Ranskill returns home to a world radically changed by the outbreak, unknown to her, of the Second World War, and not to the nostalgic image of England that she and the Carpenter used to summon up in mental pictures to entertain each other most evenings. Nevertheless she finds many class barriers still intact. The Commander of the convoy who has rescued her prophetically warns Miss Ranskill that nostalgia, translated literally from the Greek, means 'return pain', and she has much reason to remember his remark.

The contemporary reader would have understood about the innovations presenting seemingly insuperable obstacles in Miss Ranskill's path; having lost her naval escort, she encounters suspicion and hostility as she attempts to buy food without a ration-book, clothes without 'coupons'. The younger reader of today, while appreciating the humour often inherent in the situations, might also share Miss Ranskill's Kafkaesque bewilderment as to the meaning of overheard conversations:

> Miss Ranskill put a hand to her aching head. Had the language changed or had she forgotten words? Was she, perhaps, a trifle mad? Rip van Winkle could scarcely have felt more puzzled than she did. What had happened in her absence that fantastic horrors could be described so casually? Even the language was secret from her, full of strange words and alphabetical sequences.

In her brief memoir, Ursula Betts recalled her stepmother's fund of stories of the excesses of wartime committees in her village, and in this novel some of the characterisations, bordering on caricature, provide a useful corrective to the then prevalent image of nobility and self-sacrifice of the women manning the Home Front.

Throughout the novel, Barbara Euphan Todd interweaves the humour of Miss Ranskill's with serious concerns. And the reader is made conscious of the fact that the war is approaching its end, and that post-war readjustment may not be easy. Miss Ranskill recalls the difficulties suffered by ex-servicemen after the First World War:

> So many of them had journeyed through the valley of humiliation, worn smooth by the steps of commercial

travellers; and had waited diffidently on doorsteps to sell vacuum cleaners and gimcrack gadgets.

The present war's experiences meant that their sons were 'evolving slowly into a race apart'. Looking at an airman on the train, Nona wonders:

> How would they, who had seen the ten-acre meadows as inch-wide patches for a country's quilt with the warp and waft of streams and hedges no thicker than rows of stitching, keep the bounds of a counter in the years to come and employ their fingers to cut patterns of crêpe-de-Chine for customers?

Terence Rattigan was to provide a sensitive and sympathetic portrayal of this problem in the character of Freddie Page in *The Deep Blue Sea* (1952).

In *Miss Ranskill Comes Home*, there is recognition that the following generation was also at risk. Towards the end of the book, a magistrate in a Juvenile Court warns that the 'legalised crime' of reported Commando raids had lent a false glamour to such exploits to boys too young to remember peace conditions, and in a particularly prophetic passage, continues:

> All their examples are gone and their fathers are away. Old fogies like myself can't do a great deal of good, though we try our best. Yet these children must be saved or the war will be a mockery and we shall only have

bred a race of hooligans who will menace peace as the Germans have menaced it.

Rosamond Lehmann had ended her review by saying that Miss Bower had 'great gifts' and that she looked forward to her next book. It remains, however, a mystery as to why Barbara Euphan Todd did not write a further book for adults. She did continue to write books for children after the war, as well as two children's plays based on fairy stories, in collaboration with Mabel Constanduros. She died in 1976.

As an example of her step-mother's sense of humour and tenacious spirit, Ursula Betts told the following tale:

When she was no longer young, a dog of hers died and the gardener dug a grave. Out in the garden at night, she slipped and fell into it. The grave – for a dachshund – being narrow and small, she was wedged into it and could by no means raise herself. So there she spent the night (fortunately a warm May one), consoling herself, she said, by reciting the hymn – 'Teach me to live that I may dread/The grave as little as my bed.' Luckily the morning brought some workmen to a nearby plot and they heard her shouts and rescued her.

Her fictional creation, Miss Ranskill, would have given her few marks for resourcefulness with regard to her failure to escape from her predicament, but no doubt top marks for her sangfroid.

Wendy Pollard
Cambridge, 2003